Arthurian
Myths

Arthurian
Myths

General Editor: Jake Jackson

Associate Editor: Josie Karani

FLAME TREE
PUBLISHING

This is a FLAME TREE Book

FLAME TREE PUBLISHING
6 Melbray Mews
Fulham, London SW6 3NS
United Kingdom
www.flametreepublishing.com

First published 2020

ISBN: 978-1-83964-171-8

Cover illustration based on 'Sir Segwarides Rides After Sir
Tristram' by F.A. Fraser (1846–1924) from *King Arthur and
His Knights of the Round Table* by Henry Frith (1912).

All images © copyright Flame Tree Publishing 2020 except Shutterstock.
com and: antonpix, Kristina Birukova, Cube29, Marek Hlavac.

Contributors, authors, editors, translators and sources for this series include:
J. Bédier, H. Belloc, Laura Bulbeck, W.W. Comfort, Jake Jackson, Judith
John, Thomas Malory, Sarah Peverley, Chrétien de Troyes, J.L. Weston.

A copy of the CIP data for this book is available from the British Library.

Printed and bound in Turkey

Contents

Series Foreword

STRETCHING BACK to the oral traditions of thousands of years ago, tales of heroes and disaster, creation and conquest have been told by many different civilizations in many different ways. Their impact sits deep within our culture even though the detail in the tales themselves are a loose mix of historical record, transformed narrative and the distortions of hundreds of storytellers.

Today the language of mythology lives with us: our mood is jovial, our countenance is saturnine, we are narcissistic and our modern life is hermetically sealed from others. The nuances of myths and legends form part of our daily routines and help us navigate the world around us, with its half truths and biased reported facts.

The nature of a myth is that its story is already known by most of those who hear it, or read it. Every generation brings a new emphasis, but the fundamentals remain the same: a desire to understand and describe the events and relationships of the world. Many of the great stories are archetypes that help us find our own place, equipping us with tools for self-understanding, both individually and as part of a broader culture.

For Western societies it is Greek mythology that speaks to us most clearly. It greatly influenced the mythological heritage of the ancient Roman civilization and is the lens through which we still see the Celts, the Norse and many of the other great peoples and religions. The Greeks themselves learned much from their neighbours, the Egyptians, an older culture that became weak with age and incestuous leadership.

It is important to understand that what we perceive now as mythology had its own origins in perceptions of the divine and the rituals of the sacred. The earliest civilizations, in the crucible of the Middle East, in the Sumer of the third millennium BC, are the source to which many of the mythic archetypes can be traced. As humankind collected together in cities for the first time, developed writing and industrial scale agriculture, started to irrigate the rivers and attempted to control rather than be at the mercy of its environment, humanity began to write down its tentative explanations of natural events, of floods and plagues, of disease.

Early stories tell of Gods (or god-like animals in the case of tribal societies such as African, Native American or Aboriginal cultures) who are crafty and use their wits to survive, and it is reasonable to suggest that these were the first rulers of the gathering peoples of the earth, later elevated to god-like status with the distance of time. Such tales became more political as cities vied with each other for supremacy, creating new Gods, new hierarchies for their pantheons. The older Gods took on primordial roles and became the preserve of creation and destruction, leaving the new gods to deal with more current, everyday affairs. Empires rose and fell, with Babylon assuming the mantle from Sumeria in the 1800s BC, then in turn to be swept away by the Assyrians of the 1200s BC; then the Assyrians and the Egyptians were subjugated by the Greeks, the Greeks by the Romans and so on, leading to the spread and assimilation of common themes, ideas and stories throughout the world.

The survival of history is dependent on the telling of good tales, but each one must have the 'feeling' of truth, otherwise it will be ignored. Around the firesides, or embedded in a book or a computer, the myths and legends of the past are still the living materials of retold myth, not restricted to an exploration of origins. Now we have devices and global communications that give us unparalleled access to a diversity of traditions. We can find out about Native American, Indian, Chinese and tribal African mythology in a way that was denied to our ancestors, we can find connections, match the archaeology, religion and the mythologies of the world to build a comprehensive image of the human experience that is endlessly fascinating.

The stories in this book provide an introduction to the themes and concerns of the myths and legends of their respective cultures, with a short introduction to provide a linguistic, geographic and political context. This is where the myths have arrived today, but undoubtedly over the next millennia, they will transform again whilst retaining their essential truths and signs.

Jake Jackson
General Editor

Introduction to Arthurian Myths

THE MYTH OF KING ARTHUR and his knights is so well established that many believe he was a real historical figure. The original stories have been built on and expanded to encompass not just Arthur, his family and his heroic deeds, but also many of his Knights of the Round Table. Most people have their favourite character or story and Arthur is still a hugely popular figure in British culture today. So what it is that makes the myth of Arthur so popular and enduring?

Origins

It is impossible to say when the myth of King Arthur first originated. Stories of the legendary king were told and passed on orally so often that they were established in British folklore by the time the poet Aneirin wrote his medieval verse *Y Gododdin* at some point between the sixth and eleventh centuries. While the poem does not retell Arthurian legends, it makes a passing reference to a warrior who, while noble and worthy, is 'no Arthur'. The reference, with no accompanying explanation as to who Arthur was, suggests his name was already well-known. There follow many literary references to King Arthur from the sixth to the twelfth centuries, one of the most famous being Geoffrey of Monmouth in his *Historia regum Britanniae* (1138). Entitled the *Historia*, the book nevertheless includes folklore that was deeply embedded in British culture. It depicts Arthur's life from his inception by King Uther Pendragon and Igraine to his marriage and many victories in battle, his betrayal by his son, Mordred, his injury in battle and his final journey to the renowned Avalon, a magical island run by enchantresses.

Another account of Arthur's life was told in the Norman poet *Wace's Roman de Brut* in 1155. This poem is notable because it is the first written account to mention the Round Table. Wace's poem was also the first time Arthur's sword was referred to as Excalibur.

Chrétien de Troyes

However, it was not until a French courtier, Chrétien de Troyes, wrote five stories based on Arthur's knights that the original Arthurian myth was extended to include characters that have become as integral to the Arthurian myth as its original story.

Chrétien was from Troyes in the French region of Aube, near Champagne. It was likely at the court of Champagne that Chrétien developed his own knowledge of, and love for, the mythical chivalry of Arthur's court. Writing his five Arthurian stories between 1160 and 1191, they consist of *Erec and Enide; Cligès; Lancelot or the Knight of the Cart; Adventures of Yvain* and *Percevale, the Story of the Grail*. Chrétien is responsible for many Arthurian myths, including Lancelot's story, Camelot and the fabled quest for the Holy Grail.

At this time, the French court was ruled by King Henry II of England, while the French King Louis VII only directly ruled certain cities in France. While Chrétien's Arthur stories do not contain much reference to politics or courtly intrigue, he would have been well aware of the power struggles and politics of courtly life. As an example, Henry II took Eleanor of Aquitaine as his wife in 1152. Eleanor had previously been married to Louis VII until their separation in 1137 when Eleanor was unable to provide Louis with a male heir. However, such marital alliances for power – not love – that were so common in both the French and English courts do not translate into Chrétien's tales. Instead, men seek love matches and are willing to lay down their lives for the women they adore.

Chrétien's stories were immediately well-received. They were soon translated into several languages, including English, and had a profound impact on French literature. The original texts were written in French in rhyming couplets. The translations mean that some of the rhyme is lost, but the stories retain a lyrical, poetic quality that today's readers appreciate. Chrétien begins *Lancelot* with the following poetic ode to his patroness, Marie of Champagne:

> *Since my lady of Champagne wishes me to undertake to write a romance, I shall very gladly do so, being so devoted to her service as to do anything in the world for her, without any intention of flattery. But if one were to introduce any flattery upon such an occasion, he might say, and I would subscribe to it, that this lady surpasses all others who are alive, just as the south wind which blows in May or April is more lovely than any other wind.*

Chrétien's method of flattering his worthy patroness in one sentence and stating that such a woman needed no flattery in the following sentence shows his clever command of language as well as his understanding of the flowery, chivalric statements so beloved by the nobility.

One of Chrétien's wealthy and powerful patrons, Countess Marie of Champagne, commissioned him to write *Lancelot or the Knight of the Cart*. Marie was one of Louis VII and Eleanor of Aquitaine's daughters, and married the Count of Champagne in 1159 at the very tender age of 14, soon growing into a powerful and captivating woman. Chrétien's second patron was even more influential. Philip d'Alsace, Count of Flanders, was known as a 'flower of chivalry', whom Chrétien clearly admired as a great and chivalrous man. Perhaps Chrétien was flattering his wealthy patron, but it is equally likely that he genuinely saw and admired the parallels between Philip and Arthur.

Sir Thomas Malory

Another significant Arthurian author is Sir Thomas Malory. Born in Warwickshire, England, Malory spent his formative years learning about the ways of chivalry and courtly life, spending some – if not all – of his childhood in the service of noblemen. He would have been exposed to the real-life heroic quests of figures such as Kings Henry V and VI,

Sir Richard Beauchamp and the saintly warrior, Joan of Arc, whose unwavering belief that she was carrying out God's will in establishing the true French king must have resonated deeply with him.

However, Malory's conduct in much of his adult life did not reflect that of the chivalrous courtier that he would later write about in *Le Morte d'Arthur*. Indeed, the list of crimes attributed to him is long and impressive. Malory would find himself in and out of trouble with the law and he spent significant periods in prison, including the infamous Tower of London. In July 1451, the Duke of Buckingham took 60 men-at-arms to arrest Malory (possibly finding strength in numbers as Malory was previously thought to have made an attempt on Buckingham's life). Malory was on this occasion imprisoned in Coleshill with the Sheriff of Warwickshire. However, two days later – in a bold manoeuvre worthy of his stories – he escaped his prison by swimming across the moat to freedom. Eventually his crimes caught up with him and he spent much of the next decade in and out of prison.

This image of Malory as a lawbreaker is hard to reconcile with the man who penned a text of almost bard-like quality which pays homage to noble kings, chivalrous knights and romantic liaisons. It should be noted that while Malory may have been a habitual criminal, he lived in turbulent political times. Showing open support for the king could mean riches and prestige or it could result in lands and freedom being stripped away. Therefore, the true charges against Malory might have been politically motivated as the power balance in England shifted back and forth between the houses of York and Lancaster.

Malory's dubious past is perhaps one reason that he is not nearly as well-known as other British literary goliaths such as Chaucer and Shakespeare. While many can retell the legends of Arthur and his knights, few can name Malory as one of the most significant authors of Arthurian myths. Malory would complete writing *Le Morte d'Arthur* in around 1469, but his book was not published until 1485. This meant that Malory, who died in 1471, never lived to see his legacy live on for over 500 years. Famous fans from history include Edmund Spenser, John Milton, Alfred, Lord Tennyson, C.S. Lewis, John Steinbeck, Mark Twain and, of course, Walt Disney.

Le Morte d'Arthur

Le Morte d'Arthur, Malory's epic tale of Arthur and his knights, is split into eight books. In 'The Tale of King Arthur', the first book, King Uther Pendragon meets Igraine, the wife of his enemy the Duke of Tintagel, and falls suddenly and deeply in love with her. Their union is blessed with a son, Arthur, who under the advice of Merlin, is placed in the care of Sir Ector and his son, Kay.

It is not until Uther is dead, leaving the throne empty and England under threat, that the young Arthur performs perhaps his most magical and well-known feat of pulling the sword from the stone. Arthur is crowned king and is almost immediately plunged into war and rebellion from dissenting knights. Merlin acts as the young king's magical aide and war councillor, resulting in Arthur's many victories, both on the battlefield and in single combat. In this first book, Arthur also has a son, Mordred, with a married woman called Morgawse, who unfortunately turns out to be his half-sister. This regrettable act results in tragedy in later books, a tragedy that resonates throughout *Le Morte d'Arthur* when Arthur, complaining to Merlin of nightmares, is told by Merlin that he 'have gotten a child that will destroy you and all the knights of the realm'. Eventually meeting and marrying Guinevere, 'The Tale of King Arthur' culminates with Arthur forming the Knights of the Round Table, a chivalric band of noble warriors who perform adventurous quests.

In the following books, Arthur and Britain grow in power and stature. We meet several noteworthy knights, including Lancelot, Tristan, Percevale and Galahad and explore the ultimate quest for the Holy Grail, which challenges only the worthiest knights to live up to the noble and chivalric code they have sworn to uphold. The romance of Lancelot and Guinevere follows, with the final book 'The Tale of the Morte Arthur', culminating in the book's dramatic conclusion. Following Guinevere's betrayal of Arthur, she is condemned to death, only to be rescued by Lancelot and pardoned when she returns to Arthur. Arthur's nephew, Gawain, swears he will take revenge on Lancelot and incites Arthur into a mighty battle on Salisbury Plain.

During the battle Arthur is betrayed by Mordred, fulfilling the prophecy told to him by Merlin in the first book. Arthur is severely wounded and carried away to Avalon where his mortal body passes on, leaving behind only his legacy.

Key Characters and Themes

Arthurian legends may have endured for so long because they give readers the chance to vicariously live their childhood dreams. Brave knights travel the world in search of adventure and glory. Beautiful princesses meet men prepared to give them the world. Each story is given drama and glamour with codes of chivalry, courtly values, magic and enchantment. While many of the stories combine these ideas, some characters seem to epitomize certain themes from Arthurian myths. For example, Lancelot is probably most famous for his romantic – albeit adulterous – affair with Guinevere than any of his chivalric deeds. Percevale is best known for going on the original quest for the Holy Grail. Galahad – Lancelot's son by Elaine of Corbenic from bedding her after mistaking her for Guinevere – is presented as the perfect knight and joins Percevale on the Grail quest, which ends with him choosing to die and ascending into heaven.

Arthur and Merlin

The boy king, Arthur Pendragon, anointed by God, needs very little introduction. Personifying fairness, generosity and chivalry, he leads his men into dangerous and formidable battles to defend Britain from invaders seeking to corrupt and defile his people. He defeats the Saxons and extends his empire as far as Rome, becoming Emperor of Rome at the height of his powers. However, like any man destined for greatness, his legend was destined to outlive him.

From his youth, Arthur is guided by Merlin, wizard, advisor and councillor of war. Merlin is capable of great magic, has the ability to foretell the future and is himself guided by God. Merlin is instrumental in Arthur's conception and upbringing. He tells Uther that he knows 'all your heart every deal; so ye will be sworn unto me as ye be a true king anointed, to fulfil my desire, ye shall have your desire'. Merlin's desire is that Uther seduces Igraine, after which she falls pregnant with Arthur. Under Merlin's guidance, the infant is taken from his parents and brought up as the son of a knight, Sir Ector. There he remains until the fateful day in London when the child Arthur pulls the sword from the stone. A shapeshifter, Merlin often appears in different human or animal forms to guide or test his charge and others.

Magic and Christianity

An intriguing theme in Arthurian myths is the melding of magic and Christianity, usually presented in literature – and in reality – as opposites with one representing good and the other evil. In the Arthurian myths, magic and religion combine to elevate King Arthur above the rest of the mere mortals. This amalgamation of old superstitions and more modern religious beliefs could be nothing more than a useful literary technique, allowing magic to create the exciting and insurmountable quests so worthy of Arthur's knights. However, while many Britons were Christian by the fifth century, pagan superstitions were well-established and their roots ran deep. Contemporaries of early Arthurian myths might well have found comfort in this union of paganism and Christianity. The theme of Christianity is most strongly portrayed in the ever-popular quest for the Holy Grail, the fabled cup Christ used at the Last Supper, and in which his spilled blood was collected by Joseph of Arimathea.

Female Characters

While female characters are often presented as secondary to the brave deeds of Arthur and his knights, they are instrumental to many of the most well-loved and dramatic Arthurian myths. They are also presented as real women with mixed emotions and sexual appetites in a similar way to many of the male characters, rather than one-dimensional, virginal paragons. Guinevere is a prime example of a woman who is governed by such desire for Lancelot that she has an adulterous affair with him. In some stories she is even presented as cold and calculating, consorting with Mordred, her husband's son and murderer.

The enchantress Morgan le Fay, often described as Arthur's half-sister, is an apprentice of Merlin. As Thomas Malory says, 'Morgan le Fay was put to school in a nunnery, and there she learned so much that she was a great clerk of necromancy,' again lending an interesting blend of magic and religion. Le Fay often acts as Arthur's magical protector, watching over and defending him. Fiercely jealous of Guinevere because of her influence over both Arthur and Lancelot, she is often presented as the antithesis of the virtuous queen. She takes several lovers and is sometimes presented as Arthur's greatest enemy and the instrument of his downfall. However, even in these stories, they are reconciled and le Fay is the one who takes Arthur on his final journey to Avalon.

Knights of Romance

Traditionally, chivalric knights were romantic figures, often performing dramatic and extravagant gestures to win their lady loves. One of the most famous romantic knights in Arthurian legend is Lancelot. He epitomizes courtly chivalry and his entire life seems to revolve around one thing: rescuing and then winning the heart of his true love, Guinevere. Unfortunately, by this time Guinevere was married to Arthur, Lancelot's friend and mentor, meaning that Lancelot had to choose the love of his heart over his brotherhood of knights. In *Lancelot or the Knight of the Cart*, our first glimpse of the knight of romance is as an unnamed man who is trying to rescue the recently abducted Guinevere. Gawain, Arthur's nephew, has already begun the search for Guinevere and her escort, Arthur's step-brother and seneschal, Kay. Unfortunately, Kay's horse is found without a rider and Guinevere is nowhere to be seen. Onto the scene rides a dashing unnamed man, so desperate to rescue Guinevere that he has ridden his horse to death. With no other option, the unnamed hero discards all notion of honour and throws himself on the mercy of a dwarf driving a cart. The dwarf claims to know where Guinevere has been taken and, despite riding by cart being a deeply shameful for a knight, the unnamed man happily demeans himself in the name of love. On arrival in the castle in which Guinevere is being held, the unnamed man proves his love for Guinevere by performing several tasks to test his bravery and skill. Proving his love, he is revealed as Lancelot and rewarded with a night of passion with Guinevere.

Another love triangle can be seen in *Tristan and Iseult*. Here, the Cornish Knight Tristan travels to Ireland to rescue the fair princess Iseult from the clutches of Morholt the Knight. Iseult is escorted by Tristan to Ireland in order to be married to his uncle, King Mark of Cornwall. As their journey continues, Tristan and Iseult take a potion originally meant for Mark and Iseult, and the pair fall deeply in love. Iseult is wedded to King Mark as planned, but she and Tristan continue their adulterous relationship, using trickery to avoid being caught. The couple are eventually discovered, resulting in Iseult returning home with Mark and Tristan leaving her forever, taking his broken heart home to Lyonesse before roaming the lands to seek solace for his broken heart. In Brittany he meets another beautiful young woman called Iseult with the White Hands. Desperate for love, Tristan marries her but regrets his decision almost immediately. Returning to Cornwall, he is mortally wounded by a poisoned arrow and dies before Iseult can reach him, causing her to die from grief. As the text says: 'Apart the lovers could neither live nor die, for it was life and death together.'

Lancelot and Tristan, among others, can be said to epitomize the idea of courtly romance, acting against their sworn oaths as Knights of the Round Table to give all that they are for love.

Knights of Adventure

Many of Arthur's Knights of the Round Table are characterized by their love of adventure, challenges or quests. The Round Table represents the chivalric order held dear by its knights, with no head so that every man was of equal importance. One of the most famous Arthurian quests was Percevale's quest for the Holy Grail. Depicted in one of Chrétien de Troyes' books, Percevale is a true and noble knight, but even he is not worthy of finding, and benefitting from, the Grail for Arthur.

Yvain, the son of Morgan le Fay and King Urien, sets himself his own adventure when he overhears his cousin, Calogrenant, telling the story of how he was travelling the country when he needed to seek shelter. Taken in and treated with care, Calogrenant later loses face and has to flee back to the court. Hearing the tale, Yvain vows to take vengeance on the man who shamed his kin. He travels to Brocéliande where he defeats his cousin's foe, before meeting and falling in love with his widow, Laudine. As in *Lancelot*, the path of true love is never simple for a knight errant. Yvain marries Laudine but cannot turn away from his true nature as an adventurer and leaves her soon after their marriage to travel with Gawain and participate in a series of tournaments. When Yvain returns to his new wife later than expected, Laudine refuses to take him back. Briefly driven mad, Yvain is rescued by a noblewoman before embarking on six more adventures to prove his worth and his love. He then returns to his beloved Laudine as the unrecognizable Knight of the Lion, before revealing his true identity and reuniting with his wife.

Gawain, Arthur's nephew and Morgawse's son, relishes a challenge from a stranger to Arthur's court to begin his own adventurous quest. A celebrated knight who is fiercely loyal to Arthur, Gawain is eager to accept when a large stranger dressed all in green, known as the 'Green Knight', bursts into Arthur's court and challenges any knight present to chop off his head with an axe. However, there is one stipulation: in one year and one day, the Green Knight has the option to return the blow. Gawain accepts the challenge with relish, nearly severing the Green Knight's head. However, the Green Knight simply reattaches his head and tells Gawain that he will see him at the appointed time. On his way to fulfil his bargain, Gawain meets with many adventures before finally facing the Green Knight and his potential death. As he has acted with honour, the Green Knight gently nicks his neck instead of severing his head, then reveals himself as an agent of Morgan le Fay, who was testing the worth of Arthur's knights.

Many other adventures of glory and excitement are undertaken by Arthur's knights as they aim to test their skills and bravery in tournaments and quests, often the more life-threatening the better.

The Legacy of Arthur

Taking up the mantle of Arthurian authors, Alfred, Lord Tennyson wrote a cycle of 12 narrative poems based on King Arthur, entitled Idylls of the King (published between 1859–85). Harking back to Chrétien's patrons, Tennyson dedicated his work to Prince Albert, Queen Victoria's consort. Written in blank verse, the Idylls of the King spans the life of Arthur and includes the forming of the Knights of the Round Table, Guinevere and Lancelot's betrayal and Arthur's tragic death.

In 1900 Joseph Bédier wrote *Le roman de Tristan et Iseut*. His book was translated into Cornish and English in 1913 by the French poet Hilaire Belloc, known for his comic verses. In 1958, T.H. White published his homage to Thomas Malory's *Le Morte d'Arthur* in *The Once and Future King*. His book is based on Malory's account, but also includes original content, some of which was used in the Walt Disney film, *The Sword in the Stone* (1963). And who could forget the infamous *Monty Python and the Holy Grail* (1975)?

More recent adaptations based on Arthurian myths include the television shows *Merlin* (2008–12) and *Camelot* (2011), and the films *King Arthur* (2004) and *King Arthur: Legend of the Sword* (2017). In 2007, the poet Simon Armitage published his own interpretation of *Sir Gawain and the Green Knight* for a modern audience.

This is just a small selection of the many retellings of the myth of Arthur, illustrating that its popularity shows no sign of diminishing. Even some of the early texts still strongly appeal to today's readers because of their understandable English and dramatic storytelling, just as they did to their contemporary audiences. Their combination of incredible quests and endearing and imperfect characters striving to lead virtuous lives continue to intrigue and beguile audiences, and there is little doubt they will continue to do so for many years to come.

King Arthur & the Knights of the Round Table

THE LEGEND of King Arthur and the Knights of the Round Table has captured the imagination of readers, writers, artists, and composers for more than a thousand years. From its first flourishing in the Middle Ages, through each successive era, it has been a touchstone for strong leadership and accord, speaking to an elusive 'golden age' that never existed and offering consolation when things fall apart. Even in our modern age, the phenomenal number of films, TV series, novels, history books, video games, comics, websites, tourist attractions, university courses, and merchandise drawing inspiration from the Arthurian legend reveals just how powerful Arthur's story continues to be, captivating people the world over.

An essential collection of chivalric romance, swordplay, wizardry and brutal feats of courage, Thomas Malory's *Le Morte d'Arthur* is one of the world's greatest pieces of myth-making, with much gothic and modern fantasy finding its roots in this splendid mix of history, magic and literature. William Caxton was the first to publish Malory's text in 1485, and it is our curated edition of Book I of his text that we offer here. Although the entirety of the original work has not been included, you will find many popular scenes from Arthur's world within these pages.

Chapter I
How Uther Pendragon Sent for the Duke of Cornwall and Igraine his Wife, and of their Departing Suddenly Again

 I T BEFELL, in the days of Uther Pendragon, when he was king of all England, and so reigned, that there was a mighty duke in Cornwall that held war against him long time. And the duke was called the Duke of Tintagil. And so by means King Uther sent for this duke, charging him to bring his wife with him, for she was called a fair lady, and a passing wise, and her name was called Igraine.

So when the duke and his wife were come unto the king, by the means of great lords they were accorded both. The king liked and loved this lady well, and he made them great cheer out of measure, and desired to have lain by her. But she was a passing good woman, and would not assent unto the king. And then she told the duke her husband, and said, "I suppose that we were sent for that I should be dishonoured; wherefore, husband, I counsel you, that we depart from hence suddenly, that we may ride all night unto our own castle."

And in like wise as she said so they departed, that neither the king nor none of his council were ware of their departing. All so soon as King Uther knew of their departing so suddenly, he was wonderly wroth. Then he called to him his privy council, and told them of the sudden departing of the duke and his wife.

Then they advised the king to send for the duke and his wife by a great charge; and if he will not come at your summons, then may ye do your best, then have ye cause to make mighty war upon him. So that was done, and the messengers had their answers; and that was this shortly, that neither he nor his wife would not come at him.

Then was the king wonderly wroth. And then the king sent him plain word again, and bade him be ready and stuff him and garnish him, for within forty days he would fetch him out of the biggest castle that he hath.

When the duke had this warning, anon he went and furnished and garnished two strong castles of his, of the which the one hight Tintagil, and the other castle hight Terrabil. So his wife Dame Igraine he put in the castle of

Tintagil, and himself he put in the castle of Terrabil, the which had many issues and posterns out. Then in all haste came Uther with a great host, and laid a siege about the castle of Terrabil. And there he pight many pavilions, and there was great war made on both parties, and much people slain. Then for pure anger and for great love of fair Igraine the king Uther fell sick. So came to the king Uther Sir Ulfius, a noble knight, and asked the king why he was sick.

"I shall tell thee," said the king, "I am sick for anger and for love of fair Igraine, that I may not be whole."

"Well, my lord," said Sir Ulfius, "I shall seek Merlin, and he shall do you remedy, that your heart shall be pleased."

So Ulfius departed, and by adventure he met Merlin in a beggar's array, and there Merlin asked Ulfius whom he sought. And he said he had little ado to tell him.

"Well," said Merlin, "I know whom thou seekest, for thou seekest Merlin; therefore seek no farther, for I am he; and if King Uther will well reward me, and be sworn unto me to fulfil my desire, that shall be his honour and profit more than mine; for I shall cause him to have all his desire."

"All this will I undertake," said Ulfius, "that there shall be nothing reasonable but thou shalt have thy desire."

"Well," said Merlin, "he shall have his intent and desire. And therefore," said Merlin, "ride on your way, for I will not be long behind."

Chapter II
How Uther Pendragon Made War on the Duke of Cornwall, and How by the Mean of Merlin He Lay by the Duchess and Gat Arthur

THEN ULFIUS WAS GLAD and rode on more than a pace till that he came to King Uther Pendragon, and told him he had met with Merlin.

"Where is he?" said the king.

"Sir," said Ulfius, "he will not dwell long."

Therewithal Ulfius was ware where Merlin stood at the porch of the pavilion's door. And then Merlin was bound to come to the king. When King Uther saw him, he said he was welcome.

"Sir," said Merlin, "I know all your heart every deal; so ye will be sworn unto me as ye be a true king anointed, to fulfil my desire, ye shall have your desire."

Then the king was sworn upon the Four Evangelists.

"Sir," said Merlin, "this is my desire: the first night that ye shall lie by Igraine ye shall get a child on her, and when that is born, that it shall be delivered to me for to nourish there as I will have it; for it shall be your worship, and the child's avail, as mickle as the child is worth."

"I will well," said the king, "as thou wilt have it."

"Now make you ready," said Merlin, "this night ye shall lie with Igraine in the castle of Tintagil; and ye shall be like the duke her husband, Ulfius shall be like Sir Brastias, a knight of the duke's, and I will be like a knight that hight Sir Jordanus, a knight of the duke's. But wait ye make not many questions with her nor her men, but say ye are diseased, and so hie you to bed, and rise not on the morn till I come to you, for the castle of Tintagil is but ten miles hence."

So this was done as they devised. But the duke of Tintagil espied how the king rode from the siege of Terrabil, and therefore that night he issued out of the castle at a postern for to have distressed the king's host. And so, through his own issue, the duke himself was slain or ever the king came at the castle of Tintagil.

So after the death of the duke, King Uther lay with Igraine more than three hours after his death, and begat on her that night Arthur, and on day came Merlin to the king, and bade him make him ready, and so he kissed the lady Igraine and departed in all haste. But when the lady heard tell of the duke her husband, and by all record he was dead or ever King Uther came to her, then she marvelled who that might be that lay with her in likeness of her lord; so she mourned privily and held her peace. Then all the barons by one assent prayed the king of accord betwixt the lady Igraine and him; the king gave them leave, for fain would he have been accorded with her. So the king put all the trust in Ulfius to entreat between them, so by the entreaty at the last the king and she met together.

"Now will we do well," said Ulfius, "our king is a lusty knight and wifeless, and my lady Igraine is a passing fair lady; it were great joy unto us all, an it might please the king to make her his queen."

Unto that they all well accorded and moved it to the king. And anon, like a lusty knight, he assented thereto with good will, and so in all haste they were married in a morning with great mirth and joy.

And King Lot of Lothian and of Orkney then wedded Margawse that was Gawain's mother, and King Nentres of the land of Garlot wedded Elaine. All this was done at the request of King Uther. And the third sister Morgan le Fay was put to school in a nunnery, and there she learned so much that she was a great clerk of necromancy. And after she was wedded to King Uriens of the land of Gore, that was Sir Ewain's le Blanchemain's father.

Chapter III
Of the Birth of King Arthur and of His Nurture

THEN QUEEN IGRAINE **waxed daily greater and greater, so it befell after within half a year, as King Uther lay by his queen, he asked her, by the faith she owed to him, whose was the body; then she sore abashed to give answer.**

"Dismay you not," said the king, "but tell me the truth, and I shall love you the better, by the faith of my body."

"Sir," said she, "I shall tell you the truth. The same night that my lord was dead, the hour of his death, as his knights record, there came into my castle of Tintagil a man like my lord in speech and in countenance, and two knights with him in likeness of his two knights Brastias and Jordanus, and so I went unto bed with him as I ought to do with my lord, and the same night, as I shall answer unto God, this child was begotten upon me."

"That is truth," said the king, "as ye say; for it was I myself that came in the likeness, and therefore dismay you not, for I am father of the child";

and there he told her all the cause, how it was by Merlin's counsel. Then the queen made great joy when she knew who was the father of her child.

Soon came Merlin unto the king, and said, "Sir, ye must purvey you for the nourishing of your child."

"As thou wilt," said the king, "be it."

"Well," said Merlin, "I know a lord of yours in this land, that is a passing true man and a faithful, and he shall have the nourishing of your child, and his name is Sir Ector, and he is a lord of fair livelihood in many parts in England and Wales; and this lord, Sir Ector, let him be sent for, for to come and speak with you, and desire him yourself, as he loveth you, that he will put his own child to nourishing to another woman, and that his wife nourish yours. And when the child is born let it be delivered to me at yonder privy postern unchristened."

So like as Merlin devised it was done. And when Sir Ector was come he made fiaunce to the king for to nourish the child like as the king desired; and there the king granted Sir Ector great rewards. Then when the lady was delivered, the king commanded two knights and two ladies to take the child, bound in a cloth of gold, and that ye deliver him to what poor man ye meet at the postern gate of the castle. So the child was delivered unto Merlin, and so he bare it forth unto Sir Ector, and made an holy man to christen him, and named him Arthur; and so Sir Ector's wife nourished him with her own pap.

Chapter IV
Of the Death of King Uther Pendragon

THEN WITHIN TWO YEARS King Uther fell sick of a great malady. And in the meanwhile his enemies usurped upon him, and did a great battle upon his men, and slew many of his people.

"Sir," said Merlin, "ye may not lie so as ye do, for ye must to the field though ye ride on an horse-litter: for ye shall never have the better of your enemies but if your person be there, and then shall ye have the victory."

So it was done as Merlin had devised, and they carried the king forth in an horse-litter with a great host towards his enemies. And at St. Albans there met with the king a great host of the North. And that day Sir Ulfius and Sir Brastias did great deeds of arms, and King Uther's men overcame the Northern battle and slew many people, and put the remnant to flight. And then the king returned unto London, and made great joy of his victory. And then he fell passing sore sick, so that three days and three nights he was speechless: wherefore all the barons made great sorrow, and asked Merlin what counsel were best.

"There is none other remedy," said Merlin, "but God will have his will. But look ye all barons be before King Uther to-morn, and God and I shall make him to speak."

So on the morn all the barons with Merlin came to-fore the king; then Merlin said aloud unto King Uther, "Sir, shall your son Arthur be king after your days, of this realm with all the appurtenance?"

Then Uther Pendragon turned him, and said in hearing of them all, "I give him God's blessing and mine, and bid him pray for my soul, and righteously and worshipfully that he claim the crown, upon forfeiture of my blessing"; and therewith he yielded up the ghost, and then was he interred as longed to a king. Wherefore the queen, fair Igraine, made great sorrow, and all the barons.

Chapter V
How Arthur Was Chosen King, and of Wonders and Marvels of a Sword Taken out of a Stone by the Said Arthur

THEN STOOD THE REALM in great jeopardy long while, for every lord that was mighty of men made him strong, and many weened to have been king. Then Merlin went to the Archbishop of Canterbury, and counselled him for to send

for all the lords of the realm, and all the gentlemen of arms, that they should to London come by Christmas, upon pain of cursing; and for this cause, that Jesus, that was born on that night, that he would of his great mercy show some miracle, as he was come to be king of mankind, for to show some miracle who should be rightwise king of this realm.

So the Archbishop, by the advice of Merlin, sent for all the lords and gentlemen of arms that they should come by Christmas even unto London. And many of them made them clean of their life, that their prayer might be the more acceptable unto God. So in the greatest church of London, whether it were Paul's or not the French book maketh no mention, all the estates were long or day in the church for to pray. And when matins and the first mass was done, there was seen in the churchyard, against the high altar, a great stone four square, like unto a marble stone; and in midst thereof was like an anvil of steel a foot on high, and therein stuck a fair sword naked by the point, and letters there were written in gold about the sword that said thus:

Whoso pulleth out this sword of this stone and anvil,
is rightwise king born of all England.

Then the people marvelled, and told it to the Archbishop. I command, said the Archbishop, that ye keep you within your church and pray unto God still, that no man touch the sword till the high mass be all done. So when all masses were done all the lords went to behold the stone and the sword. And when they saw the scripture some assayed, such as would have been king. But none might stir the sword nor move it.

"He is not here," said the Archbishop, "that shall achieve the sword, but doubt not God will make him known. But this is my counsel," said the Archbishop, "that we let purvey ten knights, men of good fame, and they to keep this sword."

So it was ordained, and then there was made a cry, that every man should assay that would, for to win the sword. And upon New Year's

Day the barons let make a jousts and a tournament, that all knights that would joust or tourney there might play, and all this was ordained for to keep the lords together and the commons, for the Archbishop trusted that God would make him known that should win the sword.

So upon New Year's Day, when the service was done, the barons rode unto the field, some to joust and some to tourney, and so it happened that Sir Ector, that had great livelihood about London, rode unto the jousts, and with him rode Sir Kay his son, and young Arthur that was his nourished brother; and Sir Kay was made knight at All Hallowmass afore. So as they rode to the jousts-ward, Sir Kay lost his sword, for he had left it at his father's lodging, and so he prayed young Arthur for to ride for his sword.

"I will well," said Arthur, and rode fast after the sword, and when he came home, the lady and all were out to see the jousting. Then was Arthur wroth, and said to himself, "I will ride to the churchyard, and take the sword with me that sticketh in the stone, for my brother Sir Kay shall not be without a sword this day."

So when he came to the churchyard, Sir Arthur alighted and tied his horse to the stile, and so he went to the tent, and found no knights there, for they were at the jousting. And so he handled the sword by the handles, and lightly and fiercely pulled it out of the stone, and took his horse and rode his way until he came to his brother Sir Kay, and delivered him the sword. And as soon as Sir Kay saw the sword, he wist well it was the sword of the stone, and so he rode to his father Sir Ector, and said:

"Sir, lo here is the sword of the stone, wherefore I must be king of this land."

When Sir Ector beheld the sword, he returned again and came to the church, and there they alighted all three, and went into the church. And anon he made Sir Kay swear upon a book how he came to that sword.

"Sir," said Sir Kay, "by my brother Arthur, for he brought it to me."

"How gat ye this sword?" said Sir Ector to Arthur.

"Sir, I will tell you. When I came home for my brother's sword, I found nobody at home to deliver me his sword; and so I thought my brother Sir Kay should not be swordless, and so I came hither eagerly and pulled it out of the stone without any pain."

"Found ye any knights about this sword?" said Sir Ector.

"Nay," said Arthur.

"Now," said Sir Ector to Arthur, "I understand ye must be king of this land."

"Wherefore I," said Arthur, "and for what cause?"

"Sir," said Ector, "for God will have it so; for there should never man have drawn out this sword, but he that shall be rightwise king of this land. Now let me see whether ye can put the sword there as it was, and pull it out again."

"That is no mastery," said Arthur, and so he put it in the stone; wherewithal Sir Ector assayed to pull out the sword and failed.

Chapter VI
How King Arthur Pulled Out the Sword Divers Times

"**N**OW ASSAY," said Sir Ector unto Sir Kay. And anon he pulled at the sword with all his might; but it would not be. "Now shall ye assay," said Sir Ector to Arthur.

"I will well," said Arthur, and pulled it out easily. And therewithal Sir Ector knelt down to the earth, and Sir Kay. "Alas," said Arthur, "my own dear father and brother, why kneel ye to me?"

"Nay, nay, my lord Arthur, it is not so; I was never your father nor of your blood, but I wot well ye are of an higher blood than I weened ye were." And then Sir Ector told him all, how he was betaken him for to nourish him, and by whose commandment, and by Merlin's deliverance.

Then Arthur made great dole when he understood that Sir Ector was not his father.

"Sir," said Ector unto Arthur, "will ye be my good and gracious lord when ye are king?"

"Else were I to blame," said Arthur, "for ye are the man in the world that I am most beholden to, and my good lady and mother your wife, that as well as her own hath fostered me and kept. And if ever it be God's will that I be king as ye say, ye shall desire of me what I may do, and I shall not fail you."

"God forbid I should fail you Sir," said Sir Ector, "I will ask no more of you, but that ye will make my son, your foster brother, Sir Kay, seneschal of all your lands."

"That shall be done," said Arthur, "and more, by the faith of my body, that never man shall have that office but he, while he and I live."

Therewithal they went unto the Archbishop, and told him how the sword was achieved, and by whom; and on Twelfth-day all the barons came thither, and to assay to take the sword, who that would assay. But there afore them all, there might none take it out but Arthur; wherefore there were many lords wroth, and said it was great shame unto them all and the realm, to be overgoverned with a boy of no high blood born. And so they fell out at that time that it was put off till Candlemas and then all the barons should meet there again; but always the ten knights were ordained to watch the sword day and night, and so they set a pavilion over the stone and the sword, and five always watched. So at Candlemas many more great lords came thither for to have won the sword, but there might none prevail.

And right as Arthur did at Christmas, he did at Candlemas, and pulled out the sword easily, whereof the barons were sore aggrieved and put it off in delay till the high feast of Easter. And as Arthur sped before, so did he at Easter; yet there were some of the great lords had indignation that Arthur should be king, and put it off in a delay till the feast of Pentecost.

Then the Archbishop of Canterbury by Merlin's providence let purvey then of the best knights that they might get, and such knights as Uther Pendragon loved best and most trusted in his days. And such knights were put about Arthur as Sir Baudwin of Britain, Sir Kay, Sir Ulfius, Sir Brastias. All these, with many other, were always about Arthur, day and night, till the feast of Pentecost.

Chapter VII
How King Arthur Held in Wales, at a Pentecost, a Great Feast, and What Kings and Lords Came to His Feast

THEN THE KING removed into Wales, and let cry a great feast that it should be holden at Pentecost after the incoronation of him at the city of Carlion. Unto the feast came King Lot of Lothian and of Orkney, with five hundred knights with him. Also there came to the feast King Uriens of Gore with four hundred knights with him.

Also there came to that feast King Nentres of Garlot, with seven hundred knights with him. Also there came to the feast the king of Scotland with six hundred knights with him, and he was but a young man. Also there came to the feast a king that was called the King with the Hundred Knights, but he and his men were passing well beseen at all points. Also there came the king of Carados with five hundred knights.

And King Arthur was glad of their coming, for he weened that all the kings and knights had come for great love, and to have done him worship at his feast; wherefore the king made great joy, and sent the kings and knights great presents. But the kings would none receive, but rebuked the messengers shamefully, and said they had no joy to receive no gifts of a beardless boy that was come of low blood, and sent him word they would none of his gifts, but that they were come to give him gifts with hard swords betwixt the neck and the shoulders: and therefore they came thither, so they told to the messengers plainly, for it was great shame to all them to see such a boy to have a rule of so noble a realm as this land was.

With this answer the messengers departed and told to King Arthur this answer. Wherefore, by the advice of his barons, he took him to a strong tower with five hundred good men with him. And all the kings aforesaid in a manner laid a siege to-fore him, but King Arthur was well victualed. And within fifteen days there came Merlin among them into the city of Carlion. Then all the kings were passing glad of Merlin, and asked him, "For what cause is that boy Arthur made your king?"

"Sirs," said Merlin, "I shall tell you the cause, for he is King Uther Pendragon's son, born in wedlock, gotten on Igraine, the duke's wife of Tintagil."

"Then is he a bastard," they said all.

"Nay," said Merlin, "after the death of the duke, more than three hours, was Arthur begotten, and thirteen days after King Uther wedded Igraine; and therefore I prove him he is no bastard. And who saith nay, he shall be king and overcome all his enemies; and, or he die, he shall be long king of all England, and have under his obeissance Wales, Ireland, and Scotland, and more realms than I will now rehearse."

Some of the kings had marvel of Merlin's words, and deemed well that it should be as he said; and some of them laughed him to scorn, as King Lot; and more other called him a witch. But then were they accorded with Merlin, that King Arthur should come out and speak with the kings, and to come safe and to go safe, such surance there was made.

So Merlin went unto King Arthur, and told him how he had done, and bade him fear not, but come out boldly and speak with them, and spare them not, but answer them as their king and chieftain; for ye shall overcome them all, whether they will or nill.

Chapter IX
Of the First War that King Arthur Had, and How He Won the Field

THEN KING ARTHUR came out of his tower, and had under his gown a jesseraunt of double mail, and there went with him the Archbishop of Canterbury, and Sir Baudwin of Britain, and Sir Kay, and Sir Brastias: these were the men of most

worship that were with him. And when they were met there was no meekness, but stout words on both sides; but always King Arthur answered them, and said he would make them to bow an he lived. Wherefore they departed with wrath, and King Arthur bade keep them well, and they bade the king keep him well. So the king returned him to the tower again and armed him and all his knights.

"What will ye do?" said Merlin to the kings; ye were better for to stint, for ye shall not here prevail though ye were ten times so many. "Be we well advised to be afeared of a dream-reader?" said King Lot. With that Merlin vanished away, and came to King Arthur, and bade him set on them fiercely; and in the meanwhile there were three hundred good men, of the best that were with the kings, that went straight unto King Arthur, and that comforted him greatly. "Sir," said Merlin to Arthur, "fight not with the sword that ye had by miracle, till that ye see ye go unto the worse, then draw it out and do your best."

So forthwithal King Arthur set upon them in their lodging. And Sir Baudwin, Sir Kay, and Sir Brastias slew on the right hand and on the left hand that it was marvel; and always King Arthur on horseback laid on with a sword, and did marvellous deeds of arms, that many of the kings had great joy of his deeds and hardiness.

Then King Lot brake out on the back side, and the King with the Hundred Knights, and King Carados, and set on Arthur fiercely behind him. With that Sir Arthur turned with his knights, and smote behind and before, and ever Sir Arthur was in the foremost press till his horse was slain underneath him. And therewith King Lot smote down King Arthur. With that his four knights received him and set him on horseback. Then he drew his sword Excalibur, but it was so bright in his enemies' eyes, that it gave light like thirty torches. And therewith he put them a-back, and slew much people. And then the commons of Carlion arose with clubs and staves and slew many knights; but all the kings held them together with their knights that were left alive, and so fled and departed. And Merlin came unto Arthur, and counselled him to follow them no further.

Chapter X

How Merlin Counselled King Arthur to Send for King Ban and King Bors, and of their Counsel Taken for the War

SO AFTER THE FEAST and journey, King Arthur drew him unto London, and so by the counsel of Merlin, the king let call his barons to council, for Merlin had told the king that the six kings that made war upon him would in all haste be awroke on him and on his lands. Wherefore the king asked counsel at them all. They could no counsel give, but said they were big enough.

"Ye say well," said Arthur; "I thank you for your good courage, but will ye all that loveth me speak with Merlin? Ye know well that he hath done much for me, and he knoweth many things, and when he is afore you, I would that ye prayed him heartily of his best advice."

All the barons said they would pray him and desire him. So Merlin was sent for, and fair desired of all the barons to give them best counsel.

"I shall say you," said Merlin, "I warn you all, your enemies are passing strong for you, and they are good men of arms as be alive, and by this time they have gotten to them four kings more, and a mighty duke; and unless that our king have more chivalry with him than he may make within the bounds of his own realm, an he fight with them in battle, he shall be overcome and slain."

"What were best to do in this cause?" said all the barons.

"I shall tell you," said Merlin, "mine advice; there are two brethren beyond the sea, and they be kings both, and marvellous good men of their hands; and that one hight King Ban of Benwick, and that other hight King Bors of Gaul, that is France. And on these two kings warreth a mighty man of men, the King Claudas, and striveth with them for a castle, and great war is betwixt them. But this Claudas is so mighty of goods whereof he getteth good knights, that he putteth these two kings most part to the worse; wherefore this is my counsel, that our king and sovereign lord send unto the kings Ban and Bors by two trusty knights with letters well devised, that an they will come and see King Arthur and his court, and so help him in his wars, that he will be sworn unto them to help them in their wars against King Claudas. Now, what say ye unto this counsel?" said Merlin.

"This is well counselled," said the king and all the barons.

Right so in all haste there were ordained to go two knights on the message unto the two kings. So were there made letters in the pleasant wise according unto King Arthur's desire. Ulfius and Brastias were made the messengers, and so rode forth well horsed and well armed and as the guise was that time, and so passed the sea and rode toward the city of Benwick. And there besides were eight knights that espied them, and at a strait passage they met with Ulfius and Brastias, and would have taken them prisoners; so they prayed them that they might pass, for they were messengers unto King Ban and Bors sent from King Arthur.

"Therefore," said the eight knights, "ye shall die or be prisoners, for we be knights of King Claudas."

And therewith two of them dressed their spears, and Ulfius and Brastias dressed their spears, and ran together with great raundom. And Claudas' knights brake their spears, and theirs to-held and bare the two knights out of their saddles to the earth, and so left them lying, and rode their ways. And the other six knights rode afore to a passage to meet with them again, and so Ulfius and Brastias smote other two down, and so passed on their ways. And at the fourth passage there met two for two, and both were laid unto the earth; so there was none of the eight knights but he was sore hurt or bruised. And when they come to Benwick it fortuned there were both kings, Ban and Bors.

And when it was told the kings that there were come messengers, there were sent unto them two knights of worship, the one hight Lionses, lord of the country of Payarne, and Sir Phariance a worshipful knight. Anon they asked from whence they came, and they said from King Arthur, king of England; so they took them in their arms and made great joy each of other. But anon, as the two kings wist they were messengers of Arthur's, there was made no tarrying, but forthwith they spake with the knights, and welcomed them in the faithfullest wise, and said they were most welcome unto them before all the kings living; and therewith they kissed the letters and delivered them. And when Ban and Bors understood the letters, then they were more welcome than they were before. And after the haste of the letters they gave them this answer, that they would fulfil the desire of King Arthur's writing, and Ulfius and Brastias, tarry there as long as they would, they should have such cheer as might be made them in those marches. Then Ulfius and Brastias told the kings of the adventure at their passages of the eight knights.

"Ha! Ah!" said Ban and Bors, "They were my good friends. I would I had wist of them; they should not have escaped so."

So Ulfius and Brastias had good cheer and great gifts, as much as they might bear away; and had their answer by mouth and by writing, that those two kings would come unto Arthur in all the haste that they might. So the two knights rode on afore, and passed the sea, and came to their lord, and told him how they had sped, whereof King Arthur was passing glad.

"At what time suppose ye the two kings will be here?"

"Sir," said they, "afore All Hallowmass."

Then the king let purvey for a great feast, and let cry a great jousts. And by All Hallowmass the two kings were come over the sea with three hundred knights well arrayed both for the peace and for the war. And King Arthur met with them ten mile out of London, and there was great joy as could be thought or made. And on All Hallowmass at the great feast, sat in the hall the three kings, and Sir Kay seneschal served in the hall, and Sir Lucas the butler, that was Duke Corneus' son, and Sir Griflet, that was the son of Cardol, these three knights had the rule of all the service that served the kings. And anon, as they had washen and risen, all knights that would joust made them ready; by then they were ready on horseback there were seven hundred knights. And Arthur, Ban, and Bors, with the Archbishop of Canterbury, and Sir Ector, Kay's father, they were in a place covered with cloth of gold like an hall, with ladies and gentlewomen, for to behold who did best, and thereon to give judgment.

Chapter XI

Of a Great Tourney Made by King Arthur and the Two Kings Ban and Bors, and How They Went Over the Sea

AND KING ARTHUR and the two kings let depart the seven hundred knights in two parties. And there were three hundred knights of the realm of Benwick and of Gaul turned on the other side. Then they dressed their shields, and began to couch their spears many good knights.

So Griflet was the first that met with a knight, one Ladinas, and they met so eagerly that all men had wonder; and they so fought that their shields fell to pieces, and horse and man fell to the earth; and both the French knight and the English knight lay so long that all men weened they had been dead.

When Lucas the butler saw Griflet so lie, he horsed him again anon, and they two did marvellous deeds of arms with many bachelors. Also Sir Kay came out of an ambushment with five knights with him, and they six smote other six down. But Sir Kay did that day marvellous deeds of arms, that there was none did so well as he that day. Then there came Ladinas and Gracian, two knights of France, and did passing well, that all men praised them.

Then came there Sir Placidas, a good knight, and met with Sir Kay, and smote him down horse and man, where fore Sir Griflet was wroth, and met with Sir Placidas so hard, that horse and man fell to the earth. But when the five knights wist that Sir Kay had a fall, they were wroth out of wit, and therewith each of them five bare down a knight.

When King Arthur and the two kings saw them begin to wax wroth on both parties, they leapt on small hackneys, and let cry that all men should depart unto their lodging. And so they went home and unarmed them, and so to evensong and supper. And after, the three kings went into a garden, and gave the prize unto Sir Kay, and to Lucas the butler, and unto Sir Griflet. And then they went unto council, and with them

Gwenbaus, the brother unto Sir Ban and Bors, a wise clerk, and thither went Ulfius and Brastias, and Merlin. And after they had been in council, they went unto bed. And on the morn they heard mass, and to dinner, and so to their council, and made many arguments what were best to do. At the last they were concluded, that Merlin should go with a token of King Ban, and that was a ring, unto his men and King Bors'; and Gracian and Placidas should go again and keep their castles and their countries, as for [dread of King Claudas] King Ban of Benwick, and King Bors of Gaul had ordained them, and so passed the sea and came to Benwick.

And when the people saw King Ban's ring, and Gracian and Placidas, they were glad, and asked how the kings fared, and made great joy of their welfare and cording, and according unto the sovereign lords desire, the men of war made them ready in all haste possible, so that they were fifteen thousand on horse and foot, and they had great plenty of victual with them, by Merlin's provision.

But Gracian and Placidas were left to furnish and garnish the castles, for dread of King Claudas. Right so Merlin passed the sea, well victualled both by water and by land. And when he came to the sea he sent home the footmen again, and took no more with him but ten thousand men on horseback, the most part men of arms, and so shipped and passed the sea into England, and landed at Dover; and through the wit of Merlin, he had the host northward, the priviest way that could be thought, unto the forest of Bedegraine, and there in a valley he lodged them secretly.

Then rode Merlin unto Arthur and the two kings, and told them how he had sped; whereof they had great marvel, that man on earth might speed so soon, and go and come. So Merlin told them ten thousand were in the forest of Bedegraine, well armed at all points. Then was there no more to say, but to horseback went all the host as Arthur had afore purveyed. So with twenty thousand he passed by night and day, but there was made such an ordinance afore by Merlin, that there should no man of war ride nor go in no country on this side Trent water, but if he had a token from King Arthur, where through the king's enemies durst not ride as they did to-fore to espy.

Chapter XII
How Eleven Kings Gathered a Great Host Against King Arthur

AND SO within a little space the three kings came unto the castle of Bedegraine, and found there a passing fair fellowship, and well beseen, whereof they had great joy, and victual they wanted none. This was the cause of the northern host: that they were reared for the despite and rebuke the six kings had at Carlion. And those six kings by their means, gat unto them five other kings; and thus they began to gather their people.

And now they sware that for weal nor woe, they should not leave other, till they had destroyed Arthur. And then they made an oath. The first that began the oath was the Duke of Cambenet, that he would bring with him five thousand men of arms, the which were ready on horseback.

Then sware King Brandegoris of Stranggore that he would bring five thousand men of arms on horseback.

Then sware King Clariance of Northumberland he would bring three thousand men of arms.

Then sware the King of the Hundred Knights, that was a passing good man and a young, that he would bring four thousand men of arms on horseback.

Then there swore King Lot, a passing good knight, and Sir Gawain's father, that he would bring five thousand men of arms on horseback.

Also there swore King Urience, that was Sir Uwain's father, of the land of Gore, and he would bring six thousand men of arms on horseback.

Also there swore King Idres of Cornwall, that he would bring five thousand men of arms on horseback.

Also there swore King Cradelmas to bring five thousand men on horseback.

Also there swore King Agwisance of Ireland to bring five thousand men of arms on horseback.

Also there swore King Nentres to bring five thousand men of arms on horseback.

Also there swore King Carados to bring five thousand men of arms on horseback.

So their whole host was of clean men of arms on horseback fifty thousand, and a-foot ten thousand of good men's bodies. Then were they soon ready, and mounted upon horse and sent forth their fore-riders, for these eleven kings in their ways laid a siege unto the castle of Bedegraine; and so they departed and drew toward Arthur, and left few to abide at the siege, for the castle of Bedegraine was holden of King Arthur, and the men that were therein were Arthur's.

Chapter XIII
Of a Dream of the King with the Hundred Knights

SO BY MERLIN'S ADVICE there were sent fore-riders to skim the country, and they met with the fore-riders of the north, and made them to tell which way the host came, and then they told it to Arthur, and by King Ban and Bors' council they let burn and destroy all the country afore them, there they should ride.

The King with the Hundred Knights met a wonder dream two nights afore the battle, that there blew a great wind, and blew down their castles and their towns, and after that came a water and bare it all away. All that heard of the sweven said it was a token of great battle.

Then by counsel of Merlin, when they wist which way the eleven kings would ride and lodge that night, at midnight they set upon them, as they were in their pavilions. But the scout-watch by their host cried, "Lords! At arms! For here be your enemies at your hand!

Chapter XIV

How the Eleven Kings with Their Host Fought Against Arthur and His Host, and Many Great Feats of the War

THEN KING ARTHUR and King Ban and King Bors, with their good and trusty knights, set on them so fiercely that they made them overthrow their pavilions on their heads, but the eleven kings, by manly prowess of arms, took a fair champaign, but there was slain that morrowtide ten thousand good men's bodies. And so they had afore them a strong passage, yet were they fifty thousand of hardy men. Then it drew toward day.

"Now shall ye do by mine advice," said Merlin unto the three kings: "I would that King Ban and King Bors, with their fellowship of ten thousand men, were put in a wood here beside, in an ambushment, and keep them privy, and that they be laid or the light of the day come, and that they stir not till ye and your knights have fought with them long. And when it is daylight, dress your battle even afore them and the passage, that they may see all your host, for then will they be the more hardy, when they see you but about twenty thousand men, and cause them to be the gladder to suffer you and your host to come over the passage."

All the three kings and the whole barons said that Merlin said passingly well, and it was done anon as Merlin had devised. So on the morn, when either host saw other, the host of the north was well comforted. Then to Ulfius and Brastias were delivered three thousand men of arms, and they set on them fiercely in the passage, and slew on the right hand and on the left hand that it was wonder to tell.

When that the eleven kings saw that there was so few a fellowship did such deeds of arms, they were ashamed and set on them again fiercely; and there was Sir Ulfius's horse slain under him, but he did marvellously well on foot. But the Duke Eustace of Cambenet and King Clariance of Northumberland, were always grievous on Ulfius. Then

Brastias saw his fellow fared so withal he smote the duke with a spear, that horse and man fell down. That saw King Clariance and returned unto Brastias, and either smote other so that horse and man went to the earth, and so they lay long astonied, and their horses' knees brast to the hard bone. Then came Sir Kay the seneschal with six fellows with him, and did passing well. With that came the eleven kings, and there was Griflet put to the earth, horse and man, and Lucas the butler, horse and man, by King Brandegoris, and King Idres, and King Agwisance. Then waxed the medley passing hard on both parties.

When Sir Kay saw Griflet on foot, he rode on King Nentres and smote him down, and led his horse unto Sir Griflet, and horsed him again. Also Sir Kay with the same spear smote down King Lot, and hurt him passing sore. That saw the King with the Hundred Knights, and ran unto Sir Kay and smote him down, and took his horse, and gave him King Lot, whereof he said gramercy.

When Sir Griflet saw Sir Kay and Lucas the butler on foot, he took a sharp spear, great and square, and rode to Pinel, a good man of arms, and smote horse and man down, and then he took his horse, and gave him unto Sir Kay. Then King Lot saw King Nentres on foot, he ran unto Melot de la Roche, and smote him down, horse and man, and gave King Nentres the horse, and horsed him again. Also the King of the Hundred Knights saw King Idres on foot; then he ran unto Gwiniart de Bloi, and smote him down, horse and man, and gave King Idres the horse, and horsed him again; and King Lot smote down Clariance de la Forest Savage, and gave the horse unto Duke Eustace. And so when they had horsed the kings again they drew them, all eleven kings, together, and said they would be revenged of the damage that they had taken that day. The meanwhile came in Sir Ector with an eager countenance, and found Ulfius and Brastias on foot, in great peril of death, that were foul defoiled under horse-feet.

Then Arthur as a lion, ran unto King Cradelment of North Wales, and smote him through the left side, that the horse and the king fell down; and then he took the horse by the rein, and led him unto Ulfius, and said, "Have this horse, mine old friend, for great need hast thou of horse."

"Gramercy," said Ulfius.

Then Sir Arthur did so marvellously in arms, that all men had wonder. When the King with the Hundred Knights saw King Cradelment on foot, he ran unto Sir Ector, that was well horsed, Sir Kay's father, and smote horse and man down, and gave the horse unto the king, and horsed him again. And when King Arthur saw the king ride on Sir Ector's horse, he was wroth and with his sword he smote the king on the helm, that a quarter of the helm and shield fell down, and so the sword carved down unto the horse's neck, and so the king and the horse fell down to the ground. Then Sir Kay came unto Sir Morganore, seneschal with the King of the Hundred Knights, and smote him down, horse and man, and led the horse unto his father, Sir Ector; then Sir Ector ran unto a knight, hight Lardans, and smote horse and man down, and led the horse unto Sir Brastias, that great need had of an horse, and was greatly defoiled. When Brastias beheld Lucas the butler, that lay like a dead man under the horses' feet, and ever Sir Griflet did marvellously for to rescue him, and there were always fourteen knights on Sir Lucas; then Brastias smote one of them on the helm, that it went to the teeth, and he rode to another and smote him, that the arm flew into the field. Then he went to the third and smote him on the shoulder, that shoulder and arm flew in the field. And when Griflet saw rescues, he smote a knight on the temples, that head and helm went to the earth, and Griflet took the horse of that knight, and led him unto Sir Lucas, and bade him mount upon the horse and revenge his hurts. For Brastias had slain a knight to-fore and horsed Griflet.

Chapter XV
Yet of the Same Battle

THEN LUCAS SAW King Agwisance, that late had slain Moris de la Roche, and Lucas ran to him with a short spear that was great, that he gave him such a fall, that the horse fell down to the earth. Also Lucas found there on foot, Bloias de La Flandres,

and Sir Gwinas, two hardy knights, and in that woodness that Lucas was in, he slew two bachelors and horsed them again. Then waxed the battle passing hard on both parties, but Arthur was glad that his knights were horsed again, and then they fought together, that the noise and sound rang by the water and the wood. Wherefore King Ban and King Bors made them ready, and dressed their shields and harness, and they were so courageous that many knights shook and bevered for eagerness.

All this while Lucas, and Gwinas, and Briant, and Bellias of Flanders, held strong medley against six kings, that was King Lot, King Nentres, King Brandegoris, King Idres, King Uriens, and King Agwisance. So with the help of Sir Kay and of Sir Griflet they held these six kings hard, that unnethe they had any power to defend them. But when Sir Arthur saw the battle would not be ended by no manner, he fared wood as a lion, and steered his horse here and there, on the right hand, and on the left hand, that he stinted not till he had slain twenty knights. Also he wounded King Lot sore on the shoulder, and made him to leave that ground, for Sir Kay and Griflet did with King Arthur there great deeds of arms. Then Ulfius, and Brastias, and Sir Ector encountered against the Duke Eustace, and King Cradelment, and King Clariance of Northumberland, and King Carados, and against the King with the Hundred Knights. So these knights encountered with these kings, that they made them to avoid the ground.

Then King Lot made great dole for his damages and his fellows, and said unto the ten kings, "But if ye will do as I devise we shall be slain and destroyed; let me have the King with the Hundred Knights, and King Agwisance, and King Idres, and the Duke of Cambenet, and we five kings will have fifteen thousand men of arms with us, and we will go apart while ye six kings hold medley with twelve thousand; an we see that ye have foughten with them long, then will we come on fiercely, and else shall we never match them, said King Lot, but by this mean."

So they departed as they here devised, and six kings made their party strong against Arthur, and made great war long.

In the meanwhile brake the ambushment of King Ban and King Bors, and Lionses and Phariance had the vanguard, and they two knights met with King Idres and his fellowship, and there began a great medley of breaking of spears, and smiting of swords, with slaying of men and horses, and King Idres was near at discomfiture.

That saw Agwisance the king, and put Lionses and Phariance in point of death; for the Duke of Cambenet came on withal with a great fellowship. So these two knights were in great danger of their lives that they were fain to return, but always they rescued themselves and their fellowship marvellously When King Bors saw those knights put aback, it grieved him sore; then he came on so fast that his fellowship seemed as black as Inde.

When King Lot had espied King Bors, he knew him well, then he said, "O Jesu, defend us from death and horrible maims! For I see well we be in great peril of death; for I see yonder a king, one of the most worshipfullest men and one of the best knights of the world, is inclined unto his fellowship."

"What is he?" said the King with the Hundred Knights.

"It is," said King Lot, "King Bors of Gaul; I marvel how they came into this country without witting of us all."

"It was by Merlin's advice," said the knight.

"As for him," said King Carados, "I will encounter with King Bors, an ye will rescue me when myster is."

"Go on," said they all, "we will do all that we may."

Then King Carados and his host rode on a soft pace, till that they came as nigh King Bors as bow-draught; then either battle let their horse run as fast as they might. And Bleoberis, that was godson unto King Bors, he bare his chief standard, that was a passing good knight. Now shall we see, said King Bors, how these northern Britons can bear the arms: and King Bors encountered with a knight, and smote him throughout with a spear that he fell dead unto the earth; and after drew his sword and did marvellous deeds of arms, that all parties had great wonder thereof; and his knights failed not, but did their part, and King Carados was smitten to the earth. With that came the King with the Hundred Knights and rescued King Carados mightily by force of arms, for he was a passing good knight of a king, and but a young man.

Chapter XVI
Yet More of the Same Battle

B Y THEN CAME into the field King Ban as fierce as a lion, with bands of green and thereupon gold.

"Ha! A!" said King Lot, "we must be discomfited, for yonder I see the most valiant knight of the world, and the man of the most renown, for such two brethren as is King Ban and King Bors are not living, wherefore we must needs void or die; and but if we avoid manly and wisely there is but death."

When King Ban came into the battle, he came in so fiercely that the strokes redounded again from the wood and the water; wherefore King Lot wept for pity and dole that he saw so many good knights take their end. But through the great force of King Ban they made both the northern battles that were departed hurtled together for great dread; and the three kings and their knights slew on ever, that it was pity on to behold that multitude of the people that fled. But King Lot, and King of the Hundred Knights, and King Morganore gathered the people together passing knightly, and did great prowess of arms, and held the battle all that day, like hard.

When the King of the Hundred Knights beheld the great damage that King Ban did, he thrust unto him with his horse, and smote him on high upon the helm, a great stroke, and astonied him sore. Then King Ban was wroth with him, and followed on him fiercely; the other saw that, and cast up his shield, and spurred his horse forward, but the stroke of King Ban fell down and carved a cantel off the shield, and the sword slid down by the hauberk behind his back, and cut through the trapping of steel and the horse even in two pieces, that the sword felt the earth. Then the King of the Hundred Knights voided the horse lightly, and with his sword he broached the horse of King Ban through and through. With that King Ban voided lightly from the dead horse, and then King Ban smote at the other so eagerly, and smote him on the helm that he fell to the earth.

Also in that ire he felled King Morganore, and there was great slaughter of good knights and much people. By then came into the press King Arthur, and found King Ban standing among dead men and dead horses, fighting on foot as a wood lion, that there came none nigh him, as far as he might reach with his sword, but he caught a grievous buffet; whereof King Arthur had great pity. And Arthur was so bloody, that by his shield there might no man know him, for all was blood and brains on his sword. And as Arthur looked by him he saw a knight that was passingly well horsed, and therewith Sir Arthur ran to him, and smote him on the helm, that his sword went unto his teeth, and the knight sank down to the earth dead, and anon Arthur took the horse by the rein, and led him unto King Ban, and said, "Fair brother, have this horse, for he have great myster thereof, and me repenteth sore of your great damage."

"It shall be soon revenged," said King Ban, "for I trust in God mine ure is not such but some of them may sore repent this."

"I will well," said Arthur, "for I see your deeds full actual; nevertheless, I might not come at you at that time."

But when King Ban was mounted on horseback, then there began new battle, the which was sore and hard, and passing great slaughter. And so through great force King Arthur, King Ban, and King Bors made their knights a little to withdraw them. But always the eleven kings with their chivalry never turned back; and so withdrew them to a little wood, and so over a little river, and there they rested them, for on the night they might have no rest on the field. And then the eleven kings and knights put them on a heap all together, as men adread and out of all comfort. But there was no man might pass them, they held them so hard together both behind and before, that King Arthur had marvel of their deeds of arms, and was passing wroth.

"Ah, Sir Arthur," said King Ban and King Bors, "blame them not, for they do as good men ought to do."

"For by my faith," said King Ban, "they are the best fighting men, and knights of most prowess, that ever I saw or heard speak of, and those eleven kings are men of great worship; and if they were longing unto you there were no king under the heaven had such eleven knights, and of such worship."

"I may not love them," said Arthur, "they would destroy me."

"That wot we well," said King Ban and King Bors, "for they are your mortal enemies, and that hath been proved aforehand; and this day they have done their part, and that is great pity of their wilfulness."

Then all the eleven kings drew them together, and then said King Lot, "Lords, ye must other ways than ye do, or else the great loss is behind; ye may see what people we have lost, and what good men we lose, because we wait always on these foot-men, and ever in saving of one of the foot-men we lose ten horsemen for him; therefore this is mine advice, let us put our footmen from us, for it is near night, for the noble Arthur will not tarry on the footmen, for they may save themselves, the wood is near hand. And when we horsemen be together, look every each of you kings let make such ordinance that none break upon pain of death. And who that seeth any man dress him to flee, lightly that he be slain, for it is better that we slay a coward, than through a coward all we to be slain."

"How say ye?" said King Lot, "Answer me all ye kings."

"It is well said," quoth King Nentres; so said the King of the Hundred Knights; the same said the King Carados, and King Uriens; so did King Idres and King Brandegoris; and so did King Cradelment, and the Duke of Cambenet; the same said King Clariance and King Agwisance, and sware they would never fail other, neither for life nor for death. And whoso that fled, but did as they did, should be slain. Then they amended their harness, and righted their shields, and took new spears and set them on their thighs, and stood still as it had been a plump of wood.

Chapter XVII
Yet More of the Same Battle, and How it Was Ended by Merlin

WHEN SIR ARTHUR and King Ban and Bors beheld them and all their knights, they praised them much for their noble cheer of chivalry, for the hardiest fighters that ever they heard or saw. With that, there dressed them a forty noble knights, and said unto the three kings, they would break their battle; these were their names: Lionses, Phariance, Ulfius, Brastias, Ector,

Kay, Lucas the butler, Griflet le Fise de Dieu, Mariet de la Roche, Guinas de Bloi, Briant de la Forest Savage, Bellaus, Morians of the Castle [of] Maidens, Flannedrius of the Castle of Ladies, Annecians that was King Bors' godson, a noble knight, Ladinas de la Rouse, Emerause, Caulas, Graciens le Castlein, one Blois de la Case, and Sir Colgrevaunce de Gorre; all these knights rode on afore with spears on their thighs, and spurred their horses mightily as the horses might run. And the eleven kings with part of their knights rushed with their horses as fast as they might with their spears, and there they did on both parties marvellous deeds of arms. So came into the thick of the press, Arthur, Ban, and Bors, and slew down right on both hands, that their horses went in blood up to the fetlocks. But ever the eleven kings and their host was ever in the visage of Arthur. Wherefore Ban and Bors had great marvel, considering the great slaughter that there was, but at the last they were driven aback over a little river.

With that came Merlin on a great black horse, and said unto Arthur, "Thou hast never done! Hast thou not done enough? Of three score thousand this day hast thou left alive but fifteen thousand, and it is time to say Ho! For God is wroth with thee, that thou wilt never have done; for yonder eleven kings at this time will not be overthrown, but an thou tarry on them any longer, thy fortune will turn and they shall increase. And therefore withdraw you unto your lodging, and rest you as soon as ye may, and reward your good knights with gold and with silver, for they have well deserved it; there may no riches be too dear for them, for of so few men as ye have, there were never men did more of prowess than they have done today, for ye have matched this day with the best fighters of the world."

"That is truth," said King Ban and Bors.

"Also," said Merlin, "withdraw you where ye list, for this three year I dare undertake they shall not dere you; and by then ye shall hear new tidings." And then Merlin said unto Arthur, "These eleven kings have more on hand than they are ware of, for the Saracens are landed in their countries, more than forty thousand, that burn and slay, and have laid siege at the castle Wandesborow, and make great destruction; therefore dread you not this three year. Also, sir, all the goods that be gotten at this battle, let it be searched, and when ye have it in your hands, let it be given freely unto these two kings, Ban and Bors, that they may reward their knights withal; and that shall cause strangers to be of better will to do you service at need. Also you be able to reward your own knights of your own goods whensomever it liketh you."

"It is well said," quoth Arthur, "and as thou hast devised, so shall it be done."

When it was delivered to Ban and Bors, they gave the goods as freely to their knights as freely as it was given to them. Then Merlin took his leave of Arthur and of the two kings, for to go and see his master Bleise, that dwelt in Northumberland; and so he departed and came to his master, that was passing glad of his coming; and there he told how Arthur and the two kings had sped at the great battle, and how it was ended, and told the names of every king and knight of worship that was there. And so Bleise wrote the battle word by word, as Merlin told him, how it began, and by whom, and in likewise how it was ended, and who had the worse. All the battles that were done in Arthur's days Merlin did his master Bleise do write; also he did do write all the battles that every worthy knight did of Arthur's court.

After this Merlin departed from his master and came to King Arthur, that was in the castle of Bedegraine, that was one of the castles that stand in the forest of Sherwood. And Merlin was so disguised that King Arthur knew him not, for he was all befurred in black sheep-skins, and a great pair of boots, and a bow and arrows, in a russet gown, and brought wild geese in his hand, and it was on the morn after Candlemas day; but King Arthur knew him not.

"Sir," said Merlin unto the king, "will ye give me a gift?"

"Wherefore," said King Arthur, "should I give thee a gift, churl?"

"Sir," said Merlin, "ye were better to give me a gift that is not in your hand than to lose great riches, for here in the same place where the great battle was, is great treasure hid in the earth."

"Who told thee so, churl?" said Arthur.

"Merlin told me so," said he.

Then Ulfius and Brastias knew him well enough, and smiled. "Sir," said these two knights, "it is Merlin that so speaketh unto you."

Then King Arthur was greatly abashed, and had marvel of Merlin, and so had King Ban and King Bors, and so they had great disport at him. So in the meanwhile there came a damosel that was an earl's daughter: his name was

Sanam, and her name was Lionors, a passing fair damosel; and so she came thither for to do homage, as other lords did after the great battle. And King Arthur set his love greatly upon her, and so did she upon him, and the king had ado with her, and gat on her a child: his name was Borre, that was after a good knight, and of the Table Round. Then there came word that the King Rience of North Wales made great war on King Leodegrance of Cameliard, for the which thing Arthur was wroth, for he loved him well, and hated King Rience, for he was always against him. So by ordinance of the three kings that were sent home unto Benwick, all they would depart for dread of King Claudas; and Phariance, and Antemes, and Gratian, and Lionses [of] Payarne, with the leaders of those that should keep the kings' lands.

Chapter XVIII
How King Arthur, King Ban, and King Bors Rescued King Leodegrance, and Other Incidents

AND THEN KING ARTHUR, and King Ban, and King Bors departed with their fellowship, a twenty thousand, and came within six days into the country of Cameliard, and there rescued King Leodegrance, and slew there much people of King Rience, unto the number of ten thousand men, and put him to flight. And then had these three kings great cheer of King Leodegrance, that thanked them of their great goodness, that they would revenge him of his enemies; and there had Arthur the first sight of Guenever, the king's daughter of Cameliard, and ever after he loved her. After they were wedded, as it telleth in the book. So, briefly to make an end, they took their leave to go into their own countries, for King Claudas did great destruction on their lands.

"Then," said Arthur, "I will go with you."

"Nay," said the kings, "ye shall not at this time, for ye have much to do yet in these lands, therefore we will depart, and with the great goods that we have gotten in these lands by your gifts, we shall wage good knights and withstand the King Claudas' malice, for by the grace of God, an we have need we will send to you for your succour; and if ye have need, send for us, and we will not tarry, by the faith of our bodies."

"It shall not," said Merlin, "need that these two kings come again in the way of war, but I know well King Arthur may not be long from you, for within a year or two ye shall have great need, and then shall he revenge you on your enemies, as ye have done on his. For these eleven kings shall die all in a day, by the great might and prowess of arms of two valiant knights (as it telleth after); their names be Balin le Savage, and Balan, his brother, that be marvellous good knights as be any living."

Now turn we to the eleven kings that returned unto a city that hight Sorhaute, the which city was within King Uriens', and there they refreshed them as well as they might, and made leeches search their wounds, and sorrowed greatly for the death of their people. With that there came a messenger and told how there was come into their lands people that were lawless as well as Saracens, a forty thousand, and have burnt and slain all the people that they may come by, without mercy, and have laid siege on the castle of Wandesborow.

"Alas," said the eleven kings, "here is sorrow upon sorrow, and if we had not warred against Arthur as we have done, he would soon revenge us. As for King Leodegrance, he loveth Arthur better than us, and as for King Rience, he hath enough to do with Leodegrance, for he hath laid siege unto him."

So they consented together to keep all the marches of Cornwall, of Wales, and of the North. So first, they put King Idres in the City of Nauntes in Britain, with four thousand men of arms, to watch both the water and the land. Also they put in the city of Windesan, King Nentres of Garlot, with four thousand knights to watch both on water and on land. Also they had of other men of war more than eight thousand, for to fortify all the fortresses in the marches of Cornwall. Also they put more knights in all the marches of Wales and Scotland, with many good men of arms, and so they kept them together the space of three year, and ever allied them with mighty kings and dukes and lords. And to them fell King Rience of North Wales, the which and Nero that was a mighty man of men. And all this while they furnished them and garnished them of good men of arms, and victual, and of all manner of habiliment that pretendeth to the war, to avenge them for the battle of Bedegraine, as it telleth in the book of adventures following.

Chapter XIX
How King Arthur Rode to Carlion, and of His Dream, and How He Saw the Questing Beast

THEN AFTER the departing of King Ban and of King Bors, King Arthur rode into Carlion. And thither came to him, King Lot's wife, of Orkney, in manner of a message, but she was sent thither to espy the court of King Arthur; and she came richly beseen, with her four sons, Gawain, Gaheris, Agravine, and Gareth, with many other knights and ladies. For she was a passing fair lady, therefore the king cast great love unto her, and desired to lie by her; so they were agreed, and he begat upon her Mordred, and she was his sister, on his mother's side, Igraine. So there she rested her a month, and at the last departed. Then the king dreamed a marvellous dream whereof he was sore adread. But all this time King Arthur knew not that King Lot's wife was his sister.

Thus was the dream of Arthur: Him thought there was come into this land griffins and serpents, and him thought they burnt and slew all the people in the land, and then him thought he fought with them, and they did him passing great harm, and wounded him full sore, but at the last he slew them. When the king awaked, he was passing heavy of his dream, and so to put it out of thoughts, he made him ready with many knights to ride a-hunting. As soon as he was in the forest the king saw a great hart afore him. This hart will I chase, said King Arthur, and so he spurred the horse, and rode after long, and so by fine force oft he was like to have smitten the hart; whereas the king had chased the hart so long, that his horse lost his breath, and fell down dead. Then a yeoman fetched the king another horse.

So the king saw the hart enbushed, and his horse dead, he set him down by a fountain, and there he fell in great thoughts. And as he sat so, him thought he heard a noise of hounds, to the sum of thirty. And with that the king saw coming toward him the strangest beast that ever he saw or heard of; so the beast went to the well and drank, and the noise was in the beast's belly like unto the questing of thirty couple hounds; but all the while the beast drank there was no noise in the beast's belly: and there with the beast departed with a great noise, whereof the king had great marvel. And so he was in a great thought, and therewith he fell asleep.

Right so there came a knight afoot unto Arthur and said, "Knight full of thought and sleepy, tell me if thou sawest a strange beast pass this way."

"Such one saw I," said King Arthur, "that is past two mile; what would ye with the beast?" said Arthur.

"Sir, I have followed that beast long time, and killed mine horse, so would God I had another to follow my quest."

Right so came one with the king's horse, and when the knight saw the horse, he prayed the king to give him the horse: "for I have followed this quest this twelvemonth, and either I shall achieve him, or bleed of the best blood of my body." Pellinore, that time king, followed the Questing Beast, and after his death Sir Palamides followed it.

Chapter XX
How King Pellinore Took Arthur's Horse and Followed the Questing Beast, and How Merlin Met with Arthur

SIR KNIGHT," said the king, "leave that quest, and suffer me to have it, and I will follow it another twelvemonth."

"Ah, fool," said the knight unto Arthur, "it is in vain thy desire, for it shall never be achieved but by me, or my next kin."

Therewith he started unto the king's horse and mounted into the saddle, and said, "Gramercy, this horse is my own."

"Well," said the king, "thou mayst take my horse by force, but an I might prove thee whether thou were better on horseback or I."

"– Well," said the knight, "seek me here when thou wilt, and here nigh this well thou shalt find me, and so passed on his way."

Then the king sat in a study, and bade his men fetch his horse as fast as ever they might. Right so came by him Merlin like a child of fourteen year of age, and saluted the king, and asked him why he was so pensive.

"I may well be pensive," said the king, "for I have seen the marvellest sight that ever I saw."

"That know I well," said Merlin, "as well as thyself, and of all thy thoughts, but thou art but a fool to take thought, for it will not amend thee. Also I know what thou art, and who was thy father, and of whom thou wert begotten; King Uther Pendragon was thy father, and begat thee on Igraine."

"That is false," said King Arthur, "how shouldest thou know it, for thou art not so old of years to know my father?"

"Yes," said Merlin, "I know it better than ye or any man living."

"I will not believe thee," said Arthur, and was wroth with the child.

So departed Merlin, and came again in the likeness of an old man of fourscore year of age, whereof the king was right glad, for he seemed to be right wise.

Then said the old man, "Why are ye so sad?"

"I may well be heavy," said Arthur, "for many things. Also here was a child, and told me many things that meseemeth he should not know, for he was not of age to know my father."

"Yes," said the old man, "the child told you truth, and more would he have told you an ye would have suffered him. But ye have done a thing late that God is displeased with you, for ye have lain by your sister, and on her ye have gotten a child that shall destroy you and all the knights of your realm."

"What are ye," said Arthur, "that tell me these tidings?"

"I am Merlin, and I was he in the child's likeness."

"Ah," said King Arthur, "ye are a marvellous man, but I marvel much of thy words that I must die in battle."

"Marvel not," said Merlin, "for it is God's will your body to be punished for your foul deeds; but I may well be sorry," said Merlin, "for I shall die a shameful death, to be put in the earth quick, and ye shall die a worshipful death."

And as they talked this, came one with the king's horse, and so the king mounted on his horse, and Merlin on another, and so rode unto Carlion. And anon the king asked Ector and Ulfius how he was begotten, and they told him Uther Pendragon was his father and Queen Igraine his mother.

Then he said to Merlin, "I will that my mother be sent for that I may speak with her; and if she say so herself then will I believe it."

In all haste, the queen was sent for, and she came and brought with her Morgan le Fay, her daughter, that was as fair a lady as any might be, and the king welcomed Igraine in the best manner.

Chapter XXI
How Ulfius Impeached Queen Igraine, Arthur's Mother, of Treason; and How a Knight Came and Desired to Have the Death of His Master Revenged

RIGHT SO CAME ULFIUS, and said openly, that the king and all might hear that were feasted that day, "Ye are the falsest lady of the world, and the most traitress unto the king's person."

"Beware," said Arthur, "what thou sayest; thou speakest a great word."

"I am well ware," said Ulfius, "what I speak, and here is my glove to prove it upon any man that will say the contrary, that this Queen Igraine is causer of your great damage, and of your great war. For, an she would have uttered it in the life of King Uther Pendragon, of the birth of you, and how ye were begotten ye had never had the mortal wars that ye have had; for the most part of your barons of your realm knew never whose son ye were, nor of whom ye were begotten; and she that bare you of her body should have made it known openly in excusing of her worship and yours, and in like wise to all the realm, wherefore I prove her false to God and to you and to all your realm, and who will say the contrary I will prove it on his body."

Then spake Igraine and said, "I am a woman and I may not fight, but rather than I should be dishonoured, there would some good man take my quarrel. More," she said, "Merlin knoweth well, and ye Sir Ulfius, how King Uther came to me in the Castle of Tintagil in the likeness of my lord, that was dead three hours to-fore, and thereby gat a child that night upon me. And after the thirteenth day King Uther wedded me, and by his commandment when the child was born it was delivered unto Merlin and nourished by him, and so I saw the child never after, nor wot not what is his name, for I knew him never yet."

"And there," Ulfius said to the queen, "Merlin is more to blame than ye."

"Well I wot," said the queen, "I bare a child by my lord King Uther, but I wot not where he is become."

Then Merlin took the king by the hand, saying, "This is your mother."

And therewith Sir Ector bare witness how he nourished him by Uther's commandment. And therewith King Arthur took his mother, Queen Igraine, in his arms and kissed her, and either wept upon other. And then the king let make a feast that lasted eight days.

Then on a day there came in the court a squire on horseback, leading a knight before him wounded to the death, and told him how "there was a knight in the forest had reared up a pavilion by a well, and hath slain my master, a good knight, his name was Miles; wherefore I beseech you that my master may be buried, and that some knight may revenge my master's death."

Then the noise was great of that knight's death in the court, and every man said his advice. Then came Griflet that was but a squire, and he was but young, of the age of the king Arthur, so he besought the king for all his service that he had done him to give the order of knighthood.

Chapter XXII
How Griflet was Made Knight, and Jousted with a Knight

"THOU ART FULL YOUNG and tender of age," said Arthur, "for to take so high an order on thee."

"Sir," said Griflet, "I beseech you make me knight."

"Sir," said Merlin, "it were great pity to lose Griflet, for he will be a passing good man when he is of age, abiding with you the term of his life. And if he adventure his body with yonder knight at the fountain, it is in great peril if ever he come again, for he is one of the best knights of the world, and the strongest man of arms."

"Well," said Arthur. So at the desire of Griflet the king made him knight. "Now," said Arthur unto Sir Griflet, "sith I have made you knight thou must give me a gift."

"What ye will," said Griflet.

"Thou shalt promise me by the faith of thy body, when thou hast jousted with the knight at the fountain, whether it fall ye be on foot or on horseback, that right so ye shall come again unto me without making any more debate."

"I will promise you," said Griflet, "as you desire."

Then took Griflet his horse in great haste, and dressed his shield and took a spear in his hand, and so he rode a great wallop till he came to the fountain, and thereby he saw a rich pavilion, and thereby under a cloth stood a fair horse well saddled and bridled, and on a tree a shield of divers colours and a great spear. Then Griflet smote on the shield with the butt of his spear, that the shield fell down to the ground.

With that the knight came out of the pavilion, and said, "Fair knight, why smote ye down my shield?"

"For I will joust with you," said Griflet.

"It is better ye do not," said the knight, "for ye are but young, and late made knight, and your might is nothing to mine."

"As for that," said Griflet, "I will joust with you."

"That is me loath," said the knight, "but sith I must needs, I will dress me thereto. Of whence be ye?" said the knight.

"Sir, I am of Arthur's court."

So the two knights ran together that Griflet's spear all to-shivered; and there withal he smote Griflet through the shield and the left side, and brake the spear that the truncheon stuck in his body, that horse and knight fell down.

Chapter XXIII
How Twelve Knights Came from Rome and Asked Truage for this Land of Arthur, and How Arthur Fought with a Knight

WHEN THE KNIGHT saw him lie so on the ground, he alighted, and was passing heavy, for he weened he had slain him, and then he unlaced his helm and gat him wind, and so with the truncheon he set him on his horse, and so betook him to God, and said he had a mighty heart, and if he might live he would prove a passing good knight. And so Sir Griflet rode to the court, where great dole was made for him. But through good leeches he was healed and saved. Right so came into the court twelve knights, and were aged men, and they came from the Emperor of Rome, and they asked of Arthur truage for this realm, other else the emperor would destroy him and his land.

"Well," said King Arthur, "ye are messengers, therefore ye may say what ye will, other else ye should die therefore. But this is mine answer: I owe the emperor no truage, nor none will I hold him, but on a fair field I shall give him my truage that shall be with a sharp spear, or else with a sharp sword, and that shall not be long, by my father's soul, Uther Pendragon."

And therewith the messengers departed passingly wroth, and King Arthur as wroth, for in evil time came they then; for the king was passingly wroth for the hurt of Sir Griflet. And so he commanded a privy man of his chamber that or it be day his best horse and armour, with all that longeth unto his person, be without the city or tomorrow day. Right so or tomorrow day he met with his man and his horse, and so mounted up and dressed his shield and took his spear, and bade his chamberlain tarry there till he came again. And so Arthur rode a soft pace till it was day, and then was he ware of three churls chasing Merlin, and would have slain him.

Then the king rode unto them, and bade them: "Flee, churls!"

Then were they afeard when they saw a knight, and fled.

"O Merlin," said Arthur, "here hadst thou been slain for all thy crafts had I not been."

"Nay," said Merlin, "not so, for I could save myself an I would; and thou art more near thy death than I am, for thou goest to the deathward, an God be not thy friend."

So as they went thus talking they came to the fountain, and the rich pavilion there by it. Then King Arthur was ware where sat a knight armed in a chair.

"Sir knight," said Arthur, "for what cause abidest thou here, that there may no knight ride this way but if he joust with thee?" said the king. "I rede thee leave that custom," said Arthur.

"This custom," said the knight, "have I used and will use maugre who saith nay, and who is grieved with my custom let him amend it that will."

"I will amend it," said Arthur.

"I shall defend thee," said the knight. Anon he took his horse and dressed his shield and took a spear, and they met so hard either in other's shields, that all to-shivered their spears. Therewith anon Arthur pulled out his sword.

"Nay, not so," said the knight; "it is fairer," said the knight, "that we twain run more together with sharp spears."

"I will well," said Arthur, "an I had any more spears."

"I have enow," said the knight; so there came a squire and brought two good spears, and Arthur chose one and he another; so they spurred their horses and came together with all their mights, that either brake their spears to their hands. Then Arthur set hand on his sword.

"Nay," said the knight, "ye shall do better, ye are a passing good jouster as ever I met withal, and once for the love of the high order of knighthood let us joust once again."

"I assent me," said Arthur.

Anon there were brought two great spears, and every knight gat a spear, and therewith they ran together that Arthur's spear all to-shivered. But the other knight hit him so hard in midst of the shield, that horse and man fell to the earth, and therewith Arthur was eager, and pulled out his sword, and said, "I will assay thee, sir knight, on foot, for I have lost the honour on horseback."

"I will be on horseback," said the knight.

Then was Arthur wroth, and dressed his shield toward him with his sword drawn. When the knight saw that, he alighted, for him thought no worship to have a knight at such avail, he to be on horseback and he on foot, and so he alighted and dressed his shield unto Arthur.

And there began a strong battle with many great strokes, and so hewed with their swords that the cantels flew in the fields, and much blood they bled both, that all the place there as they fought was overbled with blood, and thus they fought long and rested them, and then they went to the battle again, and so hurtled together like two rams that either fell to the earth. So at the last they smote together that both their swords met even together. But the sword of the knight smote King Arthur's sword in two pieces, wherefore he was heavy.

Then said the knight unto Arthur, "Thou art in my daunger whether me list to save thee or slay thee, and but thou yield thee as overcome and recreant, thou shalt die."

"As for death," said King Arthur, "welcome be it when it cometh, but to yield me unto thee as recreant I had liefer die than to be so shamed."

And therewithal the king leapt unto Pellinore, and took him by the middle and threw him down, and raced off his helm. When the knight felt that he was adread, for he was a passing big man of might.

And anon he brought Arthur under him, and raced off his helm and would have smitten off his head.

Chapter XXIV
How Merlin Saved Arthur's Life, and Threw an Enchantment on King Pellinore and Made Him to Sleep

THEREWITHAL CAME MERLIN and said, "Knight, hold thy hand, for an thou slay that knight thou puttest this realm in the greatest damage that ever was realm: for this knight is a man of more worship than thou wotest of."

"Why, who is he?" said the knight.

"It is King Arthur."

Then would he have slain him for dread of his wrath, and heaved up his sword, and therewith Merlin cast an enchantment to the knight, that he fell to the earth in a great sleep. Then Merlin took up King Arthur, and rode forth on the knight's horse.

"Alas!" said Arthur, "What hast thou done, Merlin? Hast thou slain this good knight by thy crafts? There liveth not so worshipful a knight as he was; I had liefer than the stint of my land a year that he were alive."

"Care ye not," said Merlin, "for he is wholer than ye; for he is but asleep, and will awake within three hours. I told you," said Merlin, "what a knight he was; here had ye been slain had I not been. Also there liveth not a bigger knight than he is one, and he shall hereafter do you right good service; and his name is Pellinore, and he shall have two sons that shall be passing good men; save one they shall have no fellow of prowess and of good living, and their names shall be Percivale of Wales and Lamerake of Wales, and he shall tell you the name of your own son, begotten of your sister, that shall be the destruction of all this realm."

Chapter XXV
How Arthur by the Mean Of Merlin Gat Excalibur His Sword of the Lady of the Lake

RIGHT SO the king and he departed, and went unto an hermit that was a good man and a great leech. So the hermit searched all his wounds and gave him good salves; so the king was there three days, and then were his wounds well amended that he might ride and go, and so departed.

And as they rode, Arthur said, "I have no sword."

"No force," said Merlin, "hereby is a sword that shall be yours, an I may."

So they rode till they came to a lake, the which was a fair water and broad, and in the midst of the lake Arthur was ware of an arm clothed in white samite, that held a fair sword in that hand.

"Lo!" said Merlin, "Yonder is that sword that I spake of." With that they saw a damosel going upon the lake.

"What damosel is that?" said Arthur.

"That is the Lady of the Lake," said Merlin; "and within that lake is a rock, and therein is as fair a place as any on earth, and richly beseen; and this damosel will come to you anon, and then speak ye fair to her that she will give you that sword."

Anon withal came the damosel unto Arthur, and saluted him, and he her again.

"Damosel," said Arthur, "what sword is that, that yonder the arm holdeth above the water? I would it were mine, for I have no sword."

"Sir Arthur, king," said the damosel, "that sword is mine, and if ye will give me a gift when I ask it you, ye shall have it."

"By my faith," said Arthur, "I will give you what gift ye will ask."

"Well!" said the damosel, "Go ye into yonder barge, and row yourself to the sword, and take it and the scabbard with you, and I will ask my gift when I see my time."

So Sir Arthur and Merlin alighted and tied their horses to two trees, and so they went into the ship, and when they came to the sword that the hand held, Sir Arthur took it up by the handles, and took it with him, and the arm and the hand went under the water. And so [they] came unto the land and rode forth, and then Sir Arthur saw a rich pavilion. What signifieth yonder pavilion?

"It is the knight's pavilion," said Merlin, "that ye fought with last, Sir Pellinore; but he is out, he is not there. He hath ado with a knight of yours that hight Egglame, and they have foughten together, but at the last Egglame fled, and else he had been dead, and he hath chased him even to Carlion, and we shall meet with him anon in the highway."

"That is well said," said Arthur, "now have I a sword, now will I wage battle with him, and be avenged on him."

"Sir, you shall not so," said Merlin, "for the knight is weary of fighting and chasing, so that ye shall have no worship to have ado with him; also he will not be lightly matched of one knight living, and therefore it is my counsel, let him pass, for he shall do you good service in short time, and his sons after his days. Also ye shall see that day in short space, you shall be right glad to give him your sister to wed."

"When I see him, I will do as ye advise," said Arthur.

Then Sir Arthur looked on the sword, and liked it passing well.

"Whether liketh you better," said Merlin, "the sword or the scabbard?"

"Me liketh better the sword," said Arthur.

"Ye are more unwise," said Merlin, "for the scabbard is worth ten of the swords, for whiles ye have the scabbard upon you, ye shall never lose no blood, be ye never so sore wounded; therefore keep well the scabbard always with you."

So they rode unto Carlion, and by the way they met with Sir Pellinore; but Merlin had done such a craft, that Pellinore saw not Arthur, and he passed by without any words.

"I marvel," said Arthur, "that the knight would not speak."

"Sir," said Merlin, "he saw you not, for an he had seen you, ye had not lightly departed."

So they came unto Carlion, whereof his knights were passing glad. And when they heard of his adventures, they marvelled that he would jeopard his person so, alone. But all men of worship said it was merry to be under such a chieftain, that would put his person in adventure as other poor knights did.

Chapter XXVI
How Tidings Came to Arthur that King Rience Had Overcome Eleven Kings, and How He Desired Arthur's Beard to Trim His Mantle

THIS MEANWHILE came a messenger from King Rience of North Wales, and king he was of all Ireland, and of many isles. And this was his message, greeting well King Arthur in this manner wise, saying that King Rience had discomfited and overcome eleven kings, and everych of them did him homage, and that was this, they gave him their beards clean flayed off, as much as there was; wherefore the messenger came for King Arthur's beard. For King Rience had purfled a mantle with kings' beards, and there lacked one place of the mantle; wherefore he sent for his beard, or else he would enter into his lands, and burn and slay, and never leave till he have the head and the beard.

"Well," said Arthur, "thou hast said thy message, the which is the most villainous and lewdest message that ever man heard sent unto a king; also thou mayest see my beard is full young yet to make a purfle of it. But tell thou thy king this: I owe him none homage, nor none of mine elders; but or it be long to, he shall do me homage on both his knees, or else he shall lose his head, by the faith of my body, for this is the most shamefulest message that ever I heard speak of. I have espied thy king met never yet with worshipful man, but tell him, I will have his head without he do me homage."

Then the messenger departed.

"Now is there any here," said Arthur, "that knoweth King Rience?"

Then answered a knight that hight Naram, "Sir, I know the king well; he is a passing good man of his body, as few be living, and a passing proud man, and Sir, doubt ye not he will make war on you with a mighty puissance."

"Well," said Arthur, "I shall ordain for him in short time."

Chapter XXVII
How All the Children Were Sent For that Were Born on May-Day, and How Mordred Was Saved

THEN KING ARTHUR let send for all the children born on May-day, begotten of lords and born of ladies; for Merlin told King Arthur that he that should destroy him should be born on May-day, wherefore he sent for them all, upon pain of death; and so there were found many lords' sons, and all were sent unto the king, and so was Mordred sent by King Lot's wife, and all were put in a ship to the sea, and some were four weeks old, and some less.

And so by fortune the ship drave unto a castle, and was all to-riven, and destroyed the most part, save that Mordred was cast up, and a good man found him, and nourished him till he was fourteen year old, and then he brought him to the court, as it rehearseth afterward, toward the end of the Death of Arthur. So many lords and barons of this realm were displeased, for their children were so lost, and many put the wite on Merlin more than on Arthur; so what for dread and for love, they held their peace. But when the messenger came to King Rience, then was he wood out of measure, and purveyed him for a great host, as it rehearseth after in the book of Balin le Savage, that followeth next after, how by adventure Balin gat the sword.

Yvain or the Knight with the Lion

CHRÉTIEN DE TROYES wrote in Champagne during the third quarter of the twelfth century. Of his life we know neither the beginning nor the end, but we know that between 1160 and 1172 he lived, perhaps as herald-at-arms at Troyes, where was the court of his patroness, the Countess Marie de Champagne.

It was in Troyes that Chrétien was led to write four romances, which together form the most complete expression we possess from a single author of the ideals of French chivalry. These romances, originally written in eight-syllable rhyming couplets, tell the tales respectively of Erec and Enide, Cliges, Yvain, and Lancelot.

It is true the romance of Lancelot was not completed by Chrétien, we are told, but the poem is his in such large part that one would be over-scrupulous not to call it his. The other three poems – Erec and Enide, Cliges and Yvain – are his entire.

In the following pages you will find the story of Yvain, who hears the tale of his cousin, Calogrenant.

Pentecost

ARTHUR, THE GOOD KING OF BRITAIN, whose prowess teaches us that we, too, should be brave and courteous, held a rich and royal court upon that precious feast-day which is always known by the name of Pentecost. The court was at Carduel in Wales.

When the meal was finished, the knights betook themselves whither they were summoned by the ladies, damsels, and maidens. Some told stories; others spoke of love, of the trials and sorrows, as well as of the great blessings, which often fall to the members of its order, which was rich and flourishing in those days of old. But now its followers are few, having deserted it almost to a man, so that love is much abased. For lovers used to deserve to be considered courteous, brave, generous, and honourable.

But now love is a laughing-stock, for those who have no intelligence of it assert that they love, and in that they lie. Thus they utter a mockery and lie by boasting where they have no right. But let us leave those who are still alive, to speak of those of former time. For, I take it, a courteous man, though dead, is worth more than a living knave.

So it is my pleasure to relate a matter quite worthy of heed concerning the King whose fame was such that men still speak of him far and near; and I agree with the opinion of the Bretons that his name will live on for evermore. And in connection with him we call to mind those goodly chosen knights who spent themselves for honour's sake. But upon this day of which I speak, great was their astonishment at seeing the King quit their presence; and there were some who felt chagrined, and who did not mince their words, never before having seen the King, on the occasion of such a feast, enter his own chamber either to sleep or to seek repose. But this day it came about that the Queen detained him, and he remained so long at her side that he forgot himself and fell asleep.

The Queen Could Hear Him

OUTSIDE THE CHAMBER DOOR were Dodinel, Sagremor, and Kay, my lord Gawain, my lord Yvain, and with them Calogrenant, a very comely knight, who had begun to tell them a tale, though it was not to his credit, but rather to his shame.

The Queen could hear him as he told his tale, and rising from beside the King, she came upon them so stealthily that before any caught sight of her, she had fallen, as it were, right in their midst. Calogrenant alone jumped up quickly when he saw her come.

Then Kay, who was very quarrelsome, mean, sarcastic, and abusive, said to him: "By the Lord, Calogrenant, I see you are very bold and forward now, and certainly it pleases me to see you the most courteous of us all. And I know that you are quite persuaded of your own excellence, for that is in keeping with your little sense. And of course it is natural that my lady should suppose that you surpass us all in courtesy and bravery. We failed to rise through sloth, forsooth, or because we did not care! Upon my word, it is not so, my lord; but we did not see my lady until you had risen first."

"Really, Kay," the Queen then says, "I think you would burst if you could not pour out the poison of which you are so full. You are troublesome and mean thus to annoy your companions."

"Lady," says Kay, "if we are not better for your company, at least let us not lose by it. I am not aware that I said anything for which I ought to be accused, and so I pray you say no more. It is impolite and foolish to keep up a vain dispute. This argument should go no further, nor should any one try to make more of it. But since there must be no more high words, command him to continue the tale he had begun." Thereupon Calogrenant prepares to reply in this fashion:

"My lord, little do I care about the quarrel, which matters little and affects me not. If you have vented your scorn on me, I shall never be harmed by it. You have often spoken insultingly, my lord Kay, to braver and better men than I, for you are given to this kind of thing. The manure-pile will always stink, and gadflies sting, and bees will hum, and so a bore will torment and make a nuisance of himself. However, with my lady's leave, I'll not continue my tale to-day, and I beg her to say no more about it, and kindly not give me any unwelcome command."

"Lady," says Kay, "all those who are here will be in your debt, for they are desirous to hear it out. Don't do it as a favour to me! But by the faith you owe the King, your lord and mine, command him to continue, and you will do well."

"Calogrenant," the Queen then says, "do not mind the attack of my lord Kay the seneschal. He is so accustomed to evil speech that one cannot punish him for it. I command and request you not to be angered because of him, nor should you fail on his account to say something which it will please us all to hear; if you wish to preserve my good-will, pray begin the tale anew."

"Surely, lady, it is a very unwelcome command you lay upon me. Rather than tell any more of my tale to-day, I would have one eye plucked out, if I did not fear your displeasure. Yet will I perform your behest, however distasteful it may be. Then since you will have it so, give heed. Let your heart and ears be mine. For words, though heard, are lost unless understood within the heart. Some men there are who give consent to what they hear but do not understand: these men have the hearing alone. For the moment the heart fails to understand, the word falls upon the ears simply as the wind that blows, without stopping to tarry there; rather it quickly passes on if the heart is not so awake as to be ready to receive it. For the heart alone can receive it when it comes along, and shut it up within. The ears are the path and channel by which the voice can reach the heart, while the heart receives within the bosom the voice which enters through the ear. Now, whoever will heed my words, must surrender to me his heart and ears, for I am not going to speak of a dream, an idle tale, or lie, with which many another has regaled you, but rather shall I speak of what I saw."

Lonely as a Countryman

"**IT HAPPENED SEVEN YEARS AGO THAT, lonely as a countryman, I was making my way in search of adventures, fully armed as a knight should be, when I came upon a road leading off to the right into a thick forest. The road there was very bad, full of briars and thorns. In spite of the trouble and inconvenience, I followed the road and path.**

"Almost the entire day I went thus riding until I emerged from the forest of Broceliande. Out from the forest I passed into the open country where I saw a wooden tower at the distance of half a Welsh league: it may have been so far, but it was not anymore. Proceeding faster than a walk, I drew near and saw the palisade and moat all round it, deep and wide, and standing upon the bridge, with a moulted falcon upon his wrist, I saw the master of the castle. I had no sooner saluted him than he came forward to hold my stirrup and invited me to dismount. I did so, for it was useless to deny that I was in need of a lodging-place. Then he told me more than a hundred times at once that blessed was the road by which I had come thither. Meanwhile, we crossed the bridge, and passing through the gate, found ourselves in the courtyard. In the middle of the courtyard of this vavasor, to whom may God repay such joy and honour as he bestowed upon me that night, there hung a gong not of iron or wood, I trow, but all of copper. Upon this gong the vavasor struck three times with a hammer which hung on a post close by. Those who were upstairs in the house, upon hearing his voice and the sound, came out into the yard below. Some took my horse which the good vavasor was holding; and I saw coming toward me a very fair and gentle maid. On looking at her narrowly I saw she was tall and slim and straight. Skilful she was in disarming me, which she did gently and with address; then, when she had robed me in a short mantle of scarlet stuff spotted with a peacock's plumes, all the others left us there, so that she and I remained alone. This pleased me well, for I needed naught else to look upon. Then she took me to sit down in the prettiest little field, shut in by a wall all round about. There I found her so elegant, so fair of speech and so well informed, of such pleasing manners and character, that it was a delight to be there, and I could have wished never to be compelled to move. But as ill luck would have it, when night came on, and the time for supper had arrived. The vavasor came to look for me. No more delay was possible, so I complied with his request. Of the supper I will only say that it was all after my heart, seeing that the damsel took her seat at the table just in front of me. After the supper the vavasor admitted to me that, though he had lodged many an errant knight, he knew not how long it had been since he had welcomed one in search of adventure. Then, as a favour, he begged of me to return by way of his residence, if I could make it possible. So I said to him: 'Right gladly, sire!' for a refusal would have been impolite, and that was the least I could do for such a host."

Sitting Upon a Stump

"THAT NIGHT, indeed, I was well lodged, and as soon as the morning light appeared, I found my steed ready saddled, as I had requested the night before; thus my request was carried out. My kind host and his dear daughter I commended to the Holy Spirit, and, after taking leave of all, I got away as soon as possible.

"I had not proceeded far from my stopping-place when I came to a clearing, where there were some wild bulls at large; they were fighting among themselves and making such a dreadful and horrible noise that if the truth be known, I drew back in fear, for there is no beast so fierce and dangerous as a bull. I saw sitting upon a stump, with a great club in his hand, a rustic lout, as black as a mulberry, indescribably big and hideous; indeed, so passing ugly was the creature that no word of mouth could do him justice. On drawing near to this fellow, I saw that his head was bigger than that of a horse or of any other beast; that his hair was in tufts, leaving his forehead bare for a width of more than two spans; that his ears were big and mossy, just like those of an elephant; his eyebrows were heavy and his face was flat; his eyes were those of an owl, and his nose was like a cat's; his jowls were split like a wolf, and his teeth were sharp and yellow like a wild boar's; his beard was black and his whiskers twisted; his chin merged into his chest and his backbone was long, but twisted and hunched. There he stood, leaning upon his club and accoutred in a strange garb, consisting not of cotton or wool, but rather of the hides recently flayed from two bulls or two beeves: these he wore hanging from his neck. The fellow leaped up straightway when he saw me drawing near. I do not know whether he was going to strike me or what he intended to do, but I was prepared to stand him off, until I saw him stop and stand stock-still upon a tree trunk, where he stood full seventeen feet in height. Then he gazed at me but spoke not a word, any more than a beast would have done. And I supposed that he had not his senses or was drunk. However, I made bold to say to him: 'Come, let me know whether thou art a creature of good or not.' And he replied: 'I am a man.' 'What kind of a man art thou?' 'Such as thou seest me to be: I am by no means otherwise.' 'What dost thou here?' 'I was here, tending these cattle in this wood.' 'Wert thou really tending them? By Saint Peter of Rome! They know not the command of any man. I guess one cannot possibly guard wild beasts in a plain or wood or anywhere else unless they are tied or confined inside.' 'Well, I tend and have control of these beasts so that they will never leave this neighbourhood.' 'How dost thou do that? Come, tell me now!' 'There is not one of them that dares to move when they see me coming. For when I can get hold of one I give its two horns such a wrench with my hard, strong hands that the others tremble with fear, and gather at once round about me as if to ask for mercy. No one could venture here but me, for if he should go among them he would be straightway done to death. In this way I am master of my beasts. And now thou must tell me in turn what kind of a man thou art, and what thou seekest here.' 'I am, as thou seest, a knight seeking for what I cannot find; long have I sought without success.' 'And what is this thou fain wouldst find?' 'Some adventure whereby to test my prowess and my bravery. Now I beg and urgently request thee to give me some counsel, if possible, concerning some adventure or marvellous thing.' Says he: 'Thou wilt have to do without, for I know nothing of adventure, nor did I ever hear tell of such. But if thou wouldst go to a certain spring here hard by and shouldst comply with the practice there, thou wouldst not easily come back again. Close by here thou canst easily find a path which will lead thee thither. If thou wouldst go aright, follow the straight path, otherwise thou mayst easily go astray among the many other paths. Thou shalt see the spring which boils, though the water is colder than marble. It is shadowed by the fairest tree that ever Nature formed, for its foliage is evergreen, regardless of the winter's cold, and an iron basin is hanging there by a chain long enough to reach the spring. And beside the spring thou shalt find a massive stone, as thou shalt see, but whose nature I cannot explain, never having seen its like. On the other side a chapel stands, small, but very beautiful. If thou wilt take of the water in the basin and spill it upon the stone, thou shalt see such a storm come up that not a beast will remain within this wood; every doe, star, deer, boar, and bird will issue forth. For thou shalt see such lightning-bolts descend, such blowing of gales and crashing of trees, such torrents fail, such thunder and lightning, that, if thou canst escape from them without trouble and mischance, thou wilt be more fortunate than ever any knight was yet.' I left the fellow then, after he had pointed our the way."

Clouds Let Fall Snow and Rain and Hail

"**I**T MUST HAVE BEEN AFTER NINE O'CLOCK and might have been drawing on toward noon, when I espied the tree and the chapel. I can truly say that this tree was the finest pine that ever grew on earth. I do not believe that it ever rained so hard that a drop of water could penetrate it, but would rather drip from the outer branches.**

"From the tree I saw the basin hanging, of the finest gold that was ever for sale in any fair. As for the spring, you may take my word that it was boiling like hot water. The stone was of emerald, with holes in it like a cask, and there were four rubies underneath, more radiant and red than is the morning sun when it rises in the east. Now not one word will I say which is not true.

I wished to see the marvellous appearing of the tempest and the storm; but therein I was not wise, for I would gladly have repented, if I could, when I had sprinkled the perforated stone with the water from the basin. But I fear I poured too much, for straightway I saw the heavens so break loose that from more than fourteen directions the lightning blinded my eyes, and all at once the clouds let fall snow and rain and hail. The storm was so fierce and terrible that a hundred times I thought I should be killed by the bolts which fell about me and by the trees which were rent apart. Know that I was in great distress until the uproar was appeased. But God gave me such comfort that the storm did not continue long, and all the winds died down again. The winds dared not blow against God's will. And when I saw the air clear and serene I was filled with joy again. For I have observed that joy quickly causes trouble to be forgot. As soon as the storm was completely past, I saw so many birds gathered in the pine tree (if any one will believe my words) that not a branch or twig was to be seen which was not entirely covered with birds. The tree was all the more lovely then, for all the birds sang in harmony, yet the note of each was different, so that I never heard one singing another's note. I, too, rejoiced in their joyousness, and listened to them until they had sung their service through, for I have never heard such happy song, nor do I think any one else will hear it, unless he goes to listen to what filled me with such joy and bliss that I was lost in rapture."

I Dealt Him as Hard a Blow as I Could Give

"**I STAYED THERE until I heard some knights coming, as I thought it seemed that there must be ten of them. But all the noise and commotion was made by the approach of a single knight. When I saw him coming on alone I quickly caught my steed and made no delay in mounting him.**

"And the knight, as if with evil intent, came on swifter than an eagle, looking as fierce as a lion. From as far as his voice could reach he began to challenge me, and said: 'Vassal, without provocation you have caused me shame and harm. If there was any quarrel between us you should first have challenged me, or at least sought justice before attacking me. But, sir vassal, if it be within my power, upon you shall fall the punishment for the damage which is evident. About me here lies the evidence of my woods destroyed. He who has suffered has the right to complain. And I have good reason to complain that you have driven me from my house with lightning-bolt and rain. You have made trouble for me, and cursed be he who thinks it fair. For within my own woods and town you have made such an attack upon me that resources of men of arms and of fortifications would have been of no avail to me; no man could have been secure, even if he had been in a fortress of solid stone and wood. But be assured that from this moment there shall be neither truce nor peace between us.' At these words we rushed together, each one holding his shield well gripped and covering himself with it. The knight had a good horse and a stout lance, and was doubtless a whole head taller than I. Thus, I was altogether at a disadvantage, being shorter than he, while his horse was stronger than mine. You may be sure that I will tell the facts, in order to cover up my shame. With intent to do my best, I dealt him as hard a blow as I could give, striking the top of his shield, and I put all my strength into it with such effect that my lance flew all to splinters. His lance remained entire, being very heavy and bigger than any knight's lance I ever saw. And the knight struck me with it so heavily that he knocked me over my horse's crupper and laid me flat upon the ground, where he left me ashamed and exhausted, without bestowing another glance upon me. He took my horse, but me he left, and started back by the way he came. And I, who knew not what to do, remained there in pain and with troubled thoughts. Seating myself beside the spring I rested there awhile, not daring to follow after the knight for fear of committing some rash act of madness. And, indeed, had I had the courage, I knew not what had become of him. Finally, it occurred to me that I would keep my promise to my host and would return by way of his dwelling. This idea pleased me, and so I did. I laid off all my arms in order to proceed more easily, and thus with shame I retraced my steps. When I reached his home that night, I found my host to be the same good-natured and courteous man as I had before discovered him to be. I could not observe that either his daughter or he himself welcomed me any less gladly, or did me any less honour than they had done the night before. I am indebted to them for the great honour they all did me in that house; and they even said that, so far as they knew or had heard tell, no one had ever escaped, without being killed or kept a prisoner, from the place whence I returned. Thus I went and thus I returned, feeling, as I did so, deeply ashamed. So I have foolishly told you the story which I never wished to tell again."

I Shall Go to Avenge Your Shame

"**B**Y MY HEAD," cries my lord Yvain, "you are my own cousin-german, and we ought to love each other well. But I must consider you as mad to have concealed this from me so long. If I call you mad, I beg you not to be incensed. For if I can, and if I obtain the leave, I shall go to avenge your shame."

"It is evident that we have dined," says Kay, with his ever-ready speech; "there are more words in a pot full of wine than in a whole barrel of beer. They say that a cat is merry when full. After dinner no one stirs, but each one is ready to slay Noradin, and you will take vengeance on Forre! Are your saddle-cloths ready stuffed, and your iron greaves polished, and your banners unfurled? Come now, in God's name, my lord Yvain, is it to-night or to-morrow that you start? Tell us, fair sire, when you will start for this rude test, for we would fain convoy you thither. There will be no provost or constable who will not gladly escort you. And however it may be, I beg that you will not go without taking leave of us; and if you have a bad dream to-night, by all means stay at home!" "The devil, Sir Kay," the Queen replies, "are you beside yourself that your tongue always runs on so? Cursed be your tongue which is so full of bitterness! Surely your tongue must hate you, for it says the worst it knows to every man. Damned be any tongue that never ceases to speak ill! As for your tongue, it babbles so that it makes you hated everywhere. It cannot do you greater treachery. See here: if it were mine, I would accuse it of treason. Any man that cannot be cured by punishment ought to be tied like a madman in front of the chancel in the church."

"Really, madame," says my lord Yvain, "his impudence matters not to me. In every court my lord Kay has so much ability, knowledge, and worth that he will never be deaf or dumb. He has the wit to reply wisely and courteously to all that is mean, and this he has always done. You well know if I lie in saying so. But I have no desire to dispute or to begin our foolishness again. For he who deals the first blow does not always win the fight, but rather he who gains revenge. He who fights with his companion had better fight against some stranger. I do not wish to be like the hound that stiffens up and growls when another dog yaps at him."

Three Mighty Oaths

WHILE THEY WERE TALKING thus, the King came out of his room where he had been all this time asleep. And when the knights saw him they all sprang to their feet before him, but he made them at once sit down again. He took his place beside the Queen, who repeated to him word for word, with her customary skill, the story of Calogrenant.

The King listened eagerly to it, and then he swore three mighty oaths by the soul of his father Utherpendragon, and by the soul of his son, and of his mother too, that he would go to see that spring before a fortnight should have passed; and he would see the storm and the marvels there by reaching it on the eve of my lord Saint John the Baptist's feast; there he would spend the night, and all who wished might accompany him. All the court thought well of this, for the knights and the young bachelors were very eager to make the expedition. But despite the general joy and satisfaction my lord Yvain was much chagrined, for he intended to go there all alone; so he was grieved and much put out because of the King who planned to go. The chief cause of his displeasure was that he knew that my lord Kay, to whom the favour would not be refused if he should solicit it, would secure the battle rather than he himself, or else perchance my lord Gawain would first ask for it. If either one of these two should make request, the favour would never be refused him.

But, having no desire for their company, he resolves not to wait for them, but to go off alone, if possible, whether it be to his gain or hurt. And whoever may stay behind, he intends to be on the third day in the forest of Broceliande, and there to seek if possibly he may find the narrow wooded path for which he yearns eagerly, and the plain with the strong castle, and the pleasure and delight of the courteous damsel, who is so charming and fair, and with the damsel her worthy sire, who is so honourable and nobly born that he strives to dispense honour.

Then he will see the bulls in the clearing, with the giant boor who watches them. Great is his desire to see this fellow, who is so stout and big and ugly and deformed, and as black as a smith. Then, too, he will see, if possible, the stone and the spring itself, and the basin and the birds in the pine-tree, and he will make it rain and blow. But of all this he will not boast, nor, if he can help it, shall any one know of his purpose until he shall have received from it either great humiliation or great renown: then let the facts be known.

Through Forests Long and Wide

MY LORD YVAIN gets away from the court without any one meeting him, and proceeds alone to his lodging place. There he found all his household, and gave orders to have his horse saddled; then, calling one of his squires who was privy to his every thought, he says: "Come now, follow me outside yonder, and bring me my arms. I shall go out at once through yonder gate upon my palfrey. For thy part, do not delay, for I have a long road to travel. Have my steed well shod, and bring him quickly where I am; then shalt thou lead back my palfrey. But take good care, I adjure thee, if any one questions thee about me, to give him no satisfaction. Otherwise, whatever thy confidence in me, thou need never again count on my goodwill." "Sire," he says, "all will be well, for no one shall learn anything from me. Proceed, and I shall follow you."

My lord Yvain mounts at once, intending to avenge, if possible, his cousin's disgrace before he returns. The squire ran for the arms and steed; he mounted at once without delay, since he was already equipped with shoes and nails. Then he followed his master's track until he saw him standing mounted, waiting to one side of the road in a place apart. He brought him his harness and equipment, and then accoutred him.

My lord Yvain made no delay after putting on his arms, but hastily made his way each day over the mountains and through the valleys, through the forests long and wide, through strange and wild country, passing through many gruesome spots, many a danger and many a strait, until he came directly to the path, which was full of brambles and dark enough; then he felt he was safe at last, and could not now lose his way.

Whoever may have to pay the cost, he will not stop until he sees the pine which shades the spring and stone, and the tempest of hail and rain and thunder and wind. That night, you may be sure, he had such lodging as he desired, for he found the vavasor to be even more polite and courteous than he had been told, and in the damsel he perceived a hundred times more sense and beauty than Calogrenant had spoken of, for one cannot rehearse the sum of a lady's or a good man's qualities. The moment such a man devotes himself to virtue, his story cannot be summed up or told, for no tongue could estimate the honourable deeds of such a gentleman.

Two Knights Intent Upon Each Other's Death

MY LORD YVAIN was well content with the excellent lodging he had that night, and when he entered the clearing the next day, he met the bulls and the rustic boor who showed him the way to take. But more than a hundred times he crossed himself at sight of the monster before him – how Nature had ever been able to form such a hideous, ugly creature.

Then to the spring he made his way, and found there all that he wished to see. Without hesitation and without sitting down he poured the basin full of water upon the stone, when straightway it began to blow and rain, and such a storm was caused as had been foretold. And when God had appeased the storm, the birds came to perch upon the pine, and sang their joyous songs up above the perilous spring. But before their jubilee had ceased there came the knight, more blazing with wrath than a burning log, and making as much noise as if he were chasing a lusty stag. As soon as they espied each other they rushed together and displayed the mortal hate they bore. Each one carried a stiff, stout lance, with which they dealt such mighty blows that they pierced the shields about their necks, and cut the meshes of their hauberks; their lances are splintered and sprung, while the fragments are cast high in air.

Then each attacks the other with his sword, and in the strife they cut the straps of the shields away, and cut the shields all to bits from end to end, so that the shreds hang down, no longer serving as covering or defence; for they have so split them up that they bring down the gleaming blades upon their sides, their arms, and hips. Fierce, indeed, is their assault; yet they do not budge from their standing-place any more than would two blocks of stone. Never were there two knights so intent upon each other's death. They are careful not to waste their blows, but lay them on as best they may; they strike and bend their helmets, and they send the meshes of their hauberks flying so, that they draw not a little blood, for the hauberks are so hot with their body's heat that they hardly serve as more protection than a coat. As they drive the sword-point at the face, it is marvellous that so fierce and bitter a strife should last so long. But both are possessed of such courage that one would not for aught retreat a foot before his adversary until he had wounded him to death. Yet, in this respect they were very honourable in not trying or deigning to strike or harm their steeds in any way; but they sat astride their steeds without putting foot to earth, which made the fight more elegant.

At last my lord Yvain crushed the helmet of the knight, whom the blow stunned and made so faint that he swooned away, never having received such a cruel blow before. Beneath his kerchief his head was split to the very brains, so that the meshes of his bright hauberk were stained with the brains and blood, all of which caused him such intense pain that his heart almost ceased to beat. He had good reason then to flee, for he felt that he had a mortal wound, and that further resistance would not avail. With this thought in mind he quickly made his escape toward his town, where the bridge was lowered and the gate quickly opened for him; meanwhile my lord Yvain at once spurs after him at topmost speed. As a gerfalcon swoops upon a crane when he sees him rising from afar, and then draws so near to him that he is about to seize him, yet misses him, so flees the knight, with Yvain pressing him so close that he can almost throw his arm about him, and yet cannot quite come up with him, though he is so close that he can hear him groan for the pain he feels.

While the one exerts himself in flight the other strives in pursuit of him, fearing to have wasted his effort unless he takes him alive or dead; for he still recalls the mocking words which my lord Kay had addressed to him. He had not yet carried out the pledge which he had given to his cousin; nor will they believe his word unless he returns with the evidence. The knight led him a rapid chase to the gate of his town, where they entered in; but finding no man or woman in the streets through which they passed, they both rode swiftly on till they came to the palace-gate.

A Fair and Charming Maiden

THE GATE WAS VERY HIGH and wide, yet it had such a narrow entrance-way that two men or two horses could scarcely enter abreast or pass without interference or great difficulty; for it was constructed just like a trap which is set for the rat on mischief bent, and which has a blade above ready to fall and strike and catch, and which is suddenly released whenever anything, however gently, comes in contact with the spring. In like fashion, beneath the gate there were two springs connected with a portcullis up above, edged with iron and very sharp. If anything stepped upon this contrivance the gate descended from above, and whoever below was struck by the gate was caught and mangled.

Precisely in the middle the passage lay as narrow as if it were a beaten track. Straight through it exactly the knight rushed on, with my lord Yvain madly following him apace, and so close to him that he held him by the saddle-bow behind. It was well for him that he was stretched forward, for had it not been for this piece of luck he would have been cut quite through; for his horse stepped upon the wooden spring which kept the portcullis in place. Like a hellish devil the gate dropped down, catching the saddle and the horse's haunches, which it cut off clean. But, thank God, my lord Yvain was only slightly touched when it grazed his back so closely that it cut both his spurs off even with his heels. And while he thus fell in dismay, the other with his mortal wound escaped him, as you now shall see. Farther on there was another gate just like the one they had just passed; through this the knight made his escape, and the gate descended behind him. Thus my lord Yvain was caught, very much concerned and discomfited as he finds himself shut in this hallway, which was all studded with gilded nails, and whose walls were cunningly decorated with precious paints. But about nothing was he so worried as not to know what had become of the knight. While he was in this narrow place, he heard open the door of a little adjoining room, and there came forth alone a fair and charming maiden who closed the door again after her. When she found my lord Yvain, at first she was sore dismayed. "Surely, sir knight," she says, "I fear you have come in an evil hour. If you are seen here, you will be all cut to pieces. For my lord is mortally wounded, and I know it is you who have been the death of him. My lady is in such a state of grief, and her people about her are crying so that they are ready to die with rage; and, moreover, they know you to be inside. But as yet their grief is such that they are unable to attend to you. The moment they come to attack you, they cannot fail to kill or capture you, as they may choose." And my lord Yvain replies to her: "If God will they shall never kill me, nor shall I fall into their hands." "No," she says, "for I shall do my utmost to assist you. It is not manly to cherish fear. So I hold you to be a man of courage, when you are not dismayed. And rest assured that if I could I would help you and treat you honourably, as you in turn would do for me. Once my lady sent me on an errand to the King's court, and I suppose I was not so experienced or courteous or so well behaved as a maiden ought to be; at any rate, there was not a knight there who deigned to say a word to me except you alone who stand here now; but you, in your kindness, honoured and aided me. For the honour you did me then I shall now reward you. I know full well what your name is, and I recognised you at once: your name is my lord Yvain. You may be sure and certain that if you take my advice you will never be caught or treated ill. Please take this little ring of mine, which you will return when I shall have delivered you." Then she handed him the little ring and told him that its effect was like that of the bark which covers the wood so that it cannot be seen; but it must be worn so that the stone is within the palm; then he who wears the ring upon his finger need have no concern for anything; for no one, however sharp his eyes may be, will be able to see him any more than the wood which is covered by the outside bark. All this is pleasing to my lord Yvain. And when she had told him this, she led him to a seat upon a couch covered with a quilt so rich that the Duke of Austria had none such, and she told him that if he cared for something to eat she would fetch it for him; and he replied that he would gladly do so. Running quickly into the chamber, she presently returned, bringing a roasted fowl and a cake, a cloth, a full pot of good grape-wine covered with a white drinking-cup; all this she offered to him to eat. And he, who stood in need of food, very gladly ate and drank.

The Crowd Had Clubs and Swords

BY THE TIME he had finished his meal the knights were astir inside looking for him and eager to avenge their lord, who was already stretched upon his bier. Then the damsel said to Yvain: "Friend, do you hear them all seeking you? There is a great noise and uproar brewing. But whoever may come or go, do not stir for any noise of theirs, for they can never discover you if you do not move from this couch. Presently you will see this room all full of ill-disposed and hostile people, who will think to find you here; and I make no doubt that they will bring the body here before interment, and they will begin to search for you under the seats and the beds. It will be amusing for a man who is not afraid when he sees people searching so fruitlessly, for they will all be so blind, so undone, and so misguided that they will be beside themselves with rage. I cannot tell you more just now, for I dare no longer tarry here. But I may thank God for giving me the chance and the opportunity to do some service to please you, as I yearned to do."

Then she turned away, and when she was gone all the crowd with one accord had come from both sides to the gates, armed with clubs and swords. There was a mighty crowd and press of hostile people surging about, when they espied in front of the gate the half of the horse which had been cut down. Then they felt very sure that when the gates were opened they would find inside him whose life they wished to take. Then they caused to be drawn up those gates which had been the death of many men. But since no spring or trap was laid for their passage they all came through abreast. Then they found at the threshold the other half of the horse that had been killed; but none of them had sharp enough eyes to see my lord Yvain, whom they would gladly have killed; and he saw them beside themselves with rage and fury, as they said: "How can this be? For there is no door or window here through which anything could escape, unless it be a bird, a squirrel, or marmot, or some other even smaller animal; for the windows are barred, and the gates were closed as soon as my lord passed through. The body is in here, dead or alive, since there is no sign of it outside there; we can see more than half of the saddle in here, but of him we see nothing, except the spurs which fell down severed from his feet. Now let us cease this idle talk, and search in all these comers, for he is surely in here still, or else we are all enchanted, or the evil spirits have filched him away from us." Thus they all, aflame with rage, sought him about the room, beating upon the walls, and beds, and seats. But the couch upon which he lay was spared and missed the blows, so that he was not struck or touched. But all about they thrashed enough, and raised an uproar in the room with their clubs, like a blind man who pounds as he goes about his search. While they were poking about under the beds and the stools, there entered one of the most beautiful ladies that any earthly creature ever saw. Word or mention was never made of such a fair Christian dame, and yet she was so crazed with grief that she was on the point of taking her life. All at once she cried out at the top of her voice, and then fell prostrate in a swoon. And when she had been picked up she began to claw herself and tear her hair, like a woman who had lost her mind. She tears her hair and rips her dress, and faints at every step she takes; nor can anything comfort her when she sees her husband borne along lifeless in the bier; for her happiness is at an end, and so she made her loud lament. The holy water and the cross and the tapers were borne in advance by the nuns from a convent; then came missals and censers and the priests, who pronounce the final absolution required for the wretched soul.

The Procession Passed

MY LORD YVAIN heard the cries and the grief that can never be described, for no one could describe it, nor was such ever set down in a book. The procession passed, but in the middle of the room a great crowd gathered about the bier, for the fresh warm blood trickled out again from the dead

man's wound, and this betokened certainly that the man was still surely present who had fought the battle and had killed and defeated him. Then they sought and searched everywhere, and turned and stirred up everything, until they were all in a sweat with the trouble and the press which had been caused by the sight of the trickling crimson blood.

Then my lord Yvain was well struck and beaten where he lay, but not for that did he stir at all. And the people became more and more distraught because of the wounds which burst open, and they marvelled why they bled, without knowing whose fault it was. And each one to his neighbour said: "The murderer is among us here, and yet we do not see him, which is passing strange and mysterious." At this the lady showed such grief that she made an attempt upon her life, and cried as if beside herself: "All God, then will the murderer not be found, the traitor who took my good lord's life? Good? Aye, the best of the good, indeed! True God, Thine will be the fault if Thou dost let him thus escape. No other man than Thou should I blame for it who dost hide him from my sight. Such a wonder was never seen, nor such injustice, as Thou dost to me in not allowing me even to see the man who must be so close to me. When I cannot see him, I may well say that some demon or spirit has interposed himself between us, so that I am under a spell. Or else he is a coward and is afraid of me: he must be a craven to stand in awe of me, and it is an act of cowardice not to show himself before me. Ah, thou spirit, craven thing! Why art thou so in fear of me, when before my lord thou weft so brave? O empty and elusive thing, why cannot I have thee in my power? Why cannot I lay hands upon thee now? But how could it ever come about that thou didst kill my lord, unless it was done by treachery? Surely my lord would never have met defeat at thy hands had he seen thee face to face. For neither God nor man ever knew of his like, nor is there any like him now. Surely, hadst thou been a mortal man, thou wouldst never have dared to withstand my lord, for no one could compare with him." Thus the lady struggles with herself, and thus she contends and exhausts herself. And her people with her, for their part, show the greatest possible grief as they carry off the body to burial. After their long efforts and search they are completely exhausted by the quest, and give it up from weariness, inasmuch as they can find no one who is in any way guilty. The nuns and priests, having already finished the service, had returned from the church and were gone to the burial. But to all this the damsel in her chamber paid no heed. Her thoughts are with my lord Yvain, and, coming quickly, she said to him: "Fair sir, these people have been seeking you in force. They have raised a great tumult here, and have poked about in all the corners more diligently than a hunting-dog goes ferreting a partridge or a quail. Doubtless you have been afraid."

"Upon my word, you are right," says he: "I never thought to be so afraid. And yet, if it were possible I should gladly look out through some window or aperture at the procession and the corpse." Yet he had no interest in either the corpse or the procession, for he would gladly have seen them all burned, even had it cost him a thousand marks. A thousand marks? Three thousand, verily, upon my word. But he said it because of the lady of the town, of whom he wished to catch a glimpse. So the damsel placed him at a little window, and repaid him as well as she could for the honour which he had done her. From this window my lord Yvain espies the fair lady, as she says: "Sire, may God have mercy upon your soul! For never, I verily believe, did any knight ever sit in saddle who was your equal in any respect. No other knight, my fair sweet lord, ever possessed your honour or courtesy. Generosity was your friend and boldness your companion. May your soul rest among the saints, my fair dear lord." Then she strikes and tears whatever she can lay her hands upon. Whatever the outcome may be, it is hard for my lord Yvain to restrain himself from running forward to seize her hands. But the damsel begs and advises him, and even urgently commands him, though with courtesy and graciousness, not to commit any rash deed, saying: "You are well off here. Do not stir for any cause until this grief shall be assuaged; let these people all depart, as they will do presently. If you act as I advise, in accordance with my views, great advantage may come to you. It will be best for you to remain seated here, and watch the people inside and out as they pass along the way without their seeing you. But take care not to speak violently, for I hold that man to be rather imprudent than brave who goes too far and loses his self-restraint and commits some deed of violence the moment he has the time and chance. So if you cherish some rash thought be careful not to utter it. The wise man conceals his imprudent thought and works out righteousness if he can. So wisely take good care not to risk your head, for which they would accept no ransom. Be considerate of yourself and remember my advice. Rest assured until I return, for I dare not stay longer now. I might stay so long, I fear, that they would suspect me when they did not see me in the crowd, and then I should suffer for it."

Then she goes off, and he remains, not knowing how to comport himself. He is loath to see them bury the corpse without his securing anything to take back as evidence that he has defeated and killed him. If he has no proof or evidence he will be held in contempt, for Kay is so mean and obstinate, so given to mockery, and so annoying, that he could never succeed in convincing him. He would go about for ever insulting him, flinging his mockery and taunts as he did the other day. These taunts are still fresh and rankling in his heart. But with her sugar and honey a new Love now softened him; he had been to hunt upon his lands and had gathered in his prey. His enemy carries off his heart, and he loves the creature who hates him most. The lady, all unaware, has well avenged her lord's death. She has secured greater revenge than she could ever have done unless she had been aided by Love, who attacks him so gently that he wounds his heart through his eyes. And this wound is more enduring than any inflicted by lance or sword. A sword-blow is cured and healed at once as soon as a doctor attends to it, but the wound of love is worst when it is nearest to its physician. This is the wound of my lord Yvain, from which he will never more recover, for Love has installed himself with him. He deserts and goes away from the places he was wont to frequent. He cares for no lodging or landlord save this one, and he is very wise in leaving a poor lodging-place in order to betake himself to him. In order to devote himself completely to him, he will have no other lodging-place, though often he is wont to seek out lowly hostelries. It is a shame that Love should ever so basely conduct himself as to select the meanest lodging-place quite as readily as the best. But now he has come where he is welcome, and where he will be treated honourably, and where he will do well to stay. This is the way Love ought to act, being such a noble creature that it is marvellous how he dares shamefully to descend to such low estate. He is like him who spreads his balm upon the ashes and dust, who mingles sugar with gall, and suet with honey. However, he did not act so this time, but rather lodged in a noble place, for which no one can reproach him. When the dead man had been buried, all the people dispersed, leaving no clerks or knights or ladies, excepting only her who makes no secret of her grief. She alone remains behind, often clutching at her throat, wringing her hands, and beating her palms, as she reads her psalms in her gilt lettered psalter. All this while my lord Yvain is at the window gazing at her, and the more he looks at her the more he loves her and is enthralled by her. He would have wished that she should cease her weeping and reading, and that she should feel inclined to converse with him. Love, who caught him at the window, filled him with this desire. But he despairs of realising his wish, for he cannot imagine or believe that his desire can be gratified. So he says: "I may consider myself a fool to wish for what I cannot have. Her lord it was whom I wounded mortally, and yet do I think I can be reconciled with her? Upon my word, such thoughts are folly, for at present she has good reason to hate me more bitterly than anything. I am right in saying 'at present', for a woman has more than one mind. That mind in which she is just now I trust she will soon change; indeed, she will change it certainly, and I am mad thus to despair. God grant that she change it soon! For I am doomed to be her slave, since such is the will of Love. Whoever does not welcome Love gladly, when he comes to him, commits treason and a felony. I admit (and let whosoever will, heed what I say) that such an one deserves no happiness or joy. But if I lose, it will not be for such a reason; rather will I love my enemy. For I ought not to feel any hate for her unless I wish to betray Love. I must love in accordance with Love's desire. And ought she to regard me as a friend? Yes, surely, since it is she whom I love. And I call her my enemy, for she hates me, though with good reason, for I killed the object of her love. So, then, am I her enemy? Surely no, but her true friend, for I never so loved any one before. I grieve for her fair tresses, surpassing gold in their radiance; I feel the pangs of anguish and torment when I see her tear and cut them, nor can her tears e'er be dried which I see falling from her eyes; by all these things I am distressed. Although they are full of ceaseless, ever-flowing tears, yet never were there such lovely eves. The sight of her weeping causes me agony, but nothing pains me so much as the sight of her face, which she lacerates without its having merited such treatment. I never saw such a face so perfectly formed, nor so fresh and delicately coloured. And then it has pierced my heart to see her clutch her throat. Surely, it is all too true that she is doing the worst she can. And yet no crystal nor any mirror is so bright and smooth. God! why is she thus possessed, and why does she not spare herself? Why does she wring her lovely hands and beat and tear her breast? Would she not be marvellously fair to look upon when in happy mood, seeing that she is so fair in her displeasure? Surely yes, I can take my oath on that. Never before in a work of beauty was Nature thus able to outdo herself, for I am sure she has gone beyond the limits of any previous attempt. How could it ever have happened then? Whence came beauty so marvellous? God must have made her with His naked hand that Nature might rest from further toil. If she should try to make a replica, she might spend her time in vain without succeeding in her task. Even God Himself, were He to try, could not succeed, I guess, in ever making such another, whatever effort He might put forth."

He Saw the Lady Go Away

THUS MY LORD YVAIN considers her who is broken with her grief, and I suppose it would never happen again that any man in prison, like my lord Yvain in fear for his life, would ever be so madly in love as to make no request on his own behalf, when perhaps no one else will speak for him. He stayed at the window until he saw the lady go away, and both the portcullises were lowered again.

Another might have grieved at this, who would prefer a free escape to tarrying longer where he was. But to him it is quite indifferent whether they be shut or opened. If they were open he surely would not go away, no, even were the lady to give him leave and pardon him freely for the death of her lord. For he is detained by Love and Shame which rise up before him on either hand: he is ashamed to go away, for no one would believe in the success of his exploit; on the other hand, he has such a strong desire to see the lady at least, if he cannot obtain any other favour, that he feels little concern about his imprisonment. He would rather die than go away. And now the damsel returns, wishing to bear him company with her solace and gaiety, and to go and fetch for him whatever he may desire. But she found him pensive and quite worn out with the love which had laid hold of him; whereupon she addressed him thus: "My lord Yvain, what sort of a time have you had to-day?"

"I have been pleasantly occupied," was his reply. "Pleasantly? In God's name, is that the truth? What? How can one enjoy himself seeing that he is hunted to death, unless he courts and wishes it?" "Of a truth," he says, "my gentle friend, I should by no means wish to die; and yet, as God beholds me, I was pleased, am pleased now, and always shall be pleased by what I saw." "Well, let us say no more of that," she makes reply, "for I can understand well enough what is the meaning of such words. I am not so foolish or inexperienced that I cannot understand such words as those; but come now after me, for I shall find some speedy means to release you from your confinement. I shall surely set you free to-night or to-morrow, if you please. Come now, I will lead you away." And he thus makes reply: "You may be sure that I will never escape secretly and like a thief. When the people are all gathered out there in the streets, I can go forth more honourably than if I did so surreptitiously." Then he followed her into the little room. The damsel, who was kind, secured and bestowed upon him all that he desired. And when the opportunity arose, she remembered what he had said to her how he had been pleased by what he saw when they were seeking him in the room with intent to kill him.

The damsel stood in such favour with her lady that she had no fear of telling her anything, regardless of the consequences, for she was her confidante and companion. Then, why should she be backward in comforting her lady and in giving her advice which should redound to her honour? The first time she said to her privily: "My lady, I greatly marvel to see you act so extravagantly. Do you think you can recover your lord by giving away thus to your grief?" "Nay, rather, if I had my wish," says she, "I would now be dead of grief." "And why?" "In order to follow after him."

"After him? God forbid, and give you again as good a lord, as is consistent with His might." "Thou didst never speak such a lie as that, for He could never give me so good a lord again." "He will give you a better one, if you will accept him, and I can prove it." "Begone! Peace! I shall never find such a one." "Indeed you shall, my lady, if you will consent. Just tell me, if you will, who is going to defend your land when King Arthur comes next week to the margin of the spring? You have already been apprised of this by letters sent you by the Dameisele Sauvage. Alas, what a kind service she did for you! you ought to be considering how you will defend your spring, and yet you cease not to weep! If it please you, my dear lady, you ought not to delay. For surely, all the knights you have are not worth, as you well know, so much as a single chamber-maid. Neither shield nor lance will ever be taken in hand by the best of them. You have plenty of craven servants, but there is not one of them brave enough to dare to mount a steed. And the King is coming with such a host that his victory will be inevitable." The lady, upon reflection, knows very well that she is giving her sincere advice, but she is unreasonable in one respect, as also are other women who are, almost without exception, guilty of their own folly, and refuse to accept what they really wish. "Begone," she says; "leave me alone. If I ever hear thee speak of this again it will go hard with thee, unless thou flee. Thou weariest me with thy idle words." "Very well, my lady," she says; "that you are a woman is evident, for woman will grow irate when she hears any one give her good advice."

Then she went away and left her alone. And the lady reflected that she had been in the wrong. She would have been very glad to know how the damsel could ever prove that it would be possible to find a better knight than her lord had ever been. She would be very glad to hear her speak, but now she has forbidden her. With this desire in mind, she waited until she returned. But the warning was of no avail, for she began to say to her at once: "My lady, is it seemly that you should thus torment yourself with grief? For God's sake now control yourself, and for shame, at least, cease your lament. It is not fitting that so great a lady should keep up her grief so long. Remember your honourable estate and your very gentle birth! Think you that all virtue ceased with the death of your lord? There are in the world a hundred as good or better men." "May God confound me, if thou dost not lie! Just name to me a single one who is reputed to be so excellent as my lord was all his life." "If I did so you would be angry with me, and would fly into a passion and you would esteem me less." "No, I will not, I assure thee." "Then may it all be for your future welfare if you would but consent, and may God so incline your will! I see no reason for holding my peace, for no one hears or heeds what we say. Doubtless you will think I am impudent, but I shall freely speak my mind. When two knights have met in an affray of arms and when one has beaten the other, which of the two do you think is the better? For my part I award the prize to the victor. Now what do you think?" "It seems to me you are laying a trap for me and intend to catch me in my words." "Upon my faith, you may rest assured that I am in the right, and I can irrefutably prove to you that he who defeated your lord is better than he was himself. He beat him and pursued him valiantly until he imprisoned him in his house." "Now," she replies, "I hear the greatest nonsense that was ever uttered. Begone, thou spirit charged with evil! Begone, thou foolish and tiresome girl! Never again utter such idle words, and never come again into my presence to speak a word on his behalf!" "Indeed, my lady, I knew full well that I should receive no thanks from you, and I said so before I spoke. But you promised me you would not be displeased, and that you would not be angry with me for it. But you have failed to keep your promise, and now, as it has turned out, you have discharged your wrath on me, and I have lost by not holding my peace."

Lord Yvain is Waiting

THEREUPON SHE GOES BACK to the room where my lord Yvain is waiting, comfortably guarded by her vigilance. But he is ill at ease when he cannot see the lady, and he pays no attention, and hears no word of the report which the damsel brings to him. The lady, too, is in great perplexity all night, being worried about how she should defend the spring; and she begins to repent of her action to the damsel, whom she

**had blamed and insulted and treated with contempt. She feels
very sure and certain that not for any reward or bribe, nor for
any affection which she may bear him, would the maiden ever
have mentioned him; and that she must love her more than him,
and that she would never give her advice which would bring her
shame or embarrassment: the maid is too loyal a friend for that.**

Thus, lo! the lady is completely changed: she fears now that she to
whom she had spoken harshly will never love her again devotedly; and
him whom she had repulsed, she now loyally and with good reason
pardons, seeing that he had done her no wrong. So she argues as if he
were in her presence there, and thus she begins her argument: "Come,"
she says, "canst thou deny that my lord was killed by thee?" "That," says
he, "I cannot deny. Indeed, I fully admit it." "Tell me, then, the reason
of thy deed. Didst thou do it to injure me, prompted by hatred or by
spite?" "May death not spare me now, if I did it to injure you." "In that
case, thou hast done me no wrong, nor art thou guilty of aught toward
him. For he would have killed thee, if he could. So it seems to me that
I have decided well and righteously."

Thus, by her own arguments she succeeds in discovering justice,
reason, and common sense, how that there is no cause for hating him;
thus she frames the matter to conform with her desire, and by her
own efforts she kindles her love, as a bush which only smokes with
the flame beneath, until some one blows it or stirs it up. If the damsel
should come in now, she would win the quarrel for which she had been
so reproached, and by which she had been so hurt. And next morning,
in fact, she appeared again, taking the subject up where she had let
it drop. Meanwhile, the lady bowed her head, knowing she had done
wrong in attacking her. But now she is anxious to make amends, and
to inquire concerning the name, character, and lineage of the knight:
so she wisely humbles herself, and says: "I wish to beg your pardon
for the insulting words of pride which in my rage I spoke to you: I
will follow your advice. So tell me now, if possible, about the knight of
whom you have spoken so much to me: what sort of a man is he, and
of what parentage? If he is suited to become my mate, and provided

he be so disposed, I promise you to make him my husband and lord of my domain. But he will have to act in such a way that no one can reproach me by saying: 'This is she who took him who killed her lord.'" "In God's name, lady, so shall it be. You will have the gentlest, noblest, and fairest lord who ever belonged to Abel's line." "What is his name?" "My lord Yvain." "Upon my word, if he is King Urien's son he is of no mean birth, but very noble, as I well know." "Indeed, my lady, you say the truth." "And when shall we be able to see him?" "In five days' time." "That would be too long; for I wish he were already come. Let him come to-night, or to-morrow, at the latest." "My lady, I think no one could fly so far in one day. But I shall send one of my squires who can run fast, and who will reach King Arthur's court at least by to-morrow night, I think; that is the place we must seek for him." "That is a very long time. The days are long. But tell him that to-morrow night he must be back here, and that he must make greater haste than usual. If he will only do his best, he can do two days' journey in one. Moreover, to-night the moon will shine; so let him turn night into day. And when he returns I will give him whatever he wishes me to give."

"Leave all care of that to me; for you shall have him in your hands the day after to-morrow at the very latest. Meanwhile you shall summon your men and confer with them about the approaching visit of the King. In order to make the customary defence of your spring it behoves you to consult with them. None of them will be so hardy as to dare to boast that he will present himself. In that case you will have a good excuse for saying that it behoves you to marry again. A certain knight, highly qualified, seeks your hand; but you do not presume to accept him without their unanimous consent. And I warrant what the outcome will be: I know them all to be such cowards that in order to put on some one else the burden which would be too heavy for them, they will fall at your feet and speak their gratitude; for thus their responsibility will be at an end. For, whoever is afraid of his own shadow willingly avoids, if possible, any meeting with lance or spear; for such games a coward has no use."

"Upon my word," the lady replies, "so I would have it, and so I consent, having already conceived the plan which you have expressed; so that is what we shall do. But why do you tarry here? Go, without delay, and take measures to bring him here, while I shall summon my liege-men." Thus concluded their conference. And the damsel pretends to send to search for my lord Yvain in his country; while every day she has him bathed, and washed, and groomed. And besides this she prepares for him a robe of red scarlet stuff, brand new and lined with spotted fur. There is nothing necessary for his equipment which she does not lend to him: a golden buckle for his neck, ornamented with precious stones which make people look well, a girdle, and a wallet made of rich gold brocade. She fitted him out perfectly, then informed her lady that the messenger had returned, having done his errand well. "How is that?" she says, "is he here? Then let him come at once, secretly and privily, while no one is here with me. See to it that no one else come in, for I should hate to see a fourth person here." At this the damsel went away, and returned to her guest again. However, her face did not reveal the joy that was in her heart; indeed, she said that her lady knew that she had been sheltering him, and was very much incensed at her.

"Further concealment is useless now. The news about you has been so divulged that my lady knows the whole story and is very angry with me, heaping me with blame and reproaches. But she has given me her word that I may take you into her presence without any harm or danger. I take it that you will have no objection to this, except for one condition (for I must not disguise the truth, or I should be unjust to you): she wishes to have you in her control, and she desires such complete possession of your body that even your heart shall not be at large." "Certainly," he said, "I readily consent to what will be no hardship to me. I am willing to be her prisoner." "So shall you be: I swear it by this right hand laid upon you!. Now come and, upon my advice, demean yourself so humbly in her presence that your imprisonment may not be grievous. Otherwise feel no concern. I do not think that your restraint will be irksome." Then the damsel leads him off, now alarming, now reassuring him, and speaking to him mysteriously about the confinement in which he is to find himself; for every lover is a prisoner. She is right in calling him a prisoner; for surely any one who loves is no longer free.

He Will Be Dearly Loved

TAKING MY LORD YVAIN by the hand, the damsel leads him where he will be dearly loved; but expecting to be ill received, it is not strange if he is afraid. They found the lady seated upon a red cushion. I assure you my lord Yvain was terrified upon entering the room, where he found the lady who spoke not a word to him. At this he was still more afraid, being overcome with fear at the thought that he had been betrayed.

He stood there to one side so long that the damsel at last spoke up and said: "Five hundred curses upon the head of him who takes into a fair lady's chamber a knight who will not draw near, and who has neither tongue nor mouth nor sense to introduce himself." Thereupon, taking him by the arm, she thrust him forward with the words: "Come, step forward, knight, and have no fear that my lady is going to snap at you; but seek her good-will and give her yours. I will join you in your prayer that she pardon you for the death of her lord, Esclados the Red." Then my lord Yvain clasped his hands, and failing upon his knees, spoke like a lover with these words: "I will not crave your pardon, lady, but rather thank you for any treatment you may inflict on me, knowing that no act of yours could ever be distasteful to me." "Is that so, sir? And what if I think to kill you now?" "My lady, if it please you, you will never hear me speak otherwise." "I never heard of such a thing as this: that you put yourself voluntarily and absolutely within my power, without the coercion of any one." "My lady, there is no force so strong, in truth, as that which commands me to conform absolutely to your desire. I do not fear to carry out any order you may be pleased to give. And if I could atone for the death, which came through no fault of mine, I would do so cheerfully." "What?" says she, "come tell me now and be forgiven, if you did no wrong in killing my lord?" "Lady," he says, "if I may say it, when your lord attacked me, why was I wrong to defend myself? When a man in self-defence kills another who is trying to kill or capture him, tell me if in any way he is to blame." "No, if one looks at it aright. And I suppose it would have been no use, if I had had you put to death. But I should be glad to learn whence you derive the force that bids you to consent unquestioningly to whatever my will may dictate. I pardon you all your misdeeds and crimes. But be seated, and tell us now what is the cause of your docility?" "My lady," he says, "the impelling force comes from my heart, which is inclined toward you. My heart has fixed me in this desire." "And what prompted your heart, my fair sweet friend?" "Lady, my eyes." "And what the eyes?" "The great beauty that I see in you." "And where is beauty's fault in that?" "Lady, in this: that it makes me love." "Love? And whom?" "You, my lady dear." "I?" "Yes, truly." "Really? And how is that?" "To such an extent that my heart will not stir from you, nor is it elsewhere to be found; to such an extent that I cannot think of anything else, and I surrender myself altogether to you, whom I love more than I love myself, and for whom, if you will, I am equally ready to die or live." "And would you dare to undertake the defence of my spring for love of me?" "Yes, my lady, against the world." "Then you may know that our peace is made."

Thus they are quickly reconciled. And the lady, having previously consulted her lords, says: "We shall proceed from here to the hall where my men are assembled, who, in view of the evident need, have advised and counselled me to take a husband at their request. And I shall do so, in view of the urgent need: here and now I give myself to you; for I should not refuse to accept as lord, such a good knight and a king's son."

Lancelot or the Knight of the Cart

SINCE MY LADY OF CHAMPAGNE wishes me to undertake to write a romance, I shall very gladly do so, being so devoted to her service as to do anything in the world for her, without any intention of flattery.

But if one were to introduce any flattery upon such an occasion, he might say, and I would subscribe to it, that this lady surpasses all others who are alive, just as the south wind which blows in May or April is more lovely than any other wind. But upon my word, I am not one to wish to flatter my lady. I will simply say: "The Countess is worth as many queens as a gem is worth of pearls and sards." Nay I shall make no comparison, and yet it is true in spite of me; I will say, however, that her command has more to do with this work than any thought or pains that I may expend upon it.

Here Chrétien begins his book about the Knight of the Cart. The material and the treatment of it are given and furnished to him by the Countess, and he is simply trying to carry out her concern and intention. Here he begins the story.

Ascension Day

UPON A CERTAIN ASCENSION DAY KING ARTHUR had come from Caerleon, and had held a very magnificent court at Camelot as was fitting on such a day.

After the feast the King did not quit his noble companions, of whom there were many in the hall. The Queen was present, too, and with her many a courteous lady able to converse in French. And Kay, who had furnished the meal, was eating with the others who had served the food.

While Kay was sitting there at meat, behold there came to court a knight, well equipped and fully armed, and thus the knight appeared before the King as he sat among his lords. He gave him no greeting, but spoke out thus: "King Arthur, I hold in captivity knights, ladies, and damsels who belong to thy dominion and household; but it is not because of any intention to restore them to thee that I make reference to them here; rather do I wish to proclaim and serve thee notice that thou hast not the strength or the resources to enable thee to secure them again. And be assured that thou shalt die before thou canst ever succour them."

The King replies that he must needs endure what he has not the power to change; nevertheless, he is filled with grief. Then the knight makes as if to go away, and turns about, without tarrying longer before the King; but after reaching the door of the hall, he does not go down the stairs, but stops and speaks from there these words:

"King, if in thy court there is a single knight in whom thou hast such confidence that thou wouldst dare to entrust to him the Queen that he might escort her after me out into the woods whither I am going, I will promise to await him there, and will surrender to thee all the prisoners whom I hold in exile in my country if he is able to defend the Queen and if he succeeds in bringing her back again."

The King Was Grieved

MANY WHO WERE in the palace heard this challenge, and the whole court was in an uproar. Kay, too, heard the news as he sat at meat with those who served. Leaving the table, he came straight to the King, and as if greatly enraged, he began to say: "O King, I have served thee long, faithfully, and loyally; now I take my leave, and shall go away, having no desire to serve thee more."

The King was grieved at what he heard, and as soon as he could, he thus replied to him: "Is this serious, or a joke?" And Kay replied: "O King, fair sire, I have no desire to jest, and I take my leave quite seriously. No other reward or wages do I wish in return for the service I have given you. My mind is quite made up to go away immediately." "Is it in anger or in spite that you wish to go?" the King inquired; "seneschal, remain at court, as you have done hitherto, and be assured that I have nothing in the world which I would not give you at once in return for your consent to stay." "Sire," says Kay, "no need of that. I would not accept for each day's pay a measure of fine pure gold."

Thereupon, the King in great dismay went off to seek the Queen. "My lady," he says, "you do not know the demand that the seneschal makes of me. He asks me for leave to go away, and says he will no longer stay at court; the reason of this I do not know. But he will do at your request what he will not do for me. Go to him now, my lady dear. Since he will not consent to stay for my sake, pray him to remain on your account, and if need be, fall at his feet, for I should never again be happy if I should lose his company." The King sends the Queen to the seneschal, and she goes to him. Finding him with the rest, she went up to him, and said: "Kay, you may be very sure that I am greatly troubled by the news I have heard of you. I am grieved to say that I have been told it is your intention to leave the King. How does this come about? What motive have you in your mind? I cannot think that you are so sensible or courteous as usual. I want to ask you to remain: stay with us here, and grant my prayer." "Lady," he says, "I give you thanks; nevertheless, I shall not remain." The Queen again makes her request, and is joined by all the other knights. And Kay informs her that he is growing tired of a service which is unprofitable. Then the Queen prostrates herself at full length before his feet. Kay beseeches her to rise, but she says that she will never do so until he grants her request. Then Kay promises her to remain, provided the King and she will grant in advance a favour he is about to ask. "Kay," she says, "he will grant it, whatever it may be. Come now, and we shall tell him that upon this condition you will remain." So Kay goes away with the Queen to the King's presence. The Queen says: "I have had hard work to detain Kay; but I have brought him here to you with the understanding that you will do what he is going to ask." The King sighed with satisfaction, and said that he would perform whatever request he might make.

"Sire," says Kay, "hear now what I desire, and what is the gift you have promised me. I esteem myself very fortunate to gain such a boon with your consent. Sire, you have pledged your word that you would entrust to me my lady here, and that we should go after the knight who awaits us in the forest.

Though the King is grieved, he trusts him with the charge, for he never went back upon his word. But it made him so ill-humoured and displeased that it plainly showed in his countenance. The Queen, for her part, was sorry too, and all those of the household say that Kay had made a proud, outrageous, and mad request. Then the King took the Queen by the hand, and said: "My lady, you must accompany Kay without making objection." And Kay said: "Hand her over to me now, and have no fear, for I shall bring her back perfectly happy and safe." The King gives her into his charge, and he takes her off. After them all the rest go out, and there is not one who is not sad. You must know that the seneschal was fully armed, and his horse was led into the middle of the courtyard, together with a palfrey, as is fitting, for the Queen. The Queen walked up to the palfrey, which was neither restive nor hard-mouthed. Grieving and sad, with a sigh the Queen mounts, saying to herself in a low voice, so that no one could hear: "Alas, alas, if you only knew it, I am sure you would never allow me without interference to be led away a step." She thought she had spoken in a very low tone; but Count Guinable heard her, who was standing by when she mounted.

When they started away, as great a lament was made by all the men and women present as if she already lay dead upon a bier. They do not believe that she will ever in her life come back. The seneschal in his impudence takes her where that other knight is awaiting her. But no one was so much concerned as to undertake to follow him; until at last my lord Gawain thus addressed the King his uncle:

"Sire," he says, "you have done a very foolish thing, which causes me great surprise; but if you will take my advice, while they are still near by, I and you will ride after them, and all those who wish to accompany us. For my part, I cannot restrain myself from going in pursuit of them at once. It would not be proper for us not to go after them, at least far enough to learn what is to become of the Queen, and how Kay is going to comport himself." "Ah, fair nephew," the King replied, "you have spoken courteously. And since you have undertaken the affair, order our horses to be led out bridled and saddled that there may be no delay in setting out."

A Horse Running Wild

THE HORSES ARE AT ONCE **brought out, all ready and with the saddles on. First the King mounts, then my lord Gawain, and all the others rapidly. Each one, wishing to be of the party, follows his own will and starts away. Some were armed, but there were not a few without their arms.**

My lord Gawain was armed, and he bade two squires lead by the bridle two extra steeds. And as they thus approached the forest, they saw Kay's horse running out; and they recognised him, and saw that both reins of the bridle were broken. The horse was running wild, the stirrup-straps all stained with blood, and the saddle-bow was broken and damaged. Every one was chagrined at this, and they nudged each other and shook their heads. My lord Gawain was riding far in advance of the rest of the party, and it was not long before he saw coming slowly a knight on a horse that was sore, painfully tired, and covered with sweat. The knight first saluted my lord Gawain, and his greeting my lord Gawain returned. Then the knight, recognising my lord Gawain, stopped and thus spoke to him: "You see, sir, my horse is in a sweat and in such case as to be no longer serviceable. I suppose that those two horses belong to you now, with the understanding that I shall return the service and the favour, I beg you to let me have one or the other of them, either as a loan or outright as a gift." And he answers him: "Choose whichever you prefer."

Gawain Follows in Pursuit

THEN HE WHO WAS IN DIRE DISTRESS did not try to select the better or the fairer or the larger of the horses, but leaped quickly upon the one which was nearer to him, and rode him off. Then the one he had just left fell dead, for he had ridden him hard that day, so that he was used up and overworked.

The knight without delay goes pricking through the forest, and my lord Gawain follows in pursuit of him with all speed, until he reaches the bottom of a hill. And when he had gone some distance, he found the horse dead which he had given to the knight, and noticed that the ground had been trampled by horses, and that broken shields and lances lay strewn about, so that it seemed that there had been a great combat between several knights, and he was very sorry and grieved not to have been there.

However, he did not stay there long, but rapidly passed on until he saw again by chance the knight all alone on foot, completely armed, with helmet laced, shield hanging from his neck, and with his sword girt on. He had overtaken a cart. In those days such a cart served the same purpose as does a pillory now; and in each good town where there are more than three thousand such carts nowadays, in those times there was only one, and this, like our pillories, had to do service for all those who commit murder or treason, and those who are guilty of any delinquency, and for thieves who have stolen others' property or have forcibly seized it on the roads. Whoever was convicted of any crime was placed upon a cart and dragged through all the streets, and he lost henceforth all his legal rights, and was never afterward heard, honoured, or welcomed in any court. The carts were so dreadful in those days that the saying was then first used:

"When thou dost see and meet a cart, cross thyself and call upon God, that no evil may befall thee." The knight on foot, and without a lance, walked behind the cart, and saw a dwarf sitting on the shafts, who held, as a driver does, a long goad in his hand. Then he cries out: "Dwarf, for God's sake, tell me now if thou hast seen my lady, the Queen, pass by here." The miserable, low-born dwarf would not give him any news of her, but replied: "If thou wilt get up into the cart I am driving thou shalt hear to-morrow what has happened to the Queen."

Then he kept on his way without giving further heed. The knight hesitated only for a couple of steps before getting in. Yet, it was unlucky for him that he shrank from the disgrace, and did not jump in at once; for he will later rue his delay. But common sense, which is inconsistent with love's dictates, bids him refrain from getting in, warning him and counselling him to do and undertake nothing for which he may reap shame and disgrace. Reason, which dares thus speak to him, reaches only his lips, but not his heart; but love is enclosed within his heart, bidding him and urging him to mount at once upon the cart. So he jumps in, since love will have it so, feeling no concern about the shame, since he is prompted by love's commands. And my lord Gawain presses on in haste after the cart, and when he finds the knight sitting in it, his surprise is great.

"Tell me," he shouted to the dwarf, "if thou knowest anything of the Queen." And he replied: "If thou art so much thy own enemy as is this knight who is sitting here, get in with him, if it be thy pleasure, and I will drive thee along with him." When my lord Gawain heard that, he considered it great foolishness, and said that he would not get in, for it would be dishonourable to exchange a horse for a cart: "Go on, and wherever thy journey lies, I will follow after thee."

The Knight Riding Upon the Cart

THEREUPON THEY START AHEAD, one mounted on his horse, the other two riding in the cart, and thus they proceed in company. Late in the afternoon they arrive at a town, which, you must know, was very rich and beautiful.

All three entered through the gate; the people are greatly amazed to see the knight borne upon the cart, and they take no pains to conceal their feelings, but small and great and old and young shout taunts at him in the streets, so that the knight hears many vile and scornful words at his expense. They all inquire: "To what punishment is this knight to be consigned? Is he to be rayed, or hanged, or drowned, or burned upon a fire of thorns? Tell us, thou dwarf, who art driving him, in what crime was he caught? Is he convicted of robbery? Is he a murderer, or a criminal?" And to all this the dwarf made no response, vouchsafing to them no reply. He conducts the knight to a lodging-place; and Gawain follows the dwarf closely to a tower, which stood on the same level over against the town. Beyond there stretched a meadow, and the tower was built close by, up on a lofty eminence of rock, whose face formed a sharp precipice. Following the horse and cart, Gawain entered the tower. In the hall they met a damsel elegantly attired, than whom there was none fairer in the land, and with her they saw coming two fair and charming maidens. As soon as they saw my lord Gawain, they received him joyously and saluted him, and then asked news about the other knight: "Dwarf, of what crime is this knight guilty, whom thou dost drive like a lame man?" He would not answer her question, but he made the knight get out of the cart, and then he withdrew, without their knowing whither he went. Then my lord Gawain dismounts, and valets come forward to relieve the two knights of their armour. The damsel ordered two green mantles to be brought, which they put on. When the hour for supper came, a sumptuous repast was set. The damsel sat at table beside my lord Gawain. They would not have changed their lodging-place to seek any other, for all that evening the damsel showed them gear honour, and provided them with fair and pleasant company.

When they had sat up long enough, two long, high beds were prepared in the middle of the hall; and there was another bed alongside, fairer and more splendid than the rest; for, as the story testifies, it possessed all the excellence that one could think of in a bed. When the time came to retire, the damsel took both the guests to whom she had offered her hospitality; she shows them the two fine, long, wide beds, and says: "These two beds are set up here for the accommodation of your bodies; but in that one yonder no one ever lay who did not merit it: it was not set up to be used by you." The knight who came riding on the cart replies at once: "Tell me," he says, "for what cause this bed is inaccessible." Being thoroughly informed of this, she answers unhesitatingly: "It is not your place to ask or make such an inquiry. Any knight is disgraced in the land after being in a cart, and it is not fitting that he should concern himself with the matter upon which you have questioned me; and most of all it is not right that he should lie upon the bed, for he would soon pay dearly for his act. So rich a couch has not been prepared for you, and you would pay dearly for ever harbouring such a thought."

He replies: "You will see about that presently.".... "Am I to see it?".... "Yes.".... "It will soon appear.".... "By my head," the knight replies, "I know not who is to pay the penalty. But whoever may object or disapprove, I intend to lie upon this bed and repose there at my ease." Then he at once disrobed in the bed, which was long and raised half an ell above the other two, and was covered with a yellow cloth of silk and a coverlet with gilded stars. The furs were not of skinned vair but of sable; the covering he had on him would have been fitting for a king. The mattress was not made of straw or rushes or of old mats. At midnight there descended from the rafters suddenly a lance, as with the intention of pinning the knight through the flanks to the coverlet and the white sheets where he lay. To the lance there was attached a pennon all ablaze. The coverlet, the bedclothes, and the bed itself all caught fire at once. And the tip of the lance passed so close to the knight's side that it cut the skin a little, without seriously wounding him.

Then the knight got up, put out the fire and, taking the lance, swung it in the middle of the hall, all this without leaving his bed; rather did he lie down again and slept as securely as at first.

The Knights Meet a Damsel Who
Has Seen Queen Guinevere

IN THE MORNING, at daybreak, the damsel of the tower had Mass celebrated on their account, and had them rise and dress. When Mass had been celebrated for them, the knight who had ridden in the cart sat down pensively at a window, which looked out upon the meadow, and he gazed upon the fields below.

The damsel came to another window close by, and there my lord Gawain conversed with her privately for a while about something, I know not what. I do not know what words were uttered, but while they were leaning on the window-sill they saw carried along the river through the fields a bier, upon which there lay a knight, and alongside three damsels walked, mourning bitterly. Behind the bier they saw a crowd approaching, with a tall knight in front, leading a fair lady by the horse's rein. The knight at the window knew that it was the Queen. He continued to gaze at her attentively and with delight as long as she was visible. And when he could no longer see her, he was minded to throw himself out and break his body down below. And he would have let himself fall out had not my lord Gawain seen him, and drawn him back, saying: "I beg you, sire, be quiet now. For God's sake, never think again of committing such a mad deed. It is wrong for you to despise your life." "He is perfectly right," the damsel says; "for will not the news of his disgrace be known everywhere? Since he has been upon the cart, he has good reason to wish to die, for he would be better dead than alive. His life henceforth is sure to be one of shame, vexation, and unhappiness." Then the knights asked for their armour, and armed themselves, the damsel treating them courteously, with distinction and generosity; for when she had joked with the knight and ridiculed him enough, she presented him with a horse and lance as a token of her goodwill. The knights then courteously and politely took leave of the damsel, first saluting her, and then going off in the direction taken by the crowd they had seen. Thus they rode out from the town without addressing them. They proceeded quickly in the direction they had seen taken by the Queen, but they did not overtake the procession, which had advanced rapidly.

After leaving the fields, the knights enter an enclosed place, and find a beaten road. They advanced through the woods until it might be six o'clock, and then at a crossroads they met a damsel, whom they both saluted, each asking and requesting her to tell them, if she knows, whither the Queen has been taken.

Replying intelligently, she said to them: "If you would pledge me your word, I could set you on the right road and path, and I would tell you the name of the country and of the knight who is conducting her; but whoever would essay to enter that country must endure sore trials, for before he could reach there he must suffer much." Then my lord Gawain replies: "Damsel, so help me God, I promise to place all my strength at your disposal and service, whenever you please, if you will tell me now the truth." And he who had been on the cart did not say that he would pledge her all his strength; but he proclaims, like one whom love makes rich, powerful and bold for any enterprise, that at once and without hesitation he will promise her anything she desires, and he puts himself altogether at her disposal. "Then I will tell you the truth," says she.

Then the damsel relates to them the following story: "In truth, my lords, Meleagant, a tall and powerful knight, son of the King of Gorre, has taken her off into the kingdom whence no foreigner returns, but where he must perforce remain in servitude and banishment." Then they ask her: "Damsel, where is this country? Where can we find the way thither?"

She replies: "That you shall quickly learn; but you may be sure that you will meet with many obstacles and difficult passages, for it is not easy to enter there except with the permission of the king, whose name is Bademagu; however, it is possible to enter by two very perilous paths and by two very difficult passage-ways. One is called the water-bridge, because the bridge is under water, and there is the same amount of water beneath it as above it, so that the bridge is exactly in the middle; and it is only a foot and a half in width and in thickness. This choice is certainly to be avoided, and yet it is the less dangerous of the two. In addition there are a number of other obstacles of which I will say nothing. The other bridge is still more impracticable and much more perilous, never having been crossed by man. It is just like a sharp sword, and therefore all the people call it 'the sword-bridge'. Now I have told you all the truth I know."

But they ask of her once again: "Damsel, deign to show us these two passages." To which the damsel makes reply: "This road here is the most direct to the water-bridge, and that one yonder leads straight to the sword-bridge."

Then the knight, who had been on the cart, says: "Sire, I am ready to share with you without prejudice: take one of these two routes, and leave the other one to me; take whichever you prefer."

"In truth," my lord Gawain replies, "both of them are hard and dangerous: I am not skilled in making such a choice, and hardly know which of them to take; but it is not right for me to hesitate when you have left the choice to me: I will choose the water-bridge." The other answers: "Then I must go uncomplainingly to the sword-bridge, which I agree to do."

Thereupon, they all three part, each one commending the others very courteously to God. And when she sees them departing, she says: "Each one of you owes me a favour of my choosing, whenever I may choose to ask it. Take care not to forget that." "We shall surely not forget it, sweet friend," both the knights call out. Then each one goes his own way, and he of the cart is occupied with deep reflections, like one who has no strength or defence against love which holds him in its sway.

His thoughts are such that he totally forgets himself, and he knows not whether he is alive or dead, forgetting even his own name, not knowing whether he is armed or not, or whither he is going or whence he came. Only one creature he has in mind, and for her his thought is so occupied that he neither sees nor hears aught else.

And his horse bears him along rapidly, following no crooked road, but the best and the most direct; and thus proceeding unguided, he brings him into an open plain. In this plain there was a ford, on the other side of which a knight stood armed, who guarded it, and in his company there was a damsel who had come on a palfrey.

The Ford

BY THIS TIME the afternoon was well advanced, and yet the knight, unchanged and unwearied, pursued his thoughts. The horse, being very thirsty, sees clearly the ford, and as soon as he sees it, hastens toward it. Then he on the other side cries out: "Knight, I am guarding the ford, and forbid you to cross." He neither gives him heed, nor hears his words, being still deep in thought.

In the meantime, his horse advanced rapidly toward the water. The knight calls out to him that he will do wisely to keep at a distance from the ford, for there is no passage that way; and he swears by the heart within his breast that he will smite him if he enters the water. But his threats are not heard, and he calls out to him a third time: "Knight, do not enter the ford against my will and prohibition; for, by my head, I shall strike you as soon as I see you in the ford." But he is so deep in thought that he does not hear him.

And the horse, quickly leaving the bank, leaps into the ford and greedily begins to drink. And the knight says he shall pay for this, that his shield and the hauberk he wears upon his back shall afford him no protection. First, he puts his horse at a gallop, and from a gallop he urges him to a run, and he strikes the knight so hard that he knocks him down flat in the ford which he had forbidden him to cross. His lance flew from his hand and the shield from his neck.

When he feels the water, he shivers, and though stunned, he jumps to his feet, like one aroused from sleep, listening and looking about him with astonishment, to see who it can be who has struck him. Then face to face with the other knight, he said: "Vassal, tell me why you have struck me, when I was not aware of your presence, and when I had done you no harm." "Upon my word, you had wronged me," the other says: "did you not treat me disdainfully when I forbade you three times to cross the ford, shouting at you as loudly as I could? You surely heard me challenge you at least two or three times, and you entered in spite of me, though I told you I should strike you as soon as I saw you in the ford." Then the knight replies to him: "Whoever heard you or saw you, let him be damned, so far as I am concerned. I was probably deep in thought when you forbade me to cross the ford. But be assured that I would make you reset it, if I could just lay one of my hands on your bridle." And the other replies: "Why, what of that? If you dare, you may seize my bridle here and now. I do not esteem your proud threats so much as a handful of ashes."

And he replies: "That suits me perfectly. However the affair may turn out, I should like to lay my hands on you." Then the other knight advances to the middle of the ford, where the other lays his left hand upon his bridle, and his right hand upon his leg, pulling, dragging, and pressing him so roughly that he remonstrates, thinking that he would pull his leg out of his body. Then he begs him to let go, saying: "Knight, if it please thee to fight me on even terms, take thy shield and horse and lance, and joust with me." He answers: "That will I not do, upon my word; for I suppose thou wouldst run away as soon as thou hadst escaped my grip."

Hearing this, he was much ashamed, and said: "Knight, mount thy horse, in confidence for I will pledge thee loyally my word that I shall not flinch or run away." Then once again he answers him: "First, thou wilt have to swear to that, and I insist upon receiving thy oath that thou wilt neither run away nor flinch, nor touch me, nor come near me until thou shalt see me on my horse; I shall be treating thee very generously, if, when thou art in my hands, I let thee go." He can do nothing but give his oath; and when the other hears him swear, he gathers up his shield and lance which were floating in the ford and by this time had drifted well down-stream; then he returns and takes his horse. After catching and mounting him, he seizes the shield by the shoulder-straps and lays his lance in rest. Then each spurs toward the other as fast as their horses can carry them. And he who had to defend the ford first attacks the other, striking him so hard that his lance is completely splintered. The other strikes him in return so that he throws him prostrate into the ford, and the water closes over him.

Having accomplished that, he draws back and dismounts, thinking he could drive and chase away a hundred such. While he draws from the scabbard his sword of steel, the other jumps up and draws his excellent flashing blade. Then they clash again, advancing and covering themselves with the shields which gleam with gold. Ceaselessly and without repose they wield their swords; they have the courage to deal so many blows that the battle finally is so protracted that the Knight of the Cart is greatly ashamed in his heart, thinking that he is making a sorry start in the way he has undertaken, when he has spent so much time in defeating a single knight. If he had met yesterday a hundred such, he does not think or believe that they could have withstood him; so now he is much grieved and wroth to be in such an exhausted state that he is missing his strokes and losing time. Then he runs at him and presses him so hard that the other knight gives way and flees. However reluctant he may be, he leaves the ford and crossing free. But the other follows him in pursuit until he falls forward upon his hands; then he of the cart runs up to him, swearing by all he sees that he shall rue the day when he upset him in the ford and disturbed his revery.

Set Him Free

T HE DAMSEL, WHOM THE KNIGHT had with him, upon hearing the threats, is in great fear, and begs him for her sake to forbear from killing him; but he tells her that he must do so, and can show him no mercy for her sake, in view of the shameful wrong that he has done him.

Then, with sword drawn, he approaches the knight who cries in sore dismay: "For God's sake and for my own, show me the mercy I ask of you." And he replies: "As God may save me, no one ever sinned so against me that I would not show him mercy once, for God's sake as is right, if he asked it of me in God's name. And so on thee I will have mercy; for I ought not to refuse thee when thou hast besought me. But first, thou shalt give me thy word to constitute thyself my prisoner whenever I may wish to summon thee." Though it was hard to do so, he promised him. At once the damsel said: "O knight, since thou hast granted the mercy he asked of thee, if ever thou hast broken any bonds, for my sake now be merciful and release this prisoner from his parole. Set him free at my request, upon condition that when the time comes, I shall do my utmost to repay thee in any way that thou shalt choose." Then he declares himself satisfied with the promise she has made, and sets the knight at liberty. Then she is ashamed and anxious, thinking that he will recognise her, which she did not wish. But he goes away at once, the knight and the damsel commending him to God, and taking leave of him.

He grants them leave to go, while he himself pursues his way, until late in the afternoon he met a damsel coming, who was very fair and charming, well attired and richly dressed. The damsel greets him prudently and courteously, and he replies: "Damsel, God grant you health and happiness." Then the damsel said to him: "Sire, my house is prepared for you, if you will accept my hospitality, but you shall find shelter there only on condition that you will lie with me; upon these terms I propose and make the offer." Not a few there are who would have thanked her five hundred times for such a gift; but he is much displeased, and made a very different answer: "Damsel, I thank you for the offer of your house, and esteem it highly, but, if you please, I should be very sorry to lie with you." "By my eyes," the damsel says, "then I retract my offer." And he, since it is unavoidable, lets her have her way, though his heart grieves to give consent. He feels only reluctance now; but greater distress will be his when it is time to go to bed. The damsel, too, who leads him away, will pass through sorrow and heaviness. For it is possible that she will love him so that she will not wish to part with him. As soon as he had granted her wish and desire, she escorts him to a fortified place, than which there was none fairer in Thessaly; for it was entirely enclosed by a high wall and a deep moat, and there was no man within except him whom she brought with her.

A Drawbridge Lowered to Let Them Pass

HERE SHE HAD CONSTRUCTED FOR HER RESIDENCE a quantity of handsome rooms, and a large and roomy hall. Riding along a river bank, they approached their lodging-place, and a drawbridge was lowered to allow them to pass. Crossing the bridge, they entered in, and found the hall open with its roof of tiles. Through the open door they pass, and see a table laid with a broad white cloth, upon which the dishes were set, and the candles burning in their stands, and the gilded silver drinking-cups, and two pots of wine, one red and one white.

Standing beside the table, at the end of a bench, they found two basins of warm water in which to wash their hands, with a richly embroidered towel, all white and clean, with which to dry their hands. No valets, servants, or squires were to be found or seen. The knight, removing his shield from about his neck, hangs it upon a hook, and, taking his lance, lays it above upon a rack. Then he dismounts from his horse, as does the damsel from hers. The knight, for his part, was pleased that she did not care to wait for him to help her to dismount. Having dismounted, she runs directly to a room and brings him a short mantle of scarlet cloth which she puts on him. The hall was by no means dark; for beside the light from the stars, there were many large twisted candles lighted there, so that the illumination was very bright. When she had thrown the mantle about his shoulders, she said to him: "Friend, here is the water and the towel; there is no one to present or offer it to you except me whom you see. Wash your hands, and then sit down, when you feel like doing so. The hour and the meal, as you can see, demand that you should do so." He washes, and then gladly and readily takes his seat, and she sits down beside him, and they eat and drink together, until the time comes to leave the table.

When they had risen from the table, the damsel said to the knight: "Sire, if you do not object, go outside and amuse yourself; but, if you please, do not stay after you think I must be in bed. Feel no concern or embarrassment; for then you may come to me at once, if you will keep the promise you have made." And he replies: "I will keep my word, and will return when I think the time has come." Then he went out, and stayed in the courtyard until he thought it was time to return and keep the promise he had made. Going back into the hall, he sees nothing of her who would be his mistress; for she was not there. Not finding or seeing her, he said: "Wherever she may be, I shall look for her until I find her." He makes no delay in his search, being bound by the promise he had made her. Entering one of the rooms, he hears a damsel cry aloud, and it was the very one with whom he was about to lie. At the same time, he sees the door of another room standing open, and stepping toward it, he sees right before his eyes a knight who had thrown her down, and was holding her naked and prostrate upon the bed. She, thinking that he had come of course to help her, cried aloud: "Help, help, thou knight, who art my guest. If thou dost not take this man away from me, I shall find no one to do so; if thou dost not succour me speedily, he will wrong me before thy eyes. Thou art the one to lie with me, in accordance with thy promise; and shall this man by force accomplish his wish before thy eyes? Gentle knight, exert thyself, and make haste to bear me aid." He sees that the other man held the damsel brutally uncovered to the waist, and he is ashamed and angered to see him assault her so; yet it is not jealousy he feels, nor will he be made a cuckold by him. At the door there stood as guards two knights completely armed and with swords drawn. Behind them there stood four men-at-arms, each armed with an axe the sort with which you could split a cow down the back as easily as a root of juniper or broom.

The knight hesitated at the door, and thought: "God, what can I do? I am engaged in no less an affair than the quest of Queen Guinevere. I ought not to have the heart of a hare, when for her sake I have engaged in such a quest. If cowardice puts its heart in me, and if I follow its dictates, I shall never attain what I seek. I am disgraced, if I stand here; indeed, I am ashamed even to have thought of holding back. My heart is very sad and oppressed: now I am so ashamed and distressed that I would gladly die for having hesitated here so long. I say it not in pride: but may God have mercy on me if I do not prefer to die honourably rather than live a life of shame! If my path were unobstructed, and if these men gave me leave to pass through without restraint, what honour would I gain? Truly, in that case the greatest coward alive would pass through; and all the while I hear this poor creature calling for help constantly, and reminding me of my promise, and reproaching me with bitter taunts." Then he steps to the door, thrusting in his head and shoulders; glancing up, he sees two swords descending. He draws back, and the knights could not check their strokes: they had wielded them with such force that the swords struck the floor, and both were broken in pieces. When he sees that the swords are broken, he pays less attention to the axes, fearing and dreading them much less. Rushing in among them, he strikes first one guard in the side and then another. The two who are nearest him he jostles and thrusts aside, throwing them both down flat; the third missed his stroke at him, but the fourth, who attacked him, strikes him so that he cuts his mantle and shirt, and slices the white flesh on his shoulder so that the blood trickles down from the wound. But he, without delay, and without complaining of his wound, presses on more rapidly, until he strikes between the temples him who was assaulting his hostess. Before he departs, he will try to keep his pledge to her. He makes him stand up reluctantly. Meanwhile, he who had missed striking him comes at him as fast as he can and, raising his arm again, expects to split his head to the teeth with the axe. But the other, alert to defend himself, thrusts the knight toward him in such a way that he receives the axe just where the shoulder joins the neck, so that they are cleaved apart. Then the knight seizes the axe, wresting it quickly from him who holds it; then he lets go the knight whom he still held, and looks to his own defence; for the knights from the door, and the three men with axes are all attacking him fiercely.

So he leaped quickly between the bed and the wall, and called to them: "Come on now, all of you. If there were thirty-seven of you, you would have all the fight you wish, with me so favourably placed; I shall never be overcome by you." And the damsel watching him, exclaimed: "By my eyes, you need have no thought of that henceforth where I am." Then at once she dismisses the knights and the men-at-arms, who retire from there at once, without delay or objection. And the damsel continues: "Sire you have well defended me against the men of my household. Come now, and I'll lead you on." Hand in hand they enter the hall, but he was not at all pleased, and would have willingly dispensed with her.

The Knight Has Only One Heart

IN THE MIDST OF THE HALL a bed had been set up, the sheets of which were by no means soiled, but were white and wide and well spread out. The bed was not of shredded straw or of coarse spreads. But a covering of two silk cloths had been laid upon the couch.

The damsel lay down first, but without removing her chemise. He had great trouble in removing his hose and in untying the knots. He sweated with the trouble of it all; yet, in the midst of all the trouble, his promise impels and drives him on. Is this then an actual force? Yes, virtually so; for he feels that he is in duty bound to take his place by the damsel's side. It is his promise that urges him and dictates his act. So he lies down at once, but like her, he does not remove his shirt.

He takes good care not to touch her; and when he is in bed, he turns away from her as far as possible, and speaks not a word to her, like a monk to whom speech is forbidden. Not once does he look at her, nor show her any courtesy. Why not? Because his heart does not go out to her. She was certainly very fair and winsome, but not every one is pleased and touched by what is fair and winsome. The knight has only one heart, and this one is really no longer his, but has been entrusted to some one else, so that he cannot bestow it elsewhere. Love, which holds all hearts beneath its sway, requires it to be lodged in a single place. All hearts? No, only those which it esteems. And he whom love deigns to control ought to prize himself the more. Love prized his heart so highly that it constrained it in a special manner, and made him so proud of this distinction that I am not inclined to find fault with him, if he lets alone what love forbids, and remains fixed where it desires. The maiden clearly sees and knows that he dislikes her company and would gladly dispense with it, and that, having no desire to win her love, he would not attempt to woo her.

So she said: "My lord, if you will not feel hurt, I will leave and return to bed in my own room, and you will be more comfortable. I do not believe that you are pleased with my company and society. Do not esteem me less if I tell you what I think. Now take your rest all night, for you have so well kept your promise that I have no right to make further request of you. So I commend you to God; and shall go away." Thereupon she arises: the knight does not object, but rather gladly lets her go, like one who is the devoted lover of some one else; the damsel clearly perceived this, and went to her room, where she undressed completely and retired, saying to herself:

"Of all the knights I have ever known, I never knew a single knight whom I would value the third part of an angevin in comparison with this one. As I understand the case, he has on hand a more perilous and grave affair than any ever undertaken by a knight; and may God grant that he succeed in it." Then she fell asleep, and remained in bed until the next day's dawn appeared.

At daybreak she awakes and gets up. The knight awakes too, dressing, and putting on his arms, without waiting for any help. Then the damsel comes and sees that he is already dressed. Upon seeing him, she says: "May this day be a happy one for you." "And may it be the same to you, damsel," the knight replies, adding that he is waiting anxiously for some one to bring out his horse. The maiden has some one fetch the horse, and says: "Sire, I should like to accompany you for some distance along the road, if you would agree to escort and conduct me according to the customs and practices which were observed before we were made captive in the kingdom of Logres." In those days the customs and privileges were such that, if a knight found a damsel or lorn maid alone, and if he cared for his fair name, he would no more treat her with dishonour than he would cut his own throat. And if he assaulted her, he would be disgraced for ever in every court. But if, while she was under his escort, she should be won at arms by another who engaged him in battle, then this other knight might do with her what he pleased without receiving shame or blame. This is why the damsel said she would go with him, if he had the courage and willingness to safe guard her in his company, so that no one should do her any harm.

And he says to her: "No one shall harm you, I promise you, unless he harm me first." "Then," she says, "I will go with you." She orders her palfrey to be saddled, and her command is obeyed at once. Her palfrey was brought together with the knight's horse. Without the aid of any squire, they both mount, and rapidly ride away. She talks to him, but not caring for her words, he pays no attention to what she says. He likes to think, but dislikes to talk. Love very often inflicts afresh the wound it has given him. Yet, he applied no poultice to the wound to cure it and make it comfortable, having no intention or desire to secure a poultice or to seek a physician, unless the wound becomes more painful. Yet, there is one whose remedy he would gladly seek .... They follow the roads and paths in the right direction until they come to a spring, situated in the middle of a field, and bordered by a stone basin. Some one had forgotten upon the stone a comb of gilded ivory. Never since ancient times has wise man or fool seen such a comb. In its teeth there was almost a handful of hair belonging to her who had used the comb.

The Stone Basin and the Comb

WHEN THE DAMSEL NOTICES the spring, and sees the stone, she does not wish her companion to see it; so she turns off in another direction. And he, agreeably occupied with his own thoughts, does not at once remark that she is leading him aside; but when at last he notices it, he is afraid of being beguiled, thinking that she is yielding and is going out of the way in order to avoid some danger.

"See here, damsel," he cries, "you are not going right; come this way! No one, I think, ever went straight who left this road." "Sire, this is a better way for us," the damsel says, "I am sure of it." Then he replies to her: "I don't know, damsel, what you think; but you can plainly see that the beaten path lies this way; and since I have started to follow it, I shall not turn aside. So come now, if you will, for I shall continue along this way." Then they go forward until they come near the stone basin and see the comb. The knight says: "I surely never remember to have seen so beautiful a comb as this." "Let me have it," the damsel says. "Willingly, damsel," he replies. Then he stoops over and picks it up. While holding it, he looks at it steadfastly, gazing at the hair until the damsel begins to laugh. When he sees her doing so, he begs her to tell him why she laughs. And she says: "Never mind, for I will never tell you." "Why not?" he asks. "Because I don't wish to do so." And when he hears that, he implores her like one who holds that lovers ought to keep faith mutually: "Damsel, if you love anything passionately, by that I implore and conjure and beg you not to conceal from me the reason why you laugh." "Your appeal is so strong," she says, "that I will tell you and keep nothing back. I am sure, as I am of anything, that this comb belonged to the Queen. And you may take my word that those are strands of the Queen's hair which you see to be so fair and light and radiant, and which are clinging in the teeth of the comb; they surely never grew anywhere else."

Then the knight replied: "Upon my word, there are plenty of queens and kings; what queen do you mean?" And she answered: "In truth, fair sire, it is of King Arthur's wife I speak." When he hears that, he has not strength to keep from bowing his head over his saddle-bow. And when the damsel sees him thus, she is amazed and terrified, thinking he is about to fall. Do not blame her for her fear, for she thought him in a faint. He might as well have swooned, so near was he to doing so; for in his heart he felt such grief that for a long time he lost his colour and power of speech. And the damsel dismounts, and runs as quickly as possible to support and succour him; for she would not have wished for anything to see him fall. When he saw her, he felt ashamed, and said: "Why do you need to bear me aid?" You must not suppose that the damsel told him why; for he would have been ashamed and distressed, and it would have annoyed and troubled him, if she had confessed to him the truth.

So she took good care not to tell the truth, but tactfully answered him: "Sire, I dismounted to get the comb; for I was so anxious to hold it in my hand that I could not longer wait." Willing that she should have the comb, he gives it to her, first pulling out the hair so carefully that he tears none of it. Never will the eye of man see anything receive such honour as when he begins to adore these tresses. A hundred thousand times he raises them to his eyes and mouth, to his forehead and face: he manifests his joy in every way, considering himself rich and happy now. He lays them in his bosom near his heart, between the shirt and the flesh. He would not exchange them for a cartload of emeralds and carbuncles, nor does he think that any sore or illness can afflict him now; he holds in contempt essence of pearl, treacle, and the cure for pleurisy; even for St. Martin and St. James he has no need; for he has such confidence in this hair that he requires no other aid. But what was this hair like? If I tell the truth about it, you will think I am a mad teller of lies. When the mart is full at the yearly fair of St. Denis, and when the goods are most abundantly displayed, even then the knight would not take all this wealth, unless he had found these tresses too. And if you wish to know the truth, gold a hundred thousand times refined, and melted down as many times, would be darker than is night compared with the brightest summer day we have had this year, if one were to see the gold and set it beside this hair. But why should I make a long story of it? The damsel mounts again with the comb in her possession; while he revels and delights in the tresses in his bosom.

Leaving the plain, they come to a forest and take a short cut through it until they come to a narrow place, where they have to go in single file; for it would have been impossible to ride two horses abreast. Just where the way was narrowest, they see a knight approach. As soon as she saw him, the damsel recognised him, and said: "Sir knight, do you see him who yonder comes against us all armed and ready for a battle? I know what his intention is: he thinks now that he cannot fail to take me off defenceless with him. He loves me, but he is very foolish to do so. In person, and by messenger, he has been long wooing me. But my love is not within his reach, for I would not love him under any consideration, so help me God! I would kill myself rather than bestow my love on him. I do not doubt that he is delighted now, and is as satisfied as if he had me already in his power. But now I shall see what you can do, and I shall see how brave you are, and it will become apparent whether your escort can protect me. If you can protect me now, I shall not fail to proclaim that you are brave and very worthy."

And he answered her: "Go on, go on!" which was as much as to say: "I am not concerned; there is no need of your being worried about what you have said."

The Knight is Greatly Elated

WHILE THEY WERE PROCEEDING, talking thus, the knight, who was alone, rode rapidly toward them on the run. He was the more eager to make haste, because he felt more sure of success; he felt that he was lucky now to see her whom he most dearly loves. As soon as he approaches her, he greets her with words that come from his heart.

"Welcome to her, whence-soever she comes, whom I most desire, but who has hitherto caused me least joy and most distress!" It is not fitting that she should be so stingy of her speech as not to return his greeting, at least by word of mouth. The knight is greatly elated when the damsel greets him; though she does not take the words seriously, and the effort costs her nothing. Yet, if he had at this moment been victor in a tournament, he would not have so highly esteemed himself, nor thought he had won such honour and renown. Being now more confident of his worth, he grasped the bridle rein, and said: "Now I shall lead you away: I have to-day sailed well on my course to have arrived at last at so good a port. Now my troubles are at an end: after dangers, I have reached a haven; after sorrow, I have attained happiness; after pain, I have perfect health; now I have accomplished my desire, when I find you in such case that I can without resistance lead you away with me at once." Then she says: "You have no advantage; for I am under this knight's escort." "Surely, the escort is not worth much," he says, "and I am going to lead you off at once. This knight would have time to eat a bushel of salt before he could defend you from me; I think I could never meet a knight from whom I should not win you. And since I find you here so opportunely, though he too may do his best to prevent it, yet I will take you before his very eyes, however disgruntled he may be." The other is not angered by all the pride he hears expressed, but without any impudence or boasting, he begins thus to challenge him for her: "Sire, don't be in a hurry, and don't waste your words, but speak a little reasonably. You shall not be deprived of as much of her as rightly belongs to you. You must know, however, that the damsel has come hither under my protection. Let her alone now, for you have detained her long enough!" The other gives them leave to burn him, if he does not take her away in spite of him.

Then the other says: "It would not be right for me to let you take her away; I would sooner fight with you. But if we should wish to fight, we could not possibly do it in this narrow road. Let us go to some level place – a meadow or an open field." And he replies that that will suit him perfectly: "Certainly, I agree to that: you are quite right, this road is too narrow. My horse is so much hampered here that I am afraid he will crush his flank before I can turn him around." Then with great difficulty he turns, and his horse escapes without any wound or harm. Then he says: "To be sure, I am much chagrined that we have not met in a favourable spot and in the presence of other men, for I should have been glad to have them see which is the better of us two. Come on now, let us begin our search: we shall find in the vicinity some large, broad, and open space." Then they proceed to a meadow, where there were maids, knights, and damsels playing at divers games in this pleasant place. They were not all engaged in idle sport, but were playing backgammon and chess or dice, and were evidently agreeably employed. Most were engaged in such games as these; but the others there were engaged in sports, dancing, singing, tumbling, leaping, and wrestling with each other.

A knight somewhat advanced in years was on the other side of the meadow, seared upon a sorrel Spanish steed. His bridle and saddle were of gold, and his hair was turning grey. One hand hung at his side with easy grace. The weather being fine, he was in his shirt sleeves, with a short mantle of scarlet cloth and fur slung over his shoulders, and thus he watched the games and dances. On the other side of the field, close by a path, there were twenty-three knights mounted on good Irish steeds. As soon as the three new arrivals come into view, they all cease their play and shout across the fields: "See, yonder comes the knight who was driven in the cart! Let no one continue his sport while he is in our midst. A curse upon him who cares or deigns to play so long as he is here!" Meanwhile he who loved the damsel and claimed her as his own, approached the old knight, and said: "Sire, I have attained great happiness; let all who will now hear me say that God has granted me the thing that I have always most desired; His gift would not have been so great had He crowned me as king, nor would I have been so indebted to Him, nor would I have so profited; for what I have gained is fair and good." "I know not yet if it be thine," the knight replies to his son. But the latter answers him: "Don't you know? Can't you see it, then? For God's sake, sire, have no further doubt, when you see that I have her in my possession. In this forest, whence I come, I met her as she was on her way. I think God had fetched her there for me, and I have taken her for my own." "I do not know whether this will be allowed by him whom I see coming after thee; he looks as if he is coming to demand her of thee."

During this conversation the dancing had ceased because of the knight whom they saw, nor were they gaily playing any more because of the disgust and scorn they felt for him. But the knight without delay came up quickly after the damsel, and said: "Let the damsel alone, knight, for you have no right to her! If you dare, I am willing at once to fight with you in her defence." Then the old knight remarked: "Did I not know it? Fair son, detain the damsel no longer, but let her go." He does not relish this advice, and swears that he will not give her up: "May God never grant me joy if I give her up to him! I have her, and I shall hold on to her as something that is mine own. The shoulder-strap and all the armlets of my shield shall first be broken, and I shall have lost all confidence in my strength and arms, my sword and lance, before I will surrender my mistress to him." And his father says: "I shall not let thee fight for any reason thou mayest urge. Thou art too confident of thy bravery. So obey my command." But he in his pride replies: "What? Am I a child to be terrified? Rather will I make my boast that there is not within the sea-girt land any knight, wheresoever he may dwell, so excellent that I would let him have her, and whom I should not expect speedily to defeat." The father answers: "Fair son, I do not doubt that thou dost really think so, for thou art so confident of thy strength. But I do not wish to see thee enter a contest with this knight." Then he replies: "I shall be disgraced if I follow your advice. Curse me if I heed your counsel and turn recreant because of you, and do not do my utmost in the fight. It is true that a man fares ill among his relatives: I could drive a better bargain somewhere else, for you are trying to take me in. I am sure that where I am not known, I could act with better grace. No one, who did not know me, would try to thwart my will; whereas you are annoying and tormenting me. I am vexed by your finding fault with me. You know well enough that when any one is blamed, he breaks out still more passionately. But may God never give me joy if I renounce my purpose because of you; rather will I fight in spite of you!" "By the faith I bear the Apostle St. Peter," his father says, "now I see that my request is of no avail. I waste my time in rebuking thee; but I shall soon devise such means as shall compel thee against thy will to obey my commands and submit to them." Straightway summoning all the knights to approach, he bids them lay hands upon his son whom he cannot correct, saying: "I will have him bound rather than let him fight. You here are all my men, and you owe me your devotion and service: by all the fiefs you hold from me, I hold you responsible, and I add my prayer. It seems to me that he must be mad, and that he shows excessive pride, when he refuses to respect my will." Then they promise to take care of him, and say that never, while he is in their charge, shall he wish to fight, but that he must renounce the damsel in spite of himself. Then they all join and seize him by the arms and neck. "Dost thou not think thyself foolish now?" his father asks; "confess the truth: thou hast not the strength or power to fight or joust, however distasteful and hard it may be for thee to admit it. Thou wilt be wise to consent to my will and pleasure. Dost thou know what my intention is? In order somewhat to mitigate thy disappointment, I am willing to join thee, if thou wilt, in following the knight to-day and to-morrow, through wood and plain, each one mounted on his horse. Perhaps we shall soon find him to be of such a character and bearing that I might let thee have thy way and fight with him." To this proposal the other must perforce consent. Like the man who has no alternative, he says that he will give in, provided they both shall follow him. And when the people in the field see how this adventure has turned out, they all exclaim: "Did you see? He who was mounted on the cart has gained such honour here that he is leading away the mistress of the son of my lord, and he himself is allowing it. We may well suppose that he finds in him some merit, when he lets him take her off. Now cursed a hundred times be he who ceases longer his sport on his account! Come, let us go back to our games again." Then they resume their games and dances.

They Leave in Haste

THEREUPON THE KNIGHT TURNS AWAY, without longer remaining in the field, and the damsel accompanies him. They leave in haste, while the father and his son ride after them through the mown fields until toward three o'clock, when in a very pleasant spot they come upon a church; beside the chancel there was a cemetery enclosed by a wall. The knight was both

courteous and wise to enter the church on foot and make his prayer to God, while the damsel held his horse for him until he returned.

When he had made his prayer, and while he was coming back, a very old monk suddenly presented himself; whereupon the knight politely requests him to tell him what this place is; for he does not know. And he tells him it is a cemetery. And the other says: "Take me in, so help you God!" "Gladly, sire," and he takes him in. Following the monk's lead, the knight beholds the most beautiful tombs that one could find as far as Dombes or Pampelune; and on each tomb there were letters cut, telling the names of those who were destined to be buried there. And he began in order to read the names, and came upon some which said: "Here Gawain is to lie, here Louis, and here Yvain." After these three, he read the names of many others among the most famed and cherished knights of this or any other land. Among the others, he finds one of marble, which appears to be new, and is more rich and handsome than all the rest. Calling the monk, the knight inquired: "Of what use are these tombs here?" And the monk replied: "You have already read the inscriptions; if you have understood, you must know what they say, and what is the meaning of the tombs." "Now tell me, what is this large one for?" And the hermit answered: "I will tell you. That is a very large sarcophagus, larger than any that ever was made; one so rich and well-carved was never seen. It is magnificent without, and still more so within. But you need not be concerned with that, for it can never do you any good; you will never see inside of it; for it would require seven strong men to raise the lid of stone, if any one wished to open it. And you may be sure that to raise it would require seven men stronger than you and I. There is an inscription on it which says that any one who can lift this stone of his own unaided strength will set free all the men and women who are captives in the land, whence no slave or noble can issue forth, unless he is a native of that land. No one has ever come back from there, but they are detained in foreign prisons; whereas they of the country go and come in and out as they please." At once the knight goes to grasp the stone, and raises it without the slightest trouble, more easily than ten men would do who exerted all their strength. And the monk was amazed, and nearly fell down at the sight of this marvellous thing; for he thought he would never see the like again, and said: "Sire, I am very anxious to know your name. Will you tell me what it is?" "Not I," says the knight, "upon my word." "I am certainly sorry, for that," he says; "but if you would tell me, you would do me a great favour, and might benefit yourself. Who are you, and where do you come from?"

"I am a knight, as you may see, and I was born in the kingdom of Logre. After so much information, I should prefer to be excused. Now please tell me, for your part, who is to lie within this tomb." "Sire, he who shall deliver all those who are held captive in the kingdom whence none escapes." And when he had told him all this, the knight commended him to God and all His saints. And then, for the first time, he felt free to return to the damsel. The old white-haired monk escorts him out of the church, and they resume their way. While the damsel is mounting, however, the hermit relates to her all that the knight had done inside, and then he begged her to tell him, if she knew, what his name was; but she assured him that she did not know, but that there was one sure thing she could say, namely, that there was not such a knight alive where the four winds of heaven blow.

The Inscription Upon the Stone

THEN THE DAMSEL TAKES LEAVE OF HIM, and rides swiftly after the knight. Then those who were following them come up and see the hermit standing alone before the church. The old knight in his shirt sleeves said: "Sire, tell us, have you seen a knight with a damsel in his company?"

And he replies: "I shall not be loath to tell you all I know, for they have just passed on from here. The knight was inside yonder, and did a very marvellous thing in raising the stone from the huge marble tomb, quite unaided and without the least effort. He is bent upon the rescue of the Queen, and doubtless he will rescue her, as well as all the other people. You know well that this must be so, for you have often read the inscription upon the stone. No knight was ever born of man and woman, and no knight ever sat in a saddle, who was the equal of this man." Then the father turns to his son, and says: "Son, what dost thou think about him now? Is he not a man to be respected who has performed such a feat? Now thou knowest who was wrong, and whether it was thou or I. I would not have thee fight with him for all the town of Amiens; and yet thou didst struggle hard, before any one could dissuade thee from thy purpose. Now we may as well go back, for we should be very foolish to follow him any farther." And he replies: "I agree to that. It would be useless to follow him. Since it is your pleasure, let us return." They were very wise to retrace their steps. And all the time the damsel rides close beside the knight, wishing to compel him to give heed to her. She is anxious to learn his name, and she begs and beseeches him again and again to tell her, until in his annoyance he answers her: "Have I not already told you that I belong in King Arthur's realm? I swear by God and His goodness that you shall not learn my name." Then she bids him give her leave to go, and she will turn back, which request he gladly grants.

The Damsel Departs

THEREUPON THE DAMSEL DEPARTS, and he rides on alone until it grew very late. After vespers, about compline, as he pursued his way, he saw a knight returning from the wood where he had been hunting. With helmet unlaced, he rode along upon his big grey hunter, to which he had tied the game which God had permitted him to take.

This gentleman came quickly to meet the knight, offering him hospitality. "Sire," he says, "night will soon be here. It is time for you to be reasonable and seek a place to spend the night. I have a house of mine near at hand, whither I shall take you. No one ever lodged you better than I shall do, to the extent of my resources: I shall be very glad, if you consent." "For my part, I gladly accept," he says. The gentleman at once sends his son ahead, to prepare the house and start the preparations for supper. The lad willingly executes his command forthwith, and goes off at a rapid pace, while the others, who are in no haste, follow the road leisurely until they arrive at the house.

The gentleman's wife was a very accomplished lady; and he had five sons, whom he dearly loved, three of them mere lads, and two already knights; and he had two fair and charming daughters, who were still unmarried. They were not natives of the land, but were there in durance, having been long kept there as prisoners away from their native land of Logres. When the gentleman led the knight into his yard, the lady with her sons and daughters jumped up and ran to meet them, vying in their efforts to do him honour, as they greeted him and helped him to dismount. Neither the sisters nor the five brothers paid much attention to their father, for they knew well enough that he would have it so. They honoured the knight and welcomed him; and when they had relieved him of his armour, one of his host's two daughters threw her own mantle about him, taking it from her own shoulders and throwing it about his neck. I do not need to tell how well he was served at supper; but when the meal was finished, they felt no further hesitation in speaking of various matters. First, the host began to ask him who he was, and from what land, but he did not inquire about his name. The knight promptly answered him: "I am from the kingdom of Logres, and have never been in this land before." And when the gentleman heard that, he was greatly amazed, as were his wife and children too, and each one of them was sore distressed. Then they began to say to him: "Woe that you have come here, fair sire, for only trouble will come of it! For, like us, you will be reduced to servitude and exile." "Where do you come from, then?" he asked. "Sire, we belong in your country. Many men from your country are held in servitude in this land. Cursed be the custom, together with those who keep it up! No stranger comes here who is not compelled to stay here in the land where he is detained. For whoever wishes may come in, but once in, he has to stay. About your own fate, you may be at rest, you will doubtless never escape from here." He replies: "Indeed, I shall do so, if possible." To this the gentleman replies: "How? Do you think you can escape?"

"Yes, indeed, if it be God's will; and I shall do all within my power." "In that case, doubtless all the rest would be set free; for, as soon as one succeeds in fairly escaping from this durance, then all the rest may go forth unchallenged." Then the gentleman recalled that he had been told and informed that a knight of great excellence was making his way into the country to seek for the Queen, who was held by the king's son, Meleagant; and he said to himself: "Upon my word, I believe it is he, and I'll tell him so." So he said to him: "Sire, do not conceal from me your business, if I promise to give you the best advice I know. I too shall profit by any success you may attain. Reveal to me the truth about your errand, that it may be to your advantage as well as mine. I am persuaded that you have come in search of the Queen into this land and among these heathen people, who are worse than the Saracens." And the knight replies: "For no other purpose have I come. I know not where my lady is confined, but I am striving hard to rescue her, and am in dire need of advice. Give me any counsel you can."

And he says: "Sire, you have undertaken a very grievous task. The road you are travelling will lead you straight to the sword-bridge. You surely need advice. If you would heed my counsel, you would proceed to the sword-bridge by a surer way, and I would have you escorted thither." Then he, whose mind is fixed upon the most direct way, asks him: "Is the road of which you speak as direct as the other way?" "No, it is not," he says; "it is longer, but more sure." Then he says: "I have no use for it; tell me about this road I am following!" "I am ready to do so," he replies; "but I am sure you will not fare well if you take any other than the road I recommend. To-morrow you will reach a place where you will have trouble: it is called 'the stony passage'. Shall I tell you how bad a place it is to pass? Only one horse can go through at a time; even two men could not pass abreast, and the passage is well guarded and defended. You will meet with resistance as soon as you arrive. You will sustain many a blow of sword and lance, and will have to return full measure before you succeed in passing through." And when he had completed the account, one of the gentleman's sons, who was a knight, stepped forward, saying: "Sire, if you do not object, I will go with this gentleman." Then one of the lads jumps up, and says: "I too will go." And the father gladly gives them both consent. Now the knight will not have to go alone, and he expresses his gratitude, being much pleased with the company.

Sir Gawain and the Green Knight

AFTER THE SIEGE and the assault of Troy, when that burg was destroyed and burnt to ashes, and the traitor tried for his treason, the noble Æneas and his kin sailed forth to become princes and patrons of well-nigh all the Western Isles.

Thus Romulus built Rome (and gave to the city his own name, which it bears even to this day); and Ticius turned him to Tuscany; and Langobard raised him up dwellings in Lombardy; and Felix Brutus sailed far over the French flood, and founded the kingdom of Britain, wherein have been war and waste and wonder, and bliss and bale, ofttimes since.

And in that kingdom of Britain have been wrought more gallant deeds than in any other; but of all British kings Arthur was the most valiant, as I have heard tell, therefore will I set forth a wondrous adventure that fell out in his time. And if ye will listen to me, but for a little while, I will tell it even as it stands in story stiff and strong, fixed in the letter, as it hath long been known in the land.

Camelot at Christmas Time

KING ARTHUR lay at Camelot upon a Christmas-tide, with many a gallant lord and lovely lady, and all the noble brotherhood of the Round Table. There they held rich revels with gay talk and jest; one while they would ride forth to joust and tourney, and again back to the court to make carols; 2 for there was the feast holden fifteen days with all the mirth that men could devise, song and glee, glorious to hear, in the daytime, and dancing at night. Halls and chambers were crowded with noble guests, the bravest of knights and the loveliest of ladies, and Arthur himself was the comeliest king that ever held a court. For all this fair folk were in their youth, the fairest and most fortunate under heaven, and the king himself of such fame that it were hard now to name so valiant a hero.

Now the New Year had but newly come in, and on that day a double portion was served on the high table to all the noble guests, and thither came the king with all his knights, when the service in the chapel had been sung to an end. And they greeted each other for the New Year, and gave rich gifts, the one to the other (and they that received them were not wroth, that may ye well believe!), and the maidens laughed and made mirth till it was time to get them to meat. Then they washed and sat them down to the feast in fitting rank and order, and Guinevere the queen, gaily clad, sat on the high daïs. Silken was her seat, with a fair canopy over her head, of rich tapestries of Tars, embroidered, and studded with costly gems; fair she was to look upon, with her shining grey eyes, a fairer woman might no man boast himself of having seen.

But Arthur would not eat till all were served, so full of joy and gladness was he, even as a child; he liked not either to lie long, or to sit long at meat, so worked upon him his young blood and his wild brain. And another custom he had also, that came of his nobility, that he would never eat upon an high day till he had been advised of some knightly deed, or some strange and marvellous tale, of his ancestors, or of arms, or of other ventures. Or till some stranger knight should seek of him leave to joust with one of the Round Table, that they might set their lives in jeopardy, one against another, as fortune might favour them. Such was the king's custom when he sat in hall at each high feast with his noble knights, therefore on that New Year tide, he abode, fair of face, on the throne, and made much mirth withal.

Thus the king sat before the high tables, and spake of many things; and there good Sir Gawain was seated by Guinevere the queen, and on her other side sat Agravain, à la dure main; both were the king's sister's sons and full gallant knights. And at the end of the table was Bishop Bawdewyn, and Ywain, King Urien's son, sat at the other side alone. These were worthily served on the daïs, and at the lower tables sat many valiant knights. Then they bare the first course with the blast of trumpets and waving of banners, with the sound of drums and pipes, of song and lute, that many a heart was uplifted at the melody. Many were the dainties, and rare the meats, so great was the plenty they might scarce find room on the board to set on the dishes. Each helped himself as he liked best, and to each two were twelve dishes, with great plenty of beer and wine.

The Green Knight

NOW I WILL SAY NO MORE of the service, but that ye may know there was no lack, for there drew near a venture that the folk might well have left their labour to gaze upon. As the sound of the music ceased, and the first course had been fitly served, there came in at the hall door one terrible to behold, of stature greater than any on earth; from neck to loin so strong and thickly made, and with limbs so long and so great that he seemed even as a giant. And yet he was but a man, only the mightiest that might mount a steed; broad of chest and shoulders

and slender of waist, and all his features of like fashion; but men marvelled much at his colour, for he rode even as a knight, yet was green all over.

For he was clad all in green, with a straight coat, and a mantle above; all decked and lined with fur was the cloth and the hood that was thrown back from his locks and lay on his shoulders. Hose had he of the same green, and spurs of bright gold with silken fastenings richly worked; and all his vesture was verily green. Around his waist and his saddle were bands with fair stones set upon silken work, 'twere too long to tell of all the trifles that were embroidered thereon – birds and insects in gay gauds of green and gold. All the trappings of his steed were of metal of like enamel, even the stirrups that he stood in stained of the same, and stirrups and saddle-bow alike gleamed and shone with green stones. Even the steed on which he rode was of the same hue, a green horse, great and strong, and hard to hold, with broidered bridle, meet for the rider.

The knight was thus gaily dressed in green, his hair falling around his shoulders; on his breast hung a beard, as thick and green as a bush, and the beard and the hair of his head were clipped all round above his elbows. The lower part of his sleeves were fastened with clasps in the same wise as a king's mantle. The horse's mane was crisp and plaited with many a knot folded in with gold thread about the fair green, here a twist of the hair, here another of gold. The tail was twined in like manner, and both were bound about with a band of bright green set with many a precious stone; then they were tied aloft in a cunning knot, whereon rang many bells of burnished gold. Such a steed might no other ride, nor had such ever been looked upon in that hall ere that time; and all who saw that knight spake and said that a man might scarce abide his stroke.

The knight bore no helm nor hauberk, neither gorget nor breast-plate, neither shaft nor buckler to smite nor to shield, but in one hand he had a holly-bough, that is greenest when the groves are bare, and in his other an axe, huge and uncomely, a cruel weapon in fashion, if one would picture it. The head was an ell-yard long, the metal all of green steel and gold, the blade burnished bright, with a broad edge, as well shapen to shear as a sharp razor. The steel was set into a strong staff, all bound round with iron, even to the end, and engraved with green in cunning work. A lace was twined about it, that looped at the head, and all adown the handle it was clasped with tassels on buttons of bright green richly broidered.

The knight rideth through the entrance of the hall, driving straight to the high daïs, and greeted no man, but looked ever upwards; and the first words he spake were, "Where is the ruler of this folk? I would gladly look upon that hero, and have speech with him." He cast his eyes on the knights, and mustered them up and down, striving ever to see who of them was of most renown.

The Gallant Knights

THEN WAS THERE GREAT GAZING to behold that chief, for each man marvelled what it might mean that a knight and his steed should have even such a hue as the green grass; and that seemed even greener than green enamel on bright gold. All looked on him as he stood, and drew near unto him wondering greatly what he might be; for many marvels had they seen, but none such as this, and phantasm and faërie did the folk deem it. Therefore were the gallant knights slow to answer, and gazed astounded, and sat stone still in a deep silence through that goodly hall, as if a slumber were fallen upon them. I deem it was not all for doubt, but some for courtesy that they might give ear unto his errand.

Then Arthur beheld this adventurer before his high daïs, and knightly he greeted him, for fearful was he never. "Sir," he said, "thou art welcome to this place – lord of this hall am I, and men call me Arthur. Light thee down, and tarry awhile, and what thy will is, that shall we learn after."

"Nay," quoth the stranger, "so help me He that sitteth on high, 'twas not mine errand to tarry any while in this dwelling; but the praise of this thy folk and thy city is lifted up on high, and thy warriors are holden for the best and the most valiant of those who ride mail-clad to the fight. The wisest and the worthiest of this world are they, and well proven in all knightly sports. And here, as I have heard tell, is fairest courtesy, therefore have I come hither as at this time. Ye may be sure by the branch that I bear here that I come in peace, seeking no strife. For had I willed to journey in warlike guise I have at home both hauberk and helm, shield and shining spear, and other weapons to mine hand, but since I seek no war my raiment is that of peace. But if thou be as bold as all men tell thou wilt freely grant me the boon I ask."

And Arthur answered, "Sir Knight, if thou cravest battle here thou shalt not fail for lack of a foe."

And the knight answered, "Nay, I ask no fight, in faith here on the benches are but beardless children, were I clad in armour on my steed there is no man here might match me. Therefore I ask in this court but a Christmas jest, for that it is Yule-tide, and New Year, and there are here many fain for sport. If any one in this hall holds himself so hardy, so bold both of blood and brain, as to dare strike me one stroke for another, I will give him as a gift this axe, which is heavy enough, in sooth, to handle as he may list, and I will abide the first blow, unarmed as I sit. If any knight be so bold as to prove my words let him come swiftly to me here, and take this weapon, I quit claim to it, he may keep it as his own, and I will abide his stroke, firm on the floor. Then shalt thou give me the right to deal him another, the respite of a year and a day shall he have. Now haste, and let see whether any here dare say aught."

Now if the knights had been astounded at the first, yet stiller were they all, high and low, when they had heard his words. The knight on his steed straightened himself in the saddle, and rolled his eyes fiercely round the hall, red they gleamed under his green and bushy brows. He frowned and twisted his beard, waiting to see who should rise, and when none answered he cried aloud in mockery, "What, is this Arthur's hall, and these the knights whose renown hath run through many realms? Where are now your pride and your conquests, your wrath, and anger, and mighty words? Now are the praise and the renown of the Round Table overthrown by one man's speech, since all keep silence for dread ere ever they have seen a blow!"

With that he laughed so loudly that the blood rushed to the king's fair face for very shame; he waxed wroth, as did all his knights, and sprang to his feet, and drew near to the stranger and said, "Now by heaven foolish is thy asking, and thy folly shall find its fitting answer. I know no man aghast at thy great words. Give me here thine axe and I shall grant thee the boon thou hast asked." Lightly he sprang to him and caught at his hand, and the knight, fierce of aspect, lighted down from his charger.

Then Arthur took the axe and gripped the haft, and swung it round, ready to strike. And the knight stood before him, taller by the head than any in the hall; he stood, and stroked his beard, and drew down his coat, no more dismayed for the king's threats than if one had brought him a drink of wine.

Then Gawain, who sat by the queen, leaned forward to the king and spake, "I beseech ye, my lord, let this venture be mine. Would ye but bid me rise from this seat, and stand by your side, so that my liege lady thought it not ill, then would I come to your counsel before this goodly court. For I think it not seemly when such challenges be made in your hall that ye yourself should undertake it, while there are many bold knights who sit beside ye, none are there, methinks, of readier will under heaven, or more valiant in open field. I am the weakest, I wot, and the feeblest of wit, and it will be the less loss of my life if ye seek sooth. For save that ye are mine uncle naught is there in me to praise, no virtue is there in my body save your blood, and since this challenge is such folly that it beseems ye not to take it, and I have asked it from ye first, let it fall to me, and if I bear myself ungallantly then let all this court blame me."

Then they all spake with one voice that the king should leave this venture and grant it to Gawain.

Then Arthur commanded the knight to rise, and he rose up quickly and knelt down before the king, and caught hold of the weapon; and the king loosed his hold of it, and lifted up his hand, and gave him his blessing, and bade him be strong both of heart and hand. "Keep thee well, nephew," quoth Arthur, "that thou give him but the one blow, and if thou redest him rightly I trow thou shalt well abide the stroke he may give thee after."

Gawain stepped to the stranger, axe in hand, and he, never fearing, awaited his coming. Then the Green Knight spake to Sir Gawain, "Make we our covenant ere we go further. First, I ask thee, knight, what is thy name? Tell me truly, that I may know thee."

"In faith," quoth the good knight, "Gawain am I, who give thee this buffet, let what may come of it; and at this time twelvemonth will I take another at thine hand with whatsoever weapon thou wilt, and none other."

Then the other answered again, "Sir Gawain, so may I thrive as I am fain to take this buffet at thine hand," and he quoth further, "Sir Gawain, it liketh me well that I shall take at thy fist that which I have asked here, and thou hast readily and truly rehearsed all the covenant that I asked of the king, save that thou shalt swear me, by thy troth, to seek me thyself wherever thou hopest that I may be found, and win thee such reward as thou dealest me to-day, before this folk."

"Where shall I seek thee?" quoth Gawain. "Where is thy place? By Him that made me, I wot never where thou dwellest, nor know I thee, knight, thy court, nor thy name. But teach me truly all that pertaineth thereto, and tell me thy name, and I shall use all my wit to win my way thither, and that I swear thee for sooth, and by my sure troth."

"That is enough in the New Year, it needs no more," quoth the Green Knight to the gallant Gawain, "if I tell thee truly when I have taken the blow, and thou hast smitten me; then will I teach thee of my house and home, and mine own name, then mayest thou ask thy road and keep covenant. And if I waste no words then farest thou the better, for thou canst dwell in thy land, and seek no further. But take now thy toll, and let see how thy strikest."

"Gladly will I," quoth Gawain, handling his axe.

Then the Green Knight swiftly made him ready, he bowed down his head, and laid his long locks on the crown that his bare neck might be seen. Gawain gripped his axe and raised it on high, the left foot he set forward on the floor, and let the blow fall lightly on the bare neck. The sharp edge of the blade sundered the bones, smote through the neck, and clave it in two, so that the edge of the steel bit on the ground, and the fair head fell to the earth that many struck it with their feet as it rolled forth. The blood spurted forth, and glistened on the green raiment, but the knight neither faltered nor fell; he started forward with out-stretched hand, and caught the head, and lifted it up; then he turned to his steed, and took hold of the bride, set his foot in the stirrup, and mounted. His head he held by the hair, in his hand. Then he seated himself in his saddle as if naught ailed him, and he were not headless. He turned his steed about, the grim corpse bleeding freely the while, and they who looked upon him doubted them much for the covenant.

For he held up the head in his hand, and turned the face towards them that sat on the high daïs, and it lifted up the eyelids and looked upon them and spake as ye shall hear. "Look, Gawain, that thou art ready to go as thou hast promised, and seek leally till thou find me, even as thou hast sworn in this hall in the hearing of these knights. Come thou, I charge thee, to the Green Chapel, such a stroke as thou hast dealt thou hast deserved, and it shall be promptly paid thee on New Year's morn. Many men know me as the knight of the Green Chapel, and if thou askest, thou shalt not fail to find me. Therefore it behoves thee to come, or to yield thee as recreant."

With that he turned his bridle, and galloped out at the hall door, his head in his hands, so that the sparks flew from beneath his horse's hoofs. Whither he went none knew, no more than they wist whence he had come; and the king and Gawain they gazed and laughed, for in sooth this had proved a greater marvel than any they had known aforetime.

Though Arthur the king was astonished at his heart, yet he let no sign of it be seen, but spake in courteous wise to the fair queen: "Dear lady, be not dismayed, such craft is well suited to Christmas-tide when we seek jesting, laughter and song, and fair carols of knights and ladies. But now I may well get me to meat, for I have seen a marvel I may not forget." Then he looked on Sir Gawain, and said gaily, "Now, fair nephew, hang up thine axe, since it has hewn enough," and they hung it on the dossal above the daïs, where all men might look on it for a marvel, and by its true token tell of the wonder. Then the twain sat them down together, the king and the good knight, and men served them with a double portion, as was the share of the noblest, with all manner of meat and of minstrelsy. And they spent that day in gladness, but Sir Gawain must well bethink him of the heavy venture to which he had set his hand.

The Year Passes into Many Yesterdays

THIS BEGINNING OF ADVENTURES had Arthur at the New Year; for he yearned to hear gallant tales, though his words were few when he sat at the feast. But now had they stern work on hand. Gawain was glad to begin the jest in the hall, but ye need have no marvel if the end be heavy. For though a man be merry in mind when he has well drunk, yet a year runs full swiftly, and the beginning but rarely matches the end.

For Yule was now over-past, and the year after, each season in its turn following the other. For after Christmas comes crabbed Lent, that will have fish for flesh and simpler cheer. But then the weather of the world chides with winter; the cold withdraws itself, the clouds uplift, and the rain falls in warm showers on the fair plains. Then the flowers come forth, meadows and grove are clad in green, the birds make ready to build, and sing sweetly for solace of the soft summer that follows thereafter. The blossoms bud and blow in the hedgerows rich and rank, and noble notes enough are heard in the fair woods.

After the season of summer, with the soft winds, when zephyr breathes lightly on seeds and herbs, joyous indeed is the growth that waxes thereout when the dew drips from the leaves beneath the blissful glance of the bright sun. But then comes harvest and hardens the grain, warning it to wax ripe ere the winter. The drought drives the dust on high, flying over the face of the land; the angry wind of the welkin wrestles with the sun; the leaves fall from the trees and light upon the ground, and all brown are the groves that but now were green, and ripe is the fruit that once was flower. So the year passes into many yesterdays, and winter comes again, as it needs no sage to tell us.

The Noblest Knights Set Forth

WHEN THE MICHAELMAS moon was come in with warnings of winter, Sir Gawain bethought him full oft of his perilous journey. Yet till All Hallows Day he lingered with Arthur, and on that day they made a great feast for the hero's sake, with much revel and richness of the Round Table. Courteous knights and comely ladies, all were in sorrow for the love of that knight, and though they spake no word of it, many were joyless for his sake.

And after meat, sadly Sir Gawain turned to his uncle, and spake of his journey, and said, "Liege lord of my life, leave from you I crave. Ye know well how the matter stands without more words, to-morrow am I bound to set forth in search of the Green Knight."

Then came together all the noblest knights, Ywain and Erec, and many another. Sir Dodinel le Sauvage, the Duke of Clarence, Launcelot and Lionel, and Lucan the Good, Sir Bors and Sir Bedivere, valiant knights both, and many another hero, with Sir Mador de la Porte, and they all drew near, heavy at heart, to take counsel with Sir Gawain. Much sorrow and weeping was there in the hall to think that so worthy a knight as Gawain should wend his way to seek a deadly blow, and should no more wield his sword in fight. But the knight made ever good cheer, and said, "Nay, wherefore should I shrink? What may a man do but prove his fate?"

He dwelt there all that day, and on the morn he arose and asked betimes for his armour; and they brought it unto him on this wise: first, a rich carpet was stretched on the floor (and brightly did the gold gear glitter upon it), then the knight stepped on to it, and handled the steel; clad he was in a doublet of silk, with a close hood, lined fairly throughout. Then they set the steel shoes upon his feet, and wrapped his legs with greaves, with polished knee-caps, fastened with knots of gold. Then they cased his thighs in cuisses closed with thongs, and brought him the byrny of bright steel rings sewn upon a fair stuff. Well burnished braces they set on each arm with good elbow-pieces, and gloves of mail, and all the goodly gear that should shield him in his need. And they cast over all a rich surcoat, and set the golden spurs on his heels, and girt him with a trusty sword fastened with a silken bawdrick. When he was thus clad his harness was costly, for the least loop or latchet gleamed with gold. So armed as he was he hearkened Mass and made his offering at the high altar. Then he came to the king, and the knights of his court, and courteously took leave of lords and ladies, and they kissed him, and commended him to Christ.

With that was Gringalet ready, girt with a saddle that gleamed gaily with many golden fringes, enriched and decked anew for the venture. The bridle was all barred about with bright gold buttons, and all the covertures and trappings of the steed, the crupper and the rich skirts, accorded with the saddle; spread fair with the rich red gold that glittered and gleamed in the rays of the sun.

Then the knight called for his helmet, which was well lined throughout, and set it high on his head, and hasped it behind. He wore a light kerchief over the vintail, that was broidered and studded with fair gems on a broad silken ribbon, with birds of gay colour, and many a turtle and true-lover's knot interlaced thickly, even as many a maiden had wrought diligently for seven winter long. But the circlet which crowned his helmet was yet more precious, being adorned with a device in diamonds. Then they brought him his shield, which was of bright red, with the pentangle painted thereon in gleaming gold. And why that noble prince bare the pentangle I am minded to tell you, though my tale tarry thereby. It is a sign that Solomon set ere-while, as betokening truth; for it is a figure with five points and each line overlaps the other, and nowhere hath it beginning or end, so that in English it is called "the endless knot." And therefore was it well suiting to this knight and to his arms, since Gawain was faithful in five and five-fold, for pure was he as gold, void of all villainy and endowed with all virtues. Therefore he bare the pentangle on shield and surcoat as truest of heroes and gentlest of knights.

For first he was faultless in his five senses; and his five fingers never failed him; and all his trust upon earth was in the five wounds that Christ bare on the cross, as the Creed tells. And wherever this knight found himself in stress of battle he deemed well that he drew his strength from the five joys which the Queen of Heaven had of her Child. And for this cause did he bear an image of Our Lady on the one half of his shield, that whenever he looked upon it he might not lack for aid. And the fifth five that the hero used were frankness and fellowship above all, purity and courtesy that never failed him, and compassion that surpasses all; and in these five virtues was that hero wrapped and clothed. And all these, five-fold, were linked one in the other, so that they had no end, and were fixed on five points that never failed, neither at any side were they joined or sundered, nor could ye find beginning or end. And therefore on his shield was the knot shapen, red-gold upon red, which is the pure pentangle. Now was Sir Gawain ready, and he took his lance in hand, and bade them all Farewell , he deemed it had been for ever.

Then he smote the steed with his spurs, and sprang on his way, so that sparks flew from the stones after him. All that saw him were grieved at heart, and said one to the other, "By Christ, 'tis great pity that one of such noble life should be lost! I'faith, 'twere not easy to find his equal upon earth. The king had done better to have wrought more warily. Yonder knight should have been made a duke; a gallant leader of men is he, and such a fate had beseemed him better than to be hewn in pieces at the will of an elfish man, for mere pride. Who ever knew a king to take such counsel as to risk his knights on a Christmas jest?" Many were the tears that flowed from their eyes when that goodly knight rode from the hall. He made no delaying, but went his way swiftly, and rode many a wild road, as I heard say in the book.

So rode Sir Gawain through the realm of Logres, on an errand that he held for no jest. Often he lay companionless at night, and must lack the fare that he liked. No comrade had he save his steed, and none save God with whom to take counsel. At length he drew nigh to North Wales, and left the isles of Anglesey on his left hand, crossing over the fords by the foreland over at Holyhead, till he came into the wilderness of Wirral, where but few dwell who love God and man of true heart. And ever he asked, as he fared, of all whom he met, if they had heard any tidings of a Green Knight in the country thereabout, or of a Green Chapel? And all answered him, Nay, never in their lives had they seen any man of such a hue. And the knight wended his way by many a strange road and many a rugged path, and the fashion of his countenance changed full often ere he saw the Green Chapel.

The Fairest Castle That Ever a Knight Owned

MANY A CLIFF did he climb in that unknown land, where afar from his friends he rode as a stranger. Never did he come to a stream or a ford but he found a foe before him, and that one so marvellous, so foul and fell, that it behoved him to fight. So many wonders did that knight behold, that it were too long to tell the tenth part of them. Sometimes he fought with dragons and wolves; sometimes with wild men that dwelt in the rocks; another while with bulls, and bears, and wild boars, or with giants of the high moorland that drew near to him. Had he not been a doughty knight, enduring, and of well-proved valour, and a servant of God, doubtless he had been slain, for he was oft in danger of death. Yet he cared not so much for the strife, what he deemed worse was when the cold clear water was shed from the clouds, and froze ere it fell on the fallow ground. More nights than enough he slept in his harness on the bare rocks, near slain with the sleet, while the stream leapt bubbling from the crest of the hills, and hung in hard icicles over his head.

Thus in peril and pain, and many a hardship, the knight rode alone till Christmas Eve, and in that tide he made his prayer to the Blessed Virgin that she would guide his steps and lead him to some dwelling. On that morning he rode by a hill, and came into a thick forest, wild and drear; on each side were high hills, and thick woods below them of great hoar oaks, a hundred together, of hazel and hawthorn with their trailing boughs intertwined, and rough ragged moss spreading everywhere. On the bare twigs the birds chirped piteously, for pain of the cold. The knight upon Gringalet rode lonely beneath them, through marsh and mire, much troubled at heart lest he should fail to see the service of the Lord, who on that self-same night was born of a maiden for the cure of our grief; and therefore he said, sighing, "I beseech Thee, Lord, and Mary Thy gentle Mother, for some shelter where I may hear Mass, and Thy mattins at morn. This I ask meekly, and thereto I pray my Paternoster, Ave, and Credo." Thus he rode praying, and lamenting his misdeeds, and he crossed himself, and said, "May the Cross of Christ speed me."

Now that knight had crossed himself but thrice ere he was aware in the wood of a dwelling within a moat, above a lawn, on a mound surrounded by many mighty trees that stood round the moat. 'Twas the fairest castle that ever a knight owned; built in a meadow with a park all about it, and a spiked palisade, closely driven, that enclosed the trees for more than two miles. The knight was ware of the hold from the side, as it shone through the oaks. Then he lifted off his helmet, and thanked Christ and S. Julian that they had courteously granted his prayer, and hearkened to his cry. "Now," quoth the knight, "I beseech ye, grant me fair hostel." Then he pricked Gringalet with his golden spurs, and rode gaily towards the great gate, and came swiftly to the bridge end.

The bridge was drawn up and the gates close shut; the walls were strong and thick, so that they might fear no tempest. The knight on his charger abode on the bank of the deep double ditch that surrounded the castle. The walls were set deep in the water, and rose aloft to a wondrous height; they were of hard hewn stone up to the corbels, which were adorned beneath the battlements with fair carvings, and turrets set in between with many a loophole; a better barbican Sir Gawain had never looked upon. And within he beheld the high hall, with its tower and many windows with carven cornices, and chalk-white chimneys on the turreted roofs that shone fair in the sun. And everywhere, thickly scattered on the castle battlements, were pinnacles, so many that it seemed as if it were all wrought out of paper, so white was it.

The knight on his steed deemed it fair enough, if he might come to be sheltered within it to lodge there while that the Holy-day lasted. He called aloud, and soon there came a porter of kindly countenance, who stood on the wall and greeted this knight and asked his errand.

"Good sir," quoth Gawain, "wilt thou go mine errand to the high lord of the castle, and crave for me lodging?"

"Yea, by S. Peter," quoth the porter. "In sooth I trow that ye be welcome to dwell here so long as it may like ye."

Then he went, and came again swiftly, and many folk with him to receive the knight. They let down the great drawbridge, and came forth and knelt on their knees on the cold earth to give him worthy welcome. They held wide open the great gates, and courteously he bid them rise, and rode over the bridge. Then men came to him and held his stirrup while he dismounted, and took and stabled his steed. There came down knights and squires to bring the guest with joy to the hall. When he raised his helmet there were many to take it from his hand, fain to serve him, and they took from him sword and shield.

Sir Gawain gave good greeting to the noble and the mighty men who came to do him honour. Clad in his shining armour they led him to the hall, where a great fire burnt brightly on the floor; and the lord of the household came forth from his chamber to meet the hero fitly. He spake to the knight, and said: "Ye are welcome to do here as it likes ye. All that is here is your own to have at your will and disposal."

"Gramercy!" quote Gawain, "may Christ requite ye."

As friends that were fain each embraced the other; and Gawain looked on the knight who greeted him so kindly, and thought 'twas a bold warrior that owned that burg.

Of mighty stature he was, and of high age; broad and flowing was his beard, and of a bright hue. He was stalwart of limb, and strong in his stride, his face fiery red, and his speech free: in sooth he seemed one well fitted to be a leader of valiant men.

Then the lord led Sir Gawain to a chamber, and commanded folk to wait upon him, and at his bidding there came men enough who brought the guest to a fair bower. The bedding was noble, with curtains of pure silk wrought with gold, and wondrous coverings of fair cloth all embroidered. The curtains ran on ropes with rings of red gold, and the walls were hung with carpets of Orient, and the same spread on the floor. There with mirthful speeches they took from the guest his byrny and all his shining armour, and brought him rich robes of the choicest in its stead. They were long and flowing, and became him well, and when he was clad in them all who looked on the hero thought that surely God had never made a fairer knight: he seemed as if he might be a prince without peer in the field where men strive in battle.

Then before the hearth-place, whereon the fire burned, they made ready a chair for Gawain, hung about with cloth and fair cushions; and there they cast around him a mantle of brown samite, richly embroidered and furred within with costly skins of ermine, with a hood of the same, and he seated himself in that rich seat, and warmed himself at the fire, and was cheered at heart. And while he sat thus the serving men set up a table on trestles, and covered it with a fair white cloth, and set thereon salt-cellar, and napkin, and silver spoons; and the knight washed at his will, and set him down to meat.

The folk served him courteously with many dishes seasoned of the best, a double portion. All kinds of fish were there, some baked in bread, some broiled on the embers, some sodden, some stewed and savoured with spices, with all sorts of cunning devices to his taste. And often he called it a feast, when they spake gaily to him all together, and said, "Now take ye this penance, and it shall be for your amendment." Much mirth thereof did Sir Gawain make.

Then they questioned that prince courteously of whence he came; and he told them that he was of the court of Arthur, who is the rich royal King of the Round Table, and that it was Gawain himself who was within their walls, and would keep Christmas with them, as the chance had fallen out. And when the lord of the castle heard those tidings he laughed aloud for gladness, and all men in that keep were joyful that they should be in the company of him to whom belonged all fame, and valour, and courtesy, and whose honour was praised above that of all men on earth. Each said softly to his fellow, "Now shall we see courteous bearing, and the manner of speech befitting courts. What charm lieth in gentle speech shall we learn without asking, since here we have welcomed the fine father of courtesy. God has surely shewn us His grace since He sends us such a guest as Gawain! When men shall sit and sing, blithe for Christ's birth, this knight shall bring us to the knowledge of fair manners, and it may be that hearing him we may learn the cunning speech of love."

High Feast

BY THE TIME the knight had risen from dinner it was near nightfall. Then chaplains took their way to the chapel, and rang loudly, even as they should, for the solemn evensong of the high feast. Thither went the lord, and the lady also, and entered with her maidens into a comely closet, and thither also went Gawain. Then the lord took him by the sleeve and led him to a seat, and called him by his name, and told him he was of all men in the world the most welcome. And Sir Gawain thanked him truly, and each kissed the other, and they sat gravely together throughout the service.

Then was the lady fain to look upon that knight; and she came forth from her closet with many fair maidens. The fairest of ladies was she in face, and figure, and colouring, fairer even than Guinevere, so the knight thought. She came through the chancel to greet the hero, another lady held her by the left hand, older than she, and seemingly of high estate, with many nobles about her. But unlike to look upon were those ladies, for if the younger were fair, the elder was yellow. Rich red were the cheeks of the one, rough and wrinkled those of the other; the kerchiefs of the one were broidered with many glistening pearls, her throat and neck bare, and whiter than the snow that lies on the hills; the neck of the other was swathed in a gorget, with a white wimple over her black chin. Her forehead was wrapped in silk with many folds, worked with knots, so that naught of her was seen save her black brows, her eyes, her nose and her lips, and those were bleared, and ill to look upon. A worshipful lady in sooth one might call her! In figure was she short and broad, and thickly made – far fairer to behold was she whom she led by the hand.

When Gawain beheld that fair lady, who looked at him graciously, with leave of the lord he went towards them, and, bowing low, he greeted the elder, but the younger and fairer he took lightly in his arms, and kissed her courteously, and greeted her in knightly wise. Then she hailed him as friend, and he quickly prayed to be counted as her servant, if she so willed. Then they took him between them, and talking, led him to the chamber, to the hearth, and bade them bring spices, and they brought them in plenty with the good wine that was wont to be drunk at such seasons. Then the lord sprang to his feet and bade them make merry, and took off his hood, and hung it on a spear, and bade him win the worship thereof who should make most mirth that Christmas-tide. "And I shall try, by my faith, to fool it with the best, by the help of my friends, ere I lose my raiment." Thus with gay words the lord made trial to gladden Gawain with jests that night, till it was time to bid them light the tapers, and Sir Gawain took leave of them and gat him to rest.

In the morn when all men call to mind how Christ our Lord was born on earth to die for us, there is joy, for His sake, in all dwellings of the world; and so was there here on that day. For high feast was held, with many dainties and cunningly cooked messes. On the daïs sat gallant men, clad in their best. The ancient dame sat on the high seat, with the lord of the castle beside her. Gawain and the fair lady sat together, even in the midst of the board, when the feast was served; and so throughout all the hall each sat in his degree, and was served in order. There was meat, there was mirth, there was much joy, so that to tell thereof would take me too long, though peradventure I might strive to declare it. But Gawain and that fair lady had much joy of each other's company through her sweet words and courteous converse. And there was music made before each prince, trumpets and drums, and merry piping; each man hearkened his minstrel, and they too hearkened theirs.

So they held high feast that day and the next, and the third day thereafter, and the joy on S. John's Day was fair to hearken, for 'twas the last of the feast and the guests would depart in the grey of the morning. Therefore they awoke early, and drank wine, and danced fair carols, and at last, when it was late, each man took his leave to wend early on his way. Gawain would bid his host farewell, but the lord took him by the hand, and led him to his own chamber beside the hearth, and there he thanked him for the favour he had shown him in honouring his dwelling at that high season, and gladdening his castle with his fair countenance. "I wis, sir, that while I live I shall be held the worthier that Gawain has been my guest at God's own feast."

"Gramercy, sir," quoth Gawain, "in good faith, all the honour is yours, may the High King give it you, and I am but at your will to work your behest, inasmuch as I am beholden to you in great and small by rights."

Then the lord did his best to persuade the knight to tarry with him, but Gawain answered that he might in no wise do so. Then the host asked him courteously what stern behest had driven him at the holy season from the king's court, to fare all alone, ere yet the feast was ended?

"Forsooth," quoth the knight, "ye say but the truth: 'tis a high quest and a pressing that hath brought me afield, for I am summoned myself to a certain place, and I know not whither in the world I may wend to find it; so help me Christ, I would give all the kingdom of Logres an I might find it by New Year's morn. Therefore, sir, I make request of you that ye tell me truly if ye ever heard word of the Green Chapel, where it may be found, and the Green Knight that keeps it. For I am pledged by solemn compact sworn between us to meet that knight at the New Year if so I were on life; and of that same New Year it wants but little – I'faith, I would look on that hero more joyfully than on any other fair sight! Therefore, by your will, it behoves me to leave you, for I have but barely three days, and I would as fain fall dead as fail of mine errand."

Then the lord quoth, laughing, "Now must ye needs stay, for I will show you your goal, the Green Chapel, ere your term be at an end, have ye no fear! But ye can take your ease, friend, in your bed, till the fourth day, and go forth on the first of the year and come to that place at mid-morn to do as ye will. Dwell here till New Year's Day, and then rise and set forth, and ye shall be set in the way; 'tis not two miles hence."

Then was Gawain glad, and he laughed gaily. "Now I thank you for this above all else. Now my quest is achieved I will dwell here at your will, and otherwise do as ye shall ask."

Then the lord took him, and set him beside him, and bade the ladies be fetched for their greater pleasure, tho' between themselves they had solace. The lord, for gladness, made merry jest, even as one who wist not what to do for joy; and he cried aloud to the knight, "Ye have promised to do the thing I bid ye: will ye hold to this behest, here, at once?"

"Yea, forsooth," said that true knight, "while I abide in your burg I am bound by your behest."

"Ye have travelled from far," said the host, "and since then ye have waked with me, ye are not well refreshed by rest and sleep, as I know. Ye shall therefore abide in your chamber, and lie at your ease tomorrow at Mass-tide, and go to meat when ye will with my wife, who shall sit with you, and comfort you with her company till I return; and I shall rise early and go forth to the chase." And Gawain agreed to all this courteously.

"Sir knight," quoth the host, "we shall make a covenant. Whatsoever I win in the wood shall be yours, and whatever may fall to your share, that shall ye exchange for it. Let us swear, friend, to make this exchange, however our hap may be, for worse or for better."

"I grant ye your will," quoth Gawain the good; "if ye list so to do, it liketh me well."

"Bring hither the wine-cup, the bargain is made," so said the lord of that castle. They laughed each one, and drank of the wine, and made merry, these lords and ladies, as it pleased them. Then with gay talk and merry jest they arose, and stood, and spoke softly, and kissed courteously, and took leave of each other. With burning torches, and many a serving-man, was each led to his couch; yet ere they gat them to bed the old lord oft repeated their covenant, for he knew well how to make sport.

Each Knight Rode His Way

FULL EARLY, ERE DAYLIGHT, **the folk rose up; the guests who would depart called their grooms, and they made them ready, and saddled the steeds, tightened up the girths, and trussed up their mails. The knights, all arrayed for riding, leapt up lightly, and took their bridles, and each rode his way as pleased him best.**

The lord of the land was not the last. Ready for the chase, with many of his men, he ate a sop hastily when he had heard Mass, and then with blast of the bugle fared forth to the field. He and his nobles were to horse ere daylight glimmered upon the earth.

Then the huntsmen coupled their hounds, unclosed the kennel door, and called them out. They blew three blasts gaily on the bugles, the hounds bayed fiercely, and they that would go a-hunting checked and chastised them. A hundred hunters there were of the best, so I have heard tell. Then the trackers gat them to the trysting-place and uncoupled the hounds, and forest rang again with their gay blasts.

At the first sound of the hunt the game quaked for fear, and fled, trembling, along the vale. They betook them to the heights, but the liers in wait turned them back with loud cries; the harts they let pass them, and the stags with their spreading antlers, for the lord had forbidden that they should be slain, but the hinds and the does they turned back, and drave down into the valleys. Then might ye see much shooting of arrows. As the deer fled under the boughs a broad whistling shaft smote and wounded each sorely, so that, wounded and bleeding, they fell dying on the banks. The hounds followed swiftly on their tracks, and hunters, blowing the horn, sped after them with ringing shouts as if the cliffs burst asunder. What game escaped those that shot was run down at the outer ring. Thus were they driven on the hills, and harassed at the waters, so well did the men know their work, and the greyhounds were so great and swift that they ran them down as fast as the hunters could slay them. Thus the lord passed the day in mirth and joyfulness, even to nightfall.

So the lord roamed the woods, and Gawain, that good night, lay ever a-bed, curtained about, under the costly coverlet, while the daylight gleamed on the walls. And as he lay half slumbering, he heard a little sound at the door, and he raised his head, and caught back a corner of the curtain, and waited to see what it might be. It was the lovely lady, the lord's wife; she shut the door softly behind her, and turned towards the bed; and Gawain was shamed, laid him down softly and made as if he slept. And she came lightly to the bedside, within the curtain, and sat herself down beside him, to wait till he wakened. The knight lay there awhile, and marvelled within himself what her coming might betoken; and he said to himself, "'Twere more seemly if I asked her what hath brought her hither." Then he made feint to waken, and turned towards her, and opened his eyes as one astonished, and crossed himself; and she looked on him laughing, with her cheeks red and white, lovely to behold, and small smiling lips.

"Good morrow, Sir Gawain," said that fair lady; "ye are but a careless sleeper, since one can enter thus. Now are ye taken unawares, and lest ye escape me I shall bind you in your bed; of that be ye assured!" Laughing, she spake these words.

"Good morrow, fair lady," quoth Gawain blithely. "I will do your will, as it likes me well. For I yield me readily, and pray your grace, and that is best, by my faith, since I needs must do so." Thus he jested again, laughing. "But an ye would, fair lady, grant me this grace that ye pray your prisoner to rise. I would get me from bed, and array me better, then could I talk with ye in more comfort."

"Nay, forsooth, fair sir," quoth the lady, "ye shall not rise, I will rede ye better. I shall keep ye here, since ye can do no other, and talk with my knight whom I have captured. For I know well that ye are Sir Gawain, whom all the world worships, wheresoever ye may ride. Your honour and your courtesy are praised by lords and ladies, by all who live. Now ye are here and we are alone, my lord and his men are afield; the serving men in their beds, and my maidens also, and the door shut upon us. And since in this hour I have him that all men love, I shall use my time well with speech, while it lasts. Ye are welcome to my company, for it behoves me in sooth to be your servant."

"In good faith," quoth Gawain, "I think me that I am not him of whom ye speak, for unworthy am I of such service as ye here proffer. In sooth, I were glad if I might set myself by word or service to your pleasure; a pure joy would it be to me!"

"In good faith, Sir Gawain," quoth the gay lady, "the praise and the prowess that pleases all ladies I lack them not, nor hold them light; yet are there ladies enough who would liever now have the knight in their hold, as I have ye here, to dally with your courteous words, to bring them comfort and to ease their cares, than much of the treasure and the gold that are theirs. And now, through the grace of Him who upholds the heavens, I have wholly in my power that which they all desire!"

Thus the lady, fair to look upon, made him great cheer, and Sir Gawain, with modest words, answered her again: "Madam," he quoth, "may Mary requite ye, for in good faith I have found in ye a noble frankness. Much courtesy have other folk shown me, but the honour they have done me is naught to the worship of yourself, who knoweth but good."

"By Mary," quoth the lady, "I think otherwise; for were I worth all the women alive, and had I the wealth of the world in my hand, and might choose me a lord to my liking, then, for all that I have seen in ye, Sir Knight, of beauty and courtesy and blithe semblance, and for all that I have hearkened and hold for true, there should be no knight on earth to be chosen before ye!"

"Well I wot," quoth Sir Gawain, "that ye have chosen a better; but I am proud that ye should so prize me, and as your servant do I hold ye my sovereign, and your knight am I, and may Christ reward ye."

So they talked of many matters till mid-morn was past, and ever the lady made as though she loved him, and the knight turned her speech aside. For though she were the brightest of maidens, yet had he forborne to shew her love for the danger that awaited him, and the blow that must be given without delay.

Then the lady prayed her leave from him, and he granted it readily. And she gave [the text reads "have"] him good-day, with laughing glance, but he must needs marvel at her words:

"Now He that speeds fair speech reward ye this disport; but that ye be Gawain my mind misdoubts me greatly."

"Wherefore?" quoth the knight quickly, fearing lest he had lacked in some courtesy.

And the lady spake: "So true a knight as Gawain is holden, and one so perfect in courtesy, would never have tarried so long with a lady but he would of his courtesy have craved a kiss at parting."

Then quoth Gawain, "I wot I will do even as it may please ye, and kiss at your commandment, as a true knight should who forbears to ask for fear of displeasure."

At that she came near and bent down and kissed the knight, and each commended the other to Christ, and she went forth from the chamber softly.

Then Sir Gawain arose and called his chamberlain and chose his garments, and when he was ready he gat him forth to Mass, and then went to meat, and made merry all day till the rising of the moon, and never had a knight fairer lodging than had he with those two noble ladies, the elder and the younger.

And even the lord of the land chased the hinds through holt and heath till eventide, and then with much blowing of bugles and baying of hounds they bore the game homeward; and by the time daylight was done all the folk had returned to that fair castle. And when the lord and Sir Gawain met together, then were they both well pleased. The lord commanded them all to assemble in the great hall, and the ladies to descend with their maidens, and there, before them all, he bade the men fetch in the spoil of the day's hunting, and he called unto Gawain, and counted the tale of the beasts, and showed them unto him, and said, "What think ye of this game, Sir Knight? Have I deserved of ye thanks for my woodcraft?"

"Yea, I wis," quoth the other, "here is the fairest spoil I have seen this seven year in the winter season."

"And all this do I give ye, Gawain," quoth the host, "for by accord of covenant ye may claim it as your own."

"That is sooth," quoth the other, "I grant you that same; and I have fairly won this within walls, and with as good will do I yield it to ye." With that he clasped his hands round the lord's neck and kissed him as courteously as he might. "Take ye here my spoils, no more have I won; ye should have it freely, though it were greater than this."

"'Tis good," said the host, "gramercy thereof. Yet were I fain to know where ye won this same favour, and if it were by your own wit?"

"Nay," answered Gawain, "that was not in the bond. Ask me no more: ye have taken what was yours by right, be content with that."

They laughed and jested together, and sat them down to supper, where they were served with many dainties; and after supper they sat by the hearth, and wine was served out to them; and oft in their jesting they promised to observe on the morrow the same covenant that they had made before, and whatever chance might betide to exchange their spoil, be it much or little, when they met at night. Thus they renewed their bargain before the whole court, and then the night-drink was served, and each courteously took leave of the other and gat him to bed.

By the time the cock had crowed thrice the lord of the castle had left his bed; Mass was sung and meat fitly served. The folk were forth to the wood ere the day broke, with hound and horn they rode over the plain, and uncoupled their dogs among the thorns. Soon they struck on the scent, and the hunt cheered on the hounds who were first to seize it, urging them with shouts. The others hastened to the cry, forty at once, and there rose such a clamour from the pack that the rocks rang again. The huntsmen spurred them on with shouting and blasts of the horn; and the hounds drew together to a thicket betwixt the water and a high crag in the cliff beneath the hillside. There where the rough rock fell ruggedly they, the huntsmen, fared to the finding, and cast about round the hill and the thicket behind them. The knights wist well what beast was within, and would drive him forth with the bloodhounds. And as they beat the bushes, suddenly over the beaters there rushed forth a wondrous great and fierce boar, long since had he left the herd to roam by himself. Grunting, he cast many to the ground, and fled forth at his best speed, without more mischief. The men hallooed loudly and cried, "Hay! Hay!" and blew the horns to urge on the hounds, and rode swiftly after the boar. Many a time did he turn to bay and tare the hounds, and they yelped, and howled shrilly. Then the men made ready their arrows and shot at him, but the points were turned on his thick hide, and the barbs would not bite upon him, for the shafts shivered in pieces, and the head but leapt again wherever it hit.

But when the boar felt the stroke of the arrows he waxed mad with rage, and turned on the hunters and tare many, so that, affrightened, they fled before him. But the lord on a swift steed pursued him, blowing his bugle; as a gallant knight he rode through the woodland chasing the boar till the sun grew low.

So did the hunters this day, while Sir Gawain lay in his bed lapped in rich gear; and the lady forgat not to salute him, for early was she at his side, to cheer his mood.

She came to the bedside and looked on the knight, and Gawain gave her fit greeting, and she greeted him again with ready words, and sat her by his side and laughed, and with a sweet look she spoke to him:

"Sir, if ye be Gawain, I think it a wonder that ye be so stern and cold, and care not for the courtesies of friendship, but if one teach ye to know them ye cast the lesson out of your mind. Ye have soon forgotten what I taught ye yesterday, by all the truest tokens that I knew!"

"What is that?" quoth the knight. "I trow I know not. If it be sooth that ye say, then is the blame mine own."

"But I taught ye of kissing, " quoth the fair lady. "Wherever a fair countenance is shown him, it behoves a courteous knight quickly to claim a kiss."

"Nay, my dear," said Sir Gawain, "cease that speech; that durst I not do lest I were denied, for if I were forbidden I wot I were wrong did I further entreat."

"I' faith," quoth the lady merrily, "ye may not be forbid, ye are strong enough to constrain by strength an ye will, were any so discourteous as to give ye denial."

"Yea, by Heaven," said Gawain, "ye speak well; but threats profit little in the land where I dwell, and so with a gift that is given not of good will! I am at your commandment to kiss when ye like, to take or to leave as ye list."

Then the lady bent her down and kissed him courteously.

And as they spake together she said, "I would learn somewhat from ye, an ye would not be wroth, for young ye bare and fair, and so courteous and knightly as ye are known to be, the head of all chivalry, and versed in all wisdom of love and war – 'tis ever told of true knights how they adventured their lives for their true love, and endured hardships for her favours, and avenged her with valour, and eased her sorrows, and brought joy to her bower; and ye are the fairest knight of your time, and your fame and your honour are everywhere, yet I have sat by ye here twice, and never a word have I heard of love! Ye who are so courteous and skilled in such love ought surely to teach one so young and unskilled some little craft of true love! Why are ye so unlearned who art otherwise so famous? Or is it that ye deemed me unworthy to hearken to your teaching? For shame, Sir Knight! I come hither alone and sit at your side to learn of ye some skill; teach me of your wit, while my lord is from home."

"In good faith," quoth Gawain, "great is my joy and my profit that so fair a lady as ye are should deign to come hither, and trouble ye with so poor a man, and make sport with your knight with kindly countenance, it pleaseth me much. But that I, in my turn, should take it upon me to tell of love and such like matters to ye who know more by half, or a hundred fold, of such craft than I do, or ever shall in all my lifetime, by my troth 'twere folly indeed! I will work your will to the best of my might as I am bounden, and evermore will I be your servant, so help me Christ!"

Then often with guile she questioned that knight that she might win him to woo her, but he defended himself so fairly that none might in any wise blame him, and naught but bliss and harmless jesting was there between them. They laughed and talked together till at last she kissed him, and craved her leave of him, and went her way.

Sir Gawain Marvelled Much

THEN THE KNIGHT AROSE and went forth to Mass, and afterward dinner was served and he sat and spake with the ladies all day. But the lord of the castle rode ever over the land chasing the wild boar, that fled through the thickets, slaying the best of his hounds and breaking their backs in sunder; till at last he was so weary he might run no longer, but made for a hole in a mound by a rock. He got the mound at his back and faced the hounds, whetting his white tusks and foaming at the mouth. The huntsmen stood aloof, fearing to draw nigh him; so many of them had been already wounded that they were loth to be torn with his tusks, so fierce he was and mad with rage. At length the lord himself came up, and saw the beast at bay, and the men standing aloof. Then quickly he sprang to the ground and drew out a bright blade, and waded through the stream to the boar.

When the beast was aware of the knight with weapon in hand, he set up his bristles and snorted loudly, and many feared for their lord lest he should be slain. Then the boar leapt upon the knight so that beast and man were one atop of the other in the water; but the boar had the worst of it, for the man had marked, even as he sprang, and set the point of his brand to the beast's chest, and drove it up to the hilt, so that the heart was split in twain, and the boar fell snarling, and was swept down by the water to where a hundred hounds seized on him, and the men drew him to shore for the dogs to slay.

Then was there loud blowing of horns and baying of hounds, the huntsmen smote off the boar's head, and hung the carcase by the four feet to a stout pole, and so went on their way homewards. The head they bore before the lord himself, who had slain the beast at the ford by force of his strong hand.

It seemed him o'er long ere he saw Sir Gawain in the hall, and he called, and the guest came to take that which fell to his share. And when he saw Gawain the lord laughed aloud, and bade them call the ladies and the household together, and he showed them the game, and told them the tale, how they hunted the wild boar through the woods, and of his length and breadth and height; and Sir Gawain commended his deeds and praised him for his valour, well proven, for so mighty a beast had he never seen before.

Then they handled the huge head, and the lord said aloud, "Now, Gawain, this game is your own by sure covenant, as ye right well know."

"'Tis sooth," quoth the knight, "and as truly will I give ye all I have gained." He took the host round the neck, and kissed him courteously twice. "Now are we quits," he said, "this eventide, of all the covenants that we made since I came hither."

And the lord answered, "By S. Giles, ye are the best I know; ye will be rich in a short space if ye drive such bargains!"

Then they set up the tables on trestles, and covered them with fair cloths, and lit waxen tapers on the walls. The knights sat and were served in the hall, and much game and glee was there round the hearth, with many songs, both at supper and after; song of Christmas, and new carols, with all the mirth one may think of. And ever that lovely lady sat by the knight, and with still stolen looks made such feint of pleasing him, that Gawain marvelled much, and was wroth with himself, but he could not for his courtesy return her fair glances, but dealt with her cunningly, however she might strive to wrest the thing.

When they had tarried in the hall so long as it seemed them good, they turned to the inner chamber and the wide hearthplace, and there they drank wine, and the host proffered to renew the covenant for New Year's Eve; but the knight craved leave to depart on the morrow, for it was nigh to the term when he must fulfil his pledge. But the lord would withhold him from so doing, and prayed him to tarry, and said,

"As I am a true knight I swear my troth that ye shall come to the Green Chapel to achieve your task on New Year's morn, long before prime. Therefore abide ye in your bed, and I will hunt in this wood, and hold ye to the covenant to exchange with me against all the spoil I may bring hither. For twice have I tried ye, and found ye true, and the morrow shall be the third time and the best. Make we merry now while we may, and think on joy, for misfortune may take a man whensoever it wills."

Then Gawain granted his request, and they brought them drink, and they gat them with lights to bed.

Sir Gawain lay and slept softly, but the lord, who was keen on woodcraft, was afoot early. After Mass he and his men ate a morsel, and he asked for his steed; all the knights who should ride with him were already mounted before the hall gates.

'Twas a fair frosty morning, for the sun rose red in ruddy vapour, and the welkin was clear of clouds. The hunters scattered them by a forest side, and the rocks rang again with the blast of their horns. Some came on the scent of a fox, and a hound gave tongue; the huntsmen shouted, and the pack followed in a crowd on the trail. The fox ran before them, and when they saw him they pursued him with noise and much shouting, and he wound and turned through many a thick grove, often cowering and hearkening in a hedge. At last by a little ditch he leapt out of a spinney, stole away slily by a copse path, and so out of the wood and away from the hounds. But he went, ere he wist, to a chosen tryst, and three started forth on him at once, so he must needs double back, and betake him to the wood again.

Then was it joyful to hearken to the hounds; when all the pack had met together and had sight of their game they made as loud a din as if all the lofty cliffs had fallen clattering together. The huntsmen shouted and threatened, and followed close upon him so that he might scarce escape, but Reynard was wily, and he turned and doubled upon them, and led the lord and his men over the hills, now on the slopes, now in the vales, while the knight at home slept through the cold morning beneath his costly curtains.

But the fair lady of the castle rose betimes, and clad herself in a rich mantle that reached even to the ground, left her throat and her fair neck bare, and was bordered and lined with costly furs. On her head she wore no golden circlet, but a network of precious stones, that gleamed and shone through her tresses in clusters of twenty together. Thus she came into the chamber, closed the door after her, and set open a window, and called to him gaily, "Sir Knight, how may ye sleep? The morning is so fair."

Sir Gawain was deep in slumber, and in his dream he vexed him much for the destiny that should befall him on the morrow, when he should meet the knight at the Green Chapel, and abide his blow; but when the lady spake he heard her, and came to himself, and roused from his dream and answered swiftly. The lady came laughing, and kissed him courteously, and he welcomed her fittingly with a cheerful countenance. He saw her so glorious and gaily dressed, so faultless of features and complexion, that it warmed his heart to look upon her.

They spake to each other smiling, and all was bliss and good cheer between them. They exchanged fair words, and much happiness was therein, yet was there a gulf between them, and she might win no more of her knight, for that gallant prince watched well his words – he would neither take her love, nor frankly refuse it. He cared for his courtesy, lest he be deemed churlish, and yet more for his honour lest he be traitor to his host. "God forbid," quoth he to himself, "that it should so befall." Thus with courteous words did he set aside all the special speeches that came from her lips.

Then spake the lady to the knight, "Ye deserve blame if ye hold not that lady who sits beside ye above all else in the world, if ye have not already a love whom ye hold dearer, and like better, and have sworn such firm faith to that lady that ye care not to loose it – and that am I now fain to believe. And now I pray ye straitly that ye tell me that in truth, and hide it not."

And the knight answered, "By S. John" (and he smiled as he spake) "no such love have I, nor do I think to have yet awhile."

"That is the worst word I may hear," quoth the lady, "but in sooth I have mine answer; kiss me now courteously, and I will go hence; I can but mourn as a maiden that loves much."

Sighing, she stooped down and kissed him, and then she rose up and spake as she stood, "Now, dear, at our parting do me this grace: give me some gift, if it were but thy glove, that I may bethink me of my knight, and lessen my mourning."

"Now, I wis," quoth the knight, "I would that I had here the most precious thing that I possess on earth that I might leave ye as love-token, great or small, for ye have deserved forsooth more reward than I might give ye. But it is not to your honour to have at this time a glove for reward as gift from Gawain, and I am here on a strange errand, and have no man with me, nor mails with goodly things – that mislikes me much, lady, at this time; but each man must fare as he is taken, if for sorrow and ill."

"Nay, knight highly honoured," quoth that lovesome lady, "though I have naught of yours, yet shall ye have somewhat of mine." With that she reached him a ring of red gold with a sparkling stone therein, that shone even as the sun (wit ye well, it was worth many marks); but the knight refused it, and spake readily,

"I will take no gift, lady, at this time. I have none to give, and none will I take."

She prayed him to take it, but he refused her prayer, and sware in sooth that he would not have it.

The lady was sorely vexed, and said, "If ye refuse my ring as too costly, that ye will not be so highly beholden to me, I will give you my girdle 11 as a lesser gift." With that she loosened a lace that was fastened at her side, knit upon her kirtle under her mantle. It was wrought of green silk, and gold, only braided by the fingers, and that she offered to the knight, and besought him though it were of little worth that he would take it, and he said nay, he would touch neither gold nor gear ere God give him grace to achieve the adventure for which he had come hither. "And therefore, I pray ye, displease ye not, and ask me no longer, for I may not grant it. I am dearly beholden to ye for the favour ye have shown me, and ever, in heat and cold, will I be your true servant."

"Now," said the lady, "ye refuse this silk, for it is simple in itself, and so it seems, indeed; lo, it is small to look upon and less in cost, but whoso knew the virtue that is knit therein he would, peradventure, value it more highly. For whatever knight is girded with this green lace, while he bears it knotted about him there is no man under heaven can overcome him, for he may not be slain for any magic on earth."

Then Gawain bethought him, and it came into his heart that this were a jewel for the jeopardy that awaited him when he came to the

Green Chapel to seek the return blow – could he so order it that he should escape unslain, 'twere a craft worth trying. Then he bare with her chiding, and let her say her say, and she pressed the girdle on him and prayed him to take it, and he granted her prayer, and she gave it him with good will, and besought him for her sake never to reveal it but to hide it loyally from her lord; and the knight agreed that never should any man know it, save they two alone. He thanked her often and heartily, and she kissed him for the third time.

Then she took her leave of him, and when she was gone Sir Gawain arose, and clad him in rich attire, and took the girdle, and knotted it round him, and hid it beneath his robes. Then he took his way to the chapel, and sought out a priest privily and prayed him to teach him better how his soul might be saved when he should go hence; and there he shrived him, and showed his misdeeds, both great and small, and besought mercy and craved absolution; and the priest assoiled him, and set him as clean as if Doomsday had been on the morrow. And afterwards Sir Gawain made him merry with the ladies, with carols, and all kinds of joy, as never he did but that one day, even to nightfall; and all the men marvelled at him, and said that never since he came thither had he been so merry.

Meanwhile the lord of the castle was abroad chasing the fox; awhile he lost him, and as he rode through a spinny he heard the hounds near at hand, and Reynard came creeping through a thick grove, with all the pack at his heels. Then the lord drew out his shining brand, and cast it at the beast, and the fox swerved aside for the sharp edge, and would have doubled back, but a hound was on him ere he might turn, and right before the horse's feet they all fell on him, and worried him fiercely, snarling the while.

Then the lord leapt from his saddle, and caught the fox from the jaws, and held it aloft over his head, and hallooed loudly, and many brave hounds bayed as they beheld it; and the hunters hied them thither, blowing their horns; all that bare bugles blew them at once, and all the others shouted. 'Twas the merriest meeting that ever men heard, the clamour that was raised at the death of the fox. They rewarded the hounds, stroking them and rubbing their heads, and took Reynard and stripped him of his coat; then blowing their horns, they turned them homewards, for it was nigh nightfall.

The lord was gladsome at his return, and found a bright fire on the hearth, and the knight beside it, the good Sir Gawain, who was in joyous mood for the pleasure he had had with the ladies. He wore a robe of blue, that reached even to the ground, and a surcoat richly furred, that became him well. A hood like to the surcoat fell on his shoulders, and all alike were done about with fur. He met the host in the midst of the floor, and jesting, he greeted him, and said, "Now shall I be first to fulfil our covenant which we made together when there was no lack of wine." Then he embraced the knight, and kissed him thrice, as solemnly as he might.

"Of a sooth," quoth the other, "ye have good luck in the matter of this covenant, if ye made a good exchange!"

"Yea, it matters naught of the exchange," quoth Gawain, "since what I owe is swiftly paid."

"Marry," said the other, "mine is behind, for I have hunted all this day, and naught have I got but this foul fox-skin, and that is but poor payment for three such kisses as ye have here given me."

"Enough," quoth Sir Gawain, "I thank ye, by the Rood."

Then the lord told them of his hunting, and how the fox had been slain.

With mirth and minstrelsy, and dainties at their will, they made them as merry as a folk well might till 'twas time for them to sever, for at last they must needs betake them to their beds. Then the knight took his leave of the lord, and thanked him fairly.

"For the fair sojourn that I have had here at this high feast may the High King give ye honour. I give ye myself, as one of your servants, if ye so like; for I must needs, as you know, go hence with the morn, and ye will give me, as ye promised, a guide to show me the way to the Green Chapel, an God will suffer me on New Year's Day to deal the doom of my weird."

"By my faith," quoth the host, "all that ever I promised, that shall I keep with good will." Then he gave him a servant to set him in the way, and lead him by the downs, that he should have no need to ford the stream, and should fare by the shortest road through the groves; and Gawain thanked the lord for the honour done him. Then he would take leave of the ladies, and courteously he kissed them, and spake, praying them to receive his thanks, and they made like reply; then with many sighs they commended him to Christ, and he departed courteously from that folk. Each man that he met he thanked him for his service and his solace, and the pains he had been at to do his will; and each found it as hard to part from the knight as if he had ever dwelt with him.

Then they led him with torches to his chamber, and brought him to his bed to rest. That he slept soundly I may not say, for the morrow gave him much to think on. Let him rest awhile, for he was near that which he sought, and if ye will but listen to me I will tell ye how it fared with him thereafter.

Gawain and Gringalet

NOW THE NEW YEAR DREW NIGH, and the night passed, and the day chased the darkness, as is God's will; but wild weather wakened therewith. The clouds cast the cold to the earth, with enough of the north to slay them that lacked clothing. The snow drave smartly, and the whistling wind blew from the heights, and made great drifts in the valleys. The knight, lying in his bed, listened, for though his eyes were shut, he might sleep but little, and hearkened every cock that crew.

He arose ere the day broke, by the light of a lamp that burned in his chamber, and called to his chamberlain, bidding him bring his armour and saddle his steed. The other gat him up, and fetched his garments, and robed Sir Gawain.

First he clad him in his clothes to keep off the cold, and then in his harness, which was well and fairly kept. Both hauberk and plates were well burnished, the rings of the rich byrny freed from rust, and all as fresh as at first, so that the knight was fain to thank them. Then he did on each piece, and bade them bring his steed, while he put the fairest raiment on himself; his coat with its fair cognizance, adorned with precious stones upon velvet, with broidered seams, and all furred within with costly skins. And he left not the lace, the lady's gift, that Gawain forgot not, for his own good. When he had girded on his sword he wrapped the gift twice about him, swathed around his waist. The girdle of green silk set gaily and well upon the royal red cloth, rich to behold, but the knight ware it not for pride of the pendants, polished though they were with fair gold that gleamed brightly on the ends, but to save himself from sword and knife, when it behoved him to abide his hurt without question. With that the hero went forth, and thanked that kindly folk full often.

Then was Gringalet ready, that was great and strong, and had been well cared for and tended in every wise; in fair condition was that proud steed, and fit for a journey. Then Gawain went to him, and looked on his coat, and said by his sooth, "There is a folk in this place that thinketh on honour; much joy may they have, and the lord who maintains them, and may all good betide that lovely lady all her life long. Since they for charity cherish a guest, and hold honour in their hands, may He who holds the heaven on high requite them, and also ye all. And if I might live anywhere on earth, I would give ye full reward, readily, if so I might." Then he set foot in the stirrup and bestrode his steed, and his squire gave him his shield, which he laid on his shoulder. Then he smote Gringalet with his golden spurs, and the steed pranced on the stones and would stand no longer.

By that his man was mounted, who bare his spear and lance, and Gawain quoth, "I commend this castle to Christ, may He give it ever good fortune." Then the drawbridge was let down, and the broad gates unbarred and opened on both sides; the knight crossed himself, and passed through the gateway, and praised the porter, who knelt before the prince, and gave him good-day, and commended him to God. Thus the knight went on his way with the one man who should guide him to that dread place where he should receive rueful payment.

The two went by hedges where the boughs were bare, and climbed the cliffs where the cold clings. Naught fell from the heavens, but 'twas ill beneath them; mist brooded over the moor and hung on the mountains; each hill had a cap, a great cloak, of mist. The streams foamed and bubbled between their banks, dashing sparkling on the shores where they shelved downwards. Rugged and dangerous was the way through the woods, till it was time for the sun-rising. Then were they on a high hill; the snow lay white beside them, and the man who rode with Gawain drew rein by his master.

"Sir," he said, "I have brought ye hither, and now ye are not far from the place that ye have sought so specially. But I will tell ye for sooth, since I know ye well, and ye are such a knight as I well love, would ye follow my counsel ye would fare the better. The place whither ye go is accounted full perilous, for he who liveth in that waste is the worst on earth, for he is strong and fierce, and loveth to deal mighty blows; taller is he than any man on earth, and greater of frame than any four in Arthur's court, or in any other. And this is his custom at the Green Chapel; there may no man pass by that place, however proud his arms, but he does him to death by force of his hand, for he is a discourteous knight, and shews no mercy. Be he churl or chaplain who rides by that chapel, monk or mass priest, or any man else, he thinks it as pleasant to slay them as to pass alive himself. Therefore, I tell ye, as sooth as ye sit in saddle, if ye come there and that knight know it, ye shall be slain, though ye had twenty lives; trow me that truly! He has dwelt here full long and seen many a combat; ye may not defend ye against his blows. Therefore, good Sir Gawain, let the man be, and get ye away some other road; for God's sake seek ye another land, and there may Christ speed ye! And I will hie me home again, and I promise ye further that I will swear by God and the saints, or any other oath ye please, that I will keep counsel faithfully, and never let any wit the tale that ye fled for fear of any man."

"Gramercy," quoth Gawain, but ill-pleased. "Good fortune be his who wishes me good, and that thou wouldst keep faith with me I will believe; but didst thou keep it never so truly, an I passed here and fled for fear as thou sayest, then were I a coward knight, and might not be held guiltless. So I will to the chapel let chance what may, and talk with that man, even as I may list, whether for weal or for woe as fate may have it. Fierce though he may be in fight, yet God knoweth well how to save His servants."

"Well," quoth the other, "now that ye have said so much that ye will take your own harm on yourself, and ye be pleased to lose your life, I will neither let nor keep ye. Have here your helm and the spear in your hand, and ride down this same road beside the rock till ye come to the bottom of the valley, and there look a little to the left hand, and ye shall see in that vale the chapel, and the grim man who keeps it. Now fare ye well, noble Gawain; for all the gold on earth I would not go with ye nor bear ye fellowship one step further." With that the man turned his bridle into the wood, smote the horse with his spurs as hard as he could, and galloped off, leaving the knight alone.

Quoth Gawain, "I will neither greet nor groan, but commend myself to God, and yield me to His will."

Then the knight spurred Gringalet, and rode adown the path close in by a bank beside a grove. So he rode through the rough thicket, right into the dale, and there he halted, for it seemed him wild enough. No sign of a chapel could he see, but high and burnt banks on either side and rough rugged crags with great stones above. An ill-looking place he thought it.

Then he drew in his horse and looked around to seek the chapel, but he saw none and thought it strange. Then he saw as it were a mound on a level space of land by a bank beside the stream where it ran swiftly, the water bubbled within as if boiling. The knight turned his steed to the mound, and lighted down and tied the rein to the branch of a linden; and he turned to the mound and walked round it, questioning with himself what it might be. It had a hole at the end and at either side, and was overgrown with clumps of grass, and it was hollow within as an old cave or the crevice of a crag; he knew not what it might be.

"Ah," quoth Gawain, "can this be the Green Chapel? Here might the devil say his mattins at midnight! Now I wis there is wizardry here. 'Tis an ugly oratory, all overgrown with grass, and 'twould well beseem that fellow in green to say his devotions on devil's wise. Now feel I in five wits, 'tis the foul fiend himself who hath set me this tryst, to destroy me here! This is a chapel of mischance: ill-luck betide it, 'tis the cursedest kirk that ever I came in!"

Helmet on head and lance in hand, he came up to the rough dwelling, when he heard over the high hill beyond the brook, as it were in a bank, a wondrous fierce noise, that rang in the cliff as if it would cleave asunder. 'Twas as if one ground a scythe on a grindstone, it whirred and whetted like water on a mill-wheel and rushed and rang, terrible to hear.

"By God," quoth Gawain, "I trow that gear is preparing for the knight who will meet me here. Alas! naught may help me, yet should my life be forfeit, I fear not a jot!" With that he called aloud. "Who waiteth in this place to give me tryst? Now is Gawain come hither: if any man will aught of him let him hasten hither now or never."

"Stay," quoth one on the bank above his head, "and ye shall speedily have that which I promised ye." Yet for a while the noise of whetting went on ere he appeared, and then he came forth from a cave in the crag with a fell weapon, a Danish axe newly dight, wherewith to deal the blow. An evil head it had, four feet large, no less, sharply ground, and bound to the handle by the lace that gleamed brightly. And the knight himself was all green as before, face and foot, locks and beard, but now he was afoot. When he came to the water he would not wade it, but sprang over with the pole of his axe, and strode boldly over the brent that was white with snow.

Sir Gawain went to meet him, but he made no low bow. The other said, "Now, fair sir, one may trust thee to keep tryst. Thou art welcome, Gawain, to my place. Thou hast timed thy coming as befits a true man. Thou knowest the covenant set between us: at this time twelve months agone thou didst take that which fell to thee, and I at this New Year will readily requite thee. We are in this valley, verily alone, here are no knights to sever us, do what we will. Have off thy helm from thine head, and have here thy pay; make me no more talking than I did then when thou didst strike off my head with one blow."

"Nay," quoth Gawain, "by God that gave me life, I shall make no moan whatever befall me, but make thou ready for the blow and I shall stand still and say never a word to thee, do as thou wilt."

With that he bent his head and shewed his neck all bare, and made as if he had no fear, for he would not be thought a-dread.

Then the Green Knight made him ready, and grasped his grim weapon to smite Gawain. With all his force he bore it aloft with a mighty feint of slaying him: had it fallen as straight as he aimed he who was ever doughty of deed had been slain by the blow. But Gawain swerved aside as the axe came gliding down to slay him as he stood, and shrank a little with the shoulders, for the sharp iron. The other heaved up the blade and rebuked the prince with many proud words:

"Thou art not Gawain," he said, "who is held so valiant, that never feared he man by hill or vale, but thou shrinkest for fear ere thou feelest hurt. Such cowardice did I never hear of Gawain! Neither did I flinch from thy blow, or make strife in King Arthur's hall. My head fell to my feet, and yet I fled not; but thou didst wax faint of heart ere any harm befell. Wherefore must I be deemed the braver knight."

Quoth Gawain, "I shrank once, but so will I no more, though an my head fall on the stones I cannot replace it. But haste, Sir Knight, by thy faith, and bring me to the point, deal me my destiny, and do it out of hand, for I will stand thee a stroke and move no more till thine axe have hit me – my troth on it."

"Have at thee, then," quoth the other, and heaved aloft the axe with fierce mien, as if he were mad. He struck at him fiercely but wounded him not, withholding his hand ere it might strike him.

Gawain abode the stroke, and flinched in no limb, but stood still as a stone or the stump of a tree that is fast rooted in the rocky ground with a hundred roots.

Then spake gaily the man in green, "So now thou hast thine heart whole it behoves me to smite. Hold aside thy hood that Arthur gave thee, and keep thy neck thus bent lest it cover it again."

Then Gawain said angrily, "Why talk on thus? Thou dost threaten too long. I hope thy heart misgives thee."

"For sooth," quoth the other, "so fiercely thou speakest I will no longer let thine errand wait its reward." Then he braced himself to strike, frowning with lips and brow, 'twas no marvel that it pleased but ill him who hoped for no rescue. He lifted the axe lightly and let it fall with the edge of the blade on the bare neck. Though he struck swiftly it hurt him no more than on the one side where it severed the skin. The sharp blade cut into the flesh so that the blood ran over his shoulder to the ground. And when the knight saw the blood staining the snow, he sprang forth, swift-foot, more than a spear's length, seized his helmet and set it on his head, cast his shield over his shoulder, drew out his bright sword, and spake boldly (never since he was born was he half so blithe), "Stop, Sir Knight, bid me no more blows. I have stood a stroke here without flinching, and if thou give me another, I shall requite thee, and give thee as good again. By the covenant made betwixt us in Arthur's hall but one blow falls to me here. Halt, therefore."

Then the Green Knight drew off from him and leaned on his axe, setting the shaft on the ground, and looked on Gawain as he stood all armed and faced him fearlessly – at heart it pleased him well. Then he spake merrily in a loud voice, and said to the knight, "Bold sir, be not so fierce, no man here hath done thee wrong, nor will do, save by covenant, as we made at Arthur's court. I promised thee a blow and thou hast it – hold thyself well paid! I release thee of all other claims. If I had been so minded I might perchance have given thee a rougher buffet. First I menaced thee with a feigned one, and hurt thee not for the covenant that we made in the first night, and which thou didst hold truly. All the gain didst thou give me as a true man should. The other feint I proffered thee for the morrow: my fair wife kissed thee, and thou didst give me her kisses – for both those days I gave thee two blows without scathe – true man, true return. But the third time thou didst fail, and therefore hadst thou that blow. For 'tis my weed thou wearest, that same woven girdle, my own wife wrought it, that do I wot for sooth. Now know I well thy kisses, and thy conversation, and the wooing of my wife, for 'twas mine own doing. I sent her to try thee, and in sooth I think thou art the most faultless knight that ever trode earth. As a pearl among white peas is of more worth than they, so is Gawain, i' faith, by other knights. But thou didst lack a little, Sir Knight, and wast wanting in loyalty, yet that was for no evil work, nor for wooing neither, but because thou lovedst thy life – therefore I blame thee the less."

Then the other stood a great while, still sorely angered and vexed within himself; all the blood flew to his face, and he shrank for shame as the Green Knight spake; and the first words he said were, "Cursed be ye, cowardice and covetousness, for in ye is the destruction of virtue." Then he loosed the girdle, and gave it to the knight. "Lo, take there the falsity, may foul befall it! For fear of thy blow cowardice bade me make friends with covetousness and forsake the customs of largess and loyalty, which befit all knights. Now am I faulty and false and have been afeared: from treachery and untruth come sorrow and care. I avow to thee, Sir Knight, that I have ill done; do then thy will. I shall be more wary hereafter."

Then the other laughed and said gaily, "I wot I am whole of the hurt I had, and thou hast made such free confession of thy misdeeds, and hast so borne the penance of mine axe edge, that I hold thee absolved from that sin, and purged as clean as if thou hadst never sinned since thou wast born. And this girdle that is wrought with gold and green, like my raiment, do I give thee, Sir Gawain, that thou mayest think upon this chance when thou goest forth among princes of renown, and keep this for a token of the adventure of the Green Chapel, as it chanced between chivalrous knights. And thou shalt come again with me to my dwelling and pass the rest of this feast in gladness." Then the lord laid hold of him, and said, "I wot we shall soon make peace with my wife, who was thy bitter enemy."

"Nay, forsooth," said Sir Gawain, and seized his helmet and took it off swiftly, and thanked the knight: "I have fared ill, may bliss betide thee, and may He who rules all things reward thee swiftly. Commend me to that courteous lady, thy fair wife, and to the other my honoured ladies, who have beguiled their knight with skilful craft. But 'tis no marvel if one be made a fool and brought to sorrow by women's wiles, for so was Adam beguiled by one, and Solomon by many, and Samson all too soon, for Delilah dealt him his doom; and David thereafter was wedded with Bathsheba, which brought him much sorrow – if one might love a woman and believe her not, 'twere great gain! And since all they were beguiled by women, methinks 'tis the less blame to me that I was misled! But as for thy girdle, that will I take with good will, not for gain of the gold, nor for samite, nor silk, nor the costly pendants, neither for weal nor for worship, but in sign of my frailty. I shall look upon it when I ride in renown and remind myself of the fault and faintness of the flesh; and so when pride uplifts me for prowess of arms, the sight of this lace shall humble my heart. But one thing would I pray, if it displease thee not: since thou art lord of yonder land wherein I have dwelt, tell me what thy rightful name may be, and I will ask no more."

"That will I truly," quoth the other. "Bernlak de Hautdesert am I called in this land. Morgain le Fay dwelleth in mine house, and through knowledge of clerkly craft hath she taken many. For long time was she the mistress of Merlin, who knew well all you knights of the court. Morgain the goddess is she called therefore, and there is none so haughty but she can bring him low. She sent me in this guise to yon fair hall to test the truth of the renown that is spread abroad of the valour of the Round Table. She taught me this marvel to betray your wits, to vex Guinevere and fright her to death by the man who spake with his head in his hand at the high table. That is she who is at home, that ancient lady, she is even thine aunt, Arthur's half-sister, the daughter of the Duchess of Tintagel, who afterward married King Uther. Therefore I bid thee, knight, come to thine aunt, and make merry in thine house; my folk love thee, and I wish thee as well as any man on earth, by my faith, for thy true dealing."

But Sir Gawain said nay, he would in no wise do so; so they embraced and kissed, and commended each other to the Prince of Paradise, and parted right there, on the cold ground. Gawain on his steed rode swiftly to the king's hall, and the Green Knight got him whithersoever he would.

Sir Gawain who had thus won grace of his life, rode through wild ways on Gringalet; oft he lodged in a house, and oft without, and many adventures did he have and came off victor full often, as at this time I cannot relate in tale. The hurt that he had in his neck was healed, he bare the shining girdle as a baldric bound by his side, and made fast with a knot 'neath his left arm, in token that he was taken in a fault – and thus he came in safety again to the court.

Then joy awakened in that dwelling when the king knew that the good Sir Gawain was come, for he deemed it gain. King Arthur kissed the knight, and the queen also, and many valiant knights sought to embrace him. They asked him how he had fared, and he told them all that had chanced to him – the adventure of the chapel, the fashion of the knight, the love of the lady – at last of the lace. He showed them the wound in the neck which he won for his disloyalty at the hand of the knight, the blood flew to his face for shame as he told the tale.

"Lo, lady," he quoth, and handled the lace, "this is the bond of the blame that I bear in my neck, this is the harm and the loss I have suffered, the cowardice and covetousness in which I was caught, the token of my covenant in which I was taken. And I must needs wear it so long as I live, for none may hide his harm, but undone it may not be, for if it hath clung to thee once, it may never be severed."

Then the king comforted the knight, and the court laughed loudly at the tale, and all made accord that the lords and the ladies who belonged to the Round Table, each hero among them, should wear bound about him a baldric of bright green for the sake of Sir Gawain. And to this was agreed all the honour of the Round Table, and he who ware it was honoured the more thereafter, as it is testified in the best book of romance. That in Arthur's days this adventure befell, the book of Brutus bears witness. For since that bold knight came hither first, and the siege and the assault were ceased at Troy, I wis

Many a venture herebefore
Hath fallen such as this:
May He that bare the crown of thorn
Bring us unto His bliss.

Amen.

The Romance of Tristan and Iseult

THIS STORY should suffice to attract readers who love both history and poetry, romance and heroism. But in addition they will be fascinated as they read this ancient story by the charm of the detail, the mysterious and mythic beauty of certain episodes, the happy invention of others, the freshness of the situations and sentiments, all that makes the work a unique combination of hoary age and eternal youth, of Celtic melancholy and French grace, of powerful realism and delicate psychology.

Told in many different variations since the 12th century, the romance of the Cornish knight Tristan and the Irish princess Iseult has spread throughout the world. While of course there are differences between the texts, the overall story and plot remain the same. The story begins with Tristan's birth, the sad death of his mother, and how the years began to pass.

The Childhood of Tristan

MY LORDS, IF YOU WOULD hear a high tale of love and of death, here is that of Tristan and Queen Iseult; how to their full joy, but to their sorrow also, they loved each other, and how at last they died of that love together upon one day; she by him and he by her.

Long ago, when Mark was King over Cornwall, Rivalen, King of Lyonesse, heard that Mark's enemies waged war on him; so he crossed the sea to bring him aid; and so faithfully did he serve him with counsel and sword that Mark gave him his sister Blanchefleur, whom King Rivalen loved most marvellously.

He wedded her in Tintagel Minster, but hardly was she wed when the news came to him that his old enemy Duke Morgan had fallen on Lyonesse and was wasting town and field. Then Rivalen manned his ships in haste, and took Blanchefleur with him to his far land; but she was with child. He landed below his castle of Kanoël and gave the Queen in ward to his Marshal Rohalt, and after that set off to wage his war.

Blanchefleur waited for him continually, but he did not come home, till she learnt upon a day that Duke Morgan had killed him in foul ambush. She did not weep: she made no cry or lamentation, but her limbs failed her and grew weak, and her soul was filled with a strong desire to be rid of the flesh, and though Rohalt tried to soothe her she would not hear. Three days she awaited re-union with her lord, and on the fourth she brought forth a son; and taking him in her arms she said:

"Little son, I have longed a while to see you, and now I see you the fairest thing ever a woman bore. In sadness came I hither, in sadness did I bring forth, and in sadness has your first feast day gone. And as by sadness you came into the world, your name shall be called Tristan; that is the child of sadness."

After she had said these words she kissed him, and immediately when she had kissed him she died.

Rohalt, the keeper of faith, took the child, but already Duke Morgan's men besieged the Castle of Kanoël all round about. There is a wise saying: "Fool-hardy was never hardy," and he was compelled to yield to Duke Morgan at his mercy: but for fear that Morgan might slay Rivalen's heir the Marshal hid him among his own sons.

When seven years were passed and the time had come to take the child from the women, Rohalt put Tristan under a good master, the Squire Gorvenal, and Gorvenal taught him in a few years the arts that go with barony. He taught him the use of lance and sword and 'scutcheon and bow, and how to cast stone quoits and to leap wide dykes also: and he taught him to hate every lie and felony and to keep his given word; and he taught him the various kinds of song and harp-playing, and the hunter's craft; and when the child rode among the young squires you would have said that he and his horse and his armour were all one thing. To see him so noble and so proud, broad in the shoulders, loyal, strong and right, all men glorified Rohalt in such a son. But Rohalt remembering Rivalen and Blanchefleur (of whose youth and grace all this was a resurrection) loved him indeed as a son, but in his heart revered him as his lord.

Now all his joy was snatched from him on a day when certain merchants of Norway, having lured Tristan to their ship, bore him off as a rich prize, though Tristan fought hard, as a young wolf struggles, caught in a gin. But it is a truth well proved, and every sailor knows it, that the sea will hardly bear a felon ship, and gives no aid to rapine. The sea rose and cast a dark storm round the ship and drove it eight days and eight nights at random, till the mariners caught through the mist a coast of awful cliffs and sea-ward rocks whereon the sea would have ground their hull to pieces: then they did penance, knowing that the anger of the sea came of the lad, whom they had stolen in an evil hour, and they vowed his deliverance and got ready a boat to put him, if it might be, ashore: then the wind, and sea fell and the sky shone, and as the Norway ship grew small in the offing, a quiet tide cast Tristan and the boat upon a beach of sand.

Painfully he climbed the cliff and saw, beyond, a lonely rolling heath and a forest stretching out and endless. And he wept, remembering

Gorvenal, his father, and the land of Lyonesse. Then the distant cry of a hunt, with horse and hound, came suddenly and lifted his heart, and a tall stag broke cover at the forest edge. The pack and the hunt streamed after it with a tumult of cries and winding horns, but just as the hounds were racing clustered at the haunch, the quarry turned to bay at a stones throw from Tristan; a huntsman gave him the thrust, while all around the hunt had gathered and was winding the kill. But Tristan, seeing by the gesture of the huntsman that he made to cut the neck of the stag, cried out:

"My lord, what would you do? Is it fitting to cut up so noble a beast like any farm-yard hog? Is that the custom of this country?"

And the huntsman answered:

"Fair friend, what startles you? Why yes, first I take off the head of a stag, and then I cut it into four quarters and we carry it on our saddle bows to King Mark, our lord: So do we, and so since the days of the first huntsmen have done the Cornish men. If, however, you know of some nobler custom, teach it us: take this knife and we will learn it willingly."

Then Tristan kneeled and skinned the stag before he cut it up, and quartered it all in order leaving the crow-bone all whole, as is meet, and putting aside at the end the head, the haunch, the tongue and the great heart's vein; and the huntsmen and the kennel hinds stood over him with delight, and the Master Huntsman said:

"Friend, these are good ways. In what land learnt you them? Tell us your country and your name."

"Good lord, my name is Tristan, and I learnt these ways in my country of Lyonesse."

"Tristan," said the Master Huntsman, "God reward the father that brought you up so nobly; doubtless he is a baron, rich and strong."

Now Tristan knew both speech and silence, and he answered:

"No, lord; my father is a burgess. I left his home unbeknownst upon a ship that trafficked to a far place, for I wished to learn how men lived in foreign lands. But if you will accept me of the hunt I will follow you gladly and teach you other crafts of venery."

"Fair Tristan, I marvel there should be a land where a burgess's son can know what a knight's son knows not elsewhere, but come with us since you will it; and welcome: we will bring you to King Mark, our lord."

Tristan completed his task; to the dogs he gave the heart, the head, offal and ears; and he taught the hunt how the skinning and the ordering should be done. Then he thrust the pieces upon pikes and gave them to this huntsman and to that to carry, to one the snout to another the haunch to another the flank to another the chine; and he taught them how to ride by twos in rank, according to the dignity of the pieces each might bear.

So they took the road and spoke together, till they came on a great castle and round it fields and orchards, and living waters and fish ponds and plough lands, and many ships were in its haven, for that castle stood above the sea. It was well fenced against all assault or engines of war, and its keep, which the giants had built long ago, was compact of great stones, like a chess board of vert and azure.

And when Tristan asked its name:

"Good liege," they said, "we call it Tintagel."

And Tristan cried:

"Tintagel! Blessed be thou of God, and blessed be they that dwell within thee."

(Therein, my lords, therein had Rivalen taken Blanchefleur to wife, though their son knew it not.)

When they came before the keep the horns brought the barons to the gates and King Mark himself. And when the Master Huntsman had told him all the story, and King Mark had marvelled at the good order of the cavalcade, and the cutting of the stag, and the high art of venery in all, yet most he wondered at the stranger boy, and still gazed at him, troubled and wondering whence came his tenderness, and his heart would answer him nothing; but, my lords, it was blood that spoke, and the love he had long since borne his sister Blanchefleur.

That evening, when the boards were cleared, a singer out of Wales, a master, came forward among the barons in Hall and sang a harper's song, and as this harper touched the strings of his harp, Tristan who sat at the King's feet, spoke thus to him:

"Oh master, that is the first of songs! The Bretons of old wove it once to chant the loves of Graëlent. And the melody is rare and rare are the words: master, your voice is subtle: harp us that well."

But when the Welshman had sung, he answered:

"Boy, what do you know of the craft of music? If the burgesses of Lyonesse teach their sons harp – play also, and rotes and viols too, rise, and take this harp and show your skill."

Then Tristan took the harp and sang so well that the barons softened as they heard, and King Mark marvelled at the harper from Lyonesse whither so long ago Rivalen had taken Blanchefleur away.

When the song ended, the King was silent a long space, but he said at last:

"Son, blessed be the master that taught thee, and blessed be thou of God: for God loves good singers. Their voices and the voice of the harp enter the souls of men and wake dear memories and cause them to forget many a mourning and many a sin. For our joy did you come to this roof, stay near us a long time, friend."

And Tristan answered:

"Very willingly will I serve you, sire, as your harper, your huntsman and your liege."

So did he, and for three years a mutual love grew up in their hearts. By day Tristan followed King Mark at pleas and in saddle; by night he slept in the royal room with the councillors and the peers, and if the King was sad he would harp to him to soothe his care. The barons also cherished him, and (as you shall learn) Dinas of Lidan, the seneschal, beyond all others. And more tenderly than the barons and than Dinas the King loved him. But Tristan could not forget, or Rohalt his father, or his master Gorvenal, or the land of Lyonesse.

My lords, a teller that would please, should not stretch his tale too long, and truly this tale is so various and so high that it needs no straining. Then let me shortly tell how Rohalt himself, after long wandering by sea and land, came into Cornwall, and found Tristan, and showing the King the carbuncle that once was Blanchefleur's, said:

"King Mark, here is your nephew Tristan, son of your sister Blanchefleur and of King Rivalen. Duke Morgan holds his land most wrongfully; it is time such land came back to its lord."

And Tristan (in a word) when his uncle had armed him knight, crossed the sea, and was hailed of his father's vassals, and killed Rivalen's slayer and was re-seized of his land.

Then remembering how King Mark could no longer live in joy without him, he summoned his council and his barons and said this:

"Lords of the Lyonesse, I have retaken this place and I have avenged King Rivalen by the help of God and of you. But two men Rohalt and King Mark of Cornwall nourished me, an orphan, and a wandering boy. So should I call them also fathers. Now a free man has two things thoroughly his own, his body and his land. To Rohalt then, here, I will release my land. Do you hold it, father, and your son shall hold it after you. But my body I give up to King Mark. I will leave this country, dear though it be, and in Cornwall I will serve King Mark as my lord. Such is my judgment, but you, my lords of Lyonesse, are my lieges, and owe me counsel; if then, some one of you will counsel me another thing let him rise and speak."

But all the barons praised him, though they wept; and taking with him Gorveval only, Tristan set sail for King Mark's land.

The Morholt Out of Ireland

WHEN TRISTAN came back to that land, King Mark and all his Barony were mourning; for the King of Ireland had manned a fleet to ravage Cornwall, should King Mark refuse, as he had refused these fifteen years, to pay a tribute his fathers had paid. Now that year this King had sent to Tintagel, to carry his summons, a giant knight; the Morholt, whose sister he had wed, and whom no man had yet been able to overcome: so King Mark had summoned all the barons of his land to Council, by letters sealed.

On the day assigned, when the barons were gathered in hall, and when the King had taken his throne, the Morholt said these things:

"King Mark, hear for the last time the summons of the King of

Ireland, my lord. He arraigns you to pay at last that which you have owed so long, and because you have refused it too long already he bids you give over to me this day three hundred youths and three hundred maidens drawn by lot from among the Cornish folk. But if so be that any would prove by trial of combat that the King of Ireland receives this tribute without right, I will take up his wager. Which among you, my Cornish lords, will fight to redeem this land?"

The barons glanced at each other but all were silent.

Then Tristan knelt at the feet of King Mark and said:

"Lord King, by your leave I will do battle."

And in vain would King Mark have turned him from his purpose, thinking, how could even valour save so young a knight? But he threw down his gage to the Morholt, and the Morholt took up the gage.

On the appointed day he had himself clad for a great feat of arms in a hauberk and in a steel helm, and he entered a boat and drew to the islet of St. Samson's, where the knights were to fight each to each alone. Now the Morholt had hoisted to his mast a sail of rich purple, and coming fast to land, he moored his boat on the shore. But Tristan pushed off his own boat adrift with his feet, and said:

"One of us only will go hence alive. One boat will serve."

And each rousing the other to the fray they passed into the isle.

No man saw the sharp combat; but thrice the salt sea-breeze had wafted or seemed to waft a cry of fury to the land, when at last towards the hour of noon the purple sail showed far off; the Irish boat appeared from the island shore, and there rose a clamour of "the Morholt!" When suddenly, as the boat grew larger on the sight and topped a wave, they saw that Tristan stood on the prow holding a sword in his hand. He leapt ashore, and as the mothers kissed the steel upon his feet he cried to the Morholt's men:

"My lords of Ireland, the Morholt fought well. See here, my sword is broken and a splinter of it stands fast in his head. Take you that steel, my lords; it is the tribute of Cornwall."

Then he went up to Tintagel and as he went the people he had freed waved green boughs, and rich cloths were hung at the windows. But when Tristan reached the castle with joy, songs and joy-bells sounding about him, he drooped in the arms of King Mark, for the blood ran from his wounds.

The Morholt's men, they landed in Ireland quite cast down. For when ever he came back into Whitehaven the Morholt had been wont to take joy in the sight of his clan upon the shore, of the Queen his sister, and of his niece Iseult the Fair. Tenderly had they cherished him of old, and had he taken some wound, they healed him, for they were skilled in balms and potions. But now their magic was vain, for he lay dead and the splinter of the foreign brand yet stood in his skull till Iseult plucked it out and shut it in a chest.

From that day Iseult the Fair knew and hated the name of Tristan of Lyonesse.

But over in Tintagel Tristan languished, for there trickled a poisonous blood from his wound. The doctors found that the Morholt had thrust into him a poisoned barb, and as their potions and their theriac could never heal him they left him in God's hands. So hateful a stench came from his wound that all his dearest friends fled him, all save King Mark, Gorvenal and Dinas of Lidan. They always could stay near his couch because their love overcame their abhorrence. At last Tristan had himself carried into a boat apart on the shore; and lying facing the sea he awaited death, for he thought: "I must die; but it is good to see the sun and my heart is still high. I would like to try the sea that brings all chances. ... I would have the sea bear me far off alone, to what land no matter, so that it heal me of my wound."

He begged so long that King Mark accepted his desire. He bore him into a boat with neither sail nor oar, and Tristan wished that his harp only should be placed beside him: for sails he could not lift, nor oar ply, nor sword wield; and as a seaman on some long voyage casts to the sea a beloved companion dead, so Gorvenal pushed out to sea that boat where his dear son lay; and the sea drew him away.

For seven days and seven nights the sea so drew him; at times to charm his grief, he harped; and when at last the sea brought him near a shore where fishermen had left their port that night to fish far out, they heard as they rowed a sweet and strong and living tune that ran above the sea, and feathering their oars they listened immovable.

In the first whiteness of the dawn they saw the boat at large: she went at random and nothing seemed to live in her except the voice of the harp. But as they neared, the air grew weaker and died; and when they hailed her Tristan's hands had fallen lifeless on the strings though they still trembled. The fishermen took him in and bore him back to port, to their lady who was merciful and perhaps would heal him.

It was that same port of Whitehaven where the Morholt lay, and their lady was Iseult the Fair.

She alone, being skilled in philtres, could save Tristan, but she alone wished him dead. When Tristan knew himself again (for her art restored him) he knew himself to be in the land of peril. But he was yet strong to hold his own and found good crafty words. He told a tale of how he was a seer that had taken passage on a merchant ship and sailed to Spain to learn the art of reading all the stars, – of how pirates had boarded the ship and of how, though wounded, he had fled into that boat. He was believed, nor did any of the Morholt's men know his face again, so hardly had the poison used it. But when, after forty days, Iseult of the Golden Hair had all but healed him, when already his limbs had recovered and the grace of youth returned, he knew that he must escape, and he fled and after many dangers he came again before Mark the King.

The Quest of the Lady With the Hair of Gold

MY LORDS, THERE WERE in the court of King Mark four barons the basest of men, who hated Tristan with a hard hate, for his greatness and for the tender love the King bore him. And well I know their names: Andret, Guenelon, Gondoïne and Denoalen. They knew that the King had intent to grow old childless and to leave his land to Tristan; and their envy swelled and by lies they angered the chief men of Cornwall against Tristan. They said:

"There have been too many marvels in this man's life. It was marvel enough that he beat the Morholt, but by what sorcery did he try the sea alone at the point of death, or which of us, my lords, could voyage without mast or sail? They say that warlocks can. It was sure a warlock feat, and that is a warlock harp of his pours poison daily into the King's heart. See how he has bent that heart by power and chain of sorcery! He will be king yet, my lords, and you will hold your lands of a wizard."

They brought over the greater part of the barons and these pressed King Mark to take to wife some king's daughter who should give him an heir, or else they threatened to return each man into his keep and wage him war. But the King turned against them and swore in his heart that so long as his dear nephew lived no king's daughter should come to his bed. Then in his turn did Tristan (in his shame to be thought to serve for hire) threaten that if the King did not yield to his barons, he would himself go over sea serve some great king. At this, King Mark made a term with his barons and gave them forty days to hear his decision.

On the appointed day he waited alone in his chamber and sadly mused: "Where shall I find a king's daughter so fair and yet so distant that I may feign to wish her my wife?"

Just then by his window that looked upon the sea two building swallows came in quarrelling together. Then, startled, they flew out, but had let fall from their beaks a woman's hair, long and fine, and shining like a beam of light.

King Mark took it, and called his barons and Tristan and said:

"To please you, lords, I will take a wife; but you must seek her whom I have chosen."

"Fair lord, we wish it all," they said, "and who may she be?"

"Why," said he, "she whose hair this is; nor will I take another."

"And whence, lord King, comes this Hair of Gold; who brought it and from what land?"

"It comes, my lords, from the Lady with the Hair of Gold, the swallows brought it me. They know from what country it came."

Then the barons saw themselves mocked and cheated, and they turned with sneers to Tristan, for they thought him to have counselled the trick. But Tristan, when he had looked on the Hair of Gold, remembered Iseult the Fair and smiled and said this:

"King Mark, can you not see that the doubts of these lords shame me? You have designed in vain. I will go seek the Lady with the Hair of Gold. The search is perilous: never the less, my uncle, I would once more put my body and my life into peril for you; and that your barons may know I love you loyally, I take this oath, to die on the adventure or to bring back to this castle of Tintagel the Queen with that fair hair."

He fitted out a great ship and loaded it with corn and wine, with honey and all manner of good things; he manned it with Gorvenal and a hundred young knights of high birth, chosen among the bravest, and he clothed them in coats of home-spun and in hair cloth so that they seemed merchants only: but under the deck he hid rich cloth of gold and scarlet as for a great king's messengers.

When the ship had taken the sea the helmsman asked him:

"Lord, to what land shall I steer?"

"Sir," said he, "steer for Ireland, straight for Whitehaven harbour."

At first Tristan made believe to the men of Whitehaven that his friends were merchants of England come peacefully to barter; but as these strange merchants passed the day in the useless games of draughts and chess, and seemed to know dice better than the bargain price of corn, Tristan feared discovery and knew not how to pursue his quest.

Now it chanced once upon the break of day that he heard a cry so terrible that one would have called it a demon's cry; nor had he ever heard a brute bellow in such wise, so awful and strange it seemed. He called a woman who passed by the harbour, and said:

"Tell me, lady, whence comes that voice I have heard, and hide me nothing."

"My lord," said she, "I will tell you truly. It is the roar of a dragon the most terrible and dauntless upon earth. Daily it leaves its den and stands at one of the gates of the city: Nor can any come out or go in till a maiden has been given up to it; and when it has her in its claws it devours her."

"Lady," said Tristan, "make no mock of me, but tell me straight: Can a man born of woman kill this thing?"

"Fair sir, and gentle," she said, "I cannot say; but this is sure: Twenty knights and tried have run the venture, because the King of Ireland has published it that he will give his daughter, Iseult the Fair, to whomsoever shall kill the beast; but it has devoured them all."

Tristan left the woman and returning to his ship armed himself in secret, and it was a fine sight to see so noble a charger and so good a knight come out from such a merchant-hull: but the haven was empty of folk, for the dawn had barely broken and none saw him as he rode to the gate. And hardly had he passed it, when he met suddenly five men at full gallop flying towards the town. Tristan seized one by his hair, as he passed, and dragged him over his mount's crupper and held him fast:

"God save you, my lord," said he, "and whence does the dragon come?" And when the other had shown him by what road, he let him go.

As the monster neared, he showed the head of a bear and red eyes like coals of fire and hairy tufted ears; lion's claws, a serpent's tail, and a griffin's body.

Tristan charged his horse at him so strongly that, though the beast's mane stood with fright yet he drove at the dragon: his lance struck its scales and shivered. Then Tristan drew his sword and struck at the dragon's head, but he did not so much as cut the hide. The beast felt the blow: with its claws he dragged at the shield and broke it from the arm; then, his breast unshielded, Tristan used the sword again and struck so strongly that the air rang all round about: but in vain, for he could not wound and meanwhile the dragon vomited from his nostrils two streams of loath-some flames, and Tristan's helm blackened like a cinder and his horse stumbled and fell down and died; but Tristan standing on his feet thrust his sword right into the beast's jaws, and split its heart in two.

Then he cut out the tongue and put it into his hose, but as the poison came against his flesh the hero fainted and fell in the high grass that bordered the marsh around.

Now the man he had stopped in flight was the Seneschal of Ireland and he desired Iseult the Fair: and though he was a coward, he had dared so far as to return with his companions secretly, and he found the dragon dead; so he cut off its head and bore it to the King, and claimed the great reward.

The King could credit his prowess but hardly, yet wished justice done and summoned his vassals to court, so that there, before the Barony assembled, the seneschal should furnish proof of his victory won.

When Iseult the Fair heard that she was to be given to this coward first she laughed long, and then she wailed. But on the morrow, doubting some trick, she took with her Perinis her squire and Brangien her maid, and all three rode unbeknownst towards the dragon's lair: and Iseult saw such a trail on the road as made her wonder – for the hoofs that made it had never been shod in her land. Then she came on the dragon, headless, and a dead horse beside him: nor was the horse harnessed in the fashion of Ireland. Some foreign man had slain the beast, but they knew not whether he still lived or no.

They sought him long, Iseult and Perinis and Brangien together, till at last Brangien saw the helm glittering in the marshy grass: and Tristan still breathed. Perinis put him on his horse and bore him secretly to the women's rooms. There Iseult told her mother the tale and left the hero with her, and as the Queen unharnessed him, the dragon's tongue fell from his boot of steel. Then, the Queen of Ireland revived him by the virtue of an herb and said:

"Stranger, I know you for the true slayer of the dragon: but our seneschal, a felon, cut off its head and claims my daughter Iseult for his wage; will you be ready two days hence to give him the lie in battle?"

"Queen," said he, "the time is short, but you, I think, can cure me in two days. Upon the dragon I conquered Iseult, and on the seneschal perhaps I shall reconquer her."

Then the Queen brewed him strong brews, and on the morrow Iseult the Fair got him ready a bath and anointed him with a balm her mother had conjured, and as he looked at her he thought, "So I have found the Queen of the Hair of Gold," and he smiled as he thought it. But Iseult, noting it, thought, "Why does he smile, or what have I neglected of the things due to a guest? He smiles to think I have for – gotten to burnish his armour."

She went and drew the sword from its rich sheath, but when she saw the splinter gone and the gap in the edge she thought of the Morholt's head. She balanced a moment in doubt, then she went to where she kept the steel she had found in the skull and she put it to the sword, and it fitted so that the join was hardly seen.

She ran to where Tristan lay wounded, and with the sword above him she cried:

"You are that Tristan of the Lyonesse, who killed the Morholt, my mother's brother, and now you shall die in your turn."

Tristan strained to ward the blow, but he was too weak; his wit, however, stood firm in spite of evil and he said:

"So be it, let me die: but to save yourself long memories, listen awhile. King's daughter, my life is not only in your power but is yours of right. My life is yours because you have twice returned it me. Once, long ago: for I was the wounded harper whom you healed of the poison of the Morholt's shaft. Nor repent the healing: were not these wounds had in fair fight? Did I kill the Morholt by treason? Had he not defied me and was I not held to the defence of my body? And now this second time also you have saved me. It was for you I fought the beast.

"But let us leave these things. I would but show you how my life is your own. Then if you kill me of right for the glory of it, you may ponder for long years, praising yourself that you killed a wounded guest who had wagered his life in your gaining."

Iseult replied: "I hear strange words. Why should he that killed the Morholt seek me also, his niece? Doubtless because the Morholt came for a tribute of maidens from Cornwall, so you came to boast returning that you had brought back the maiden who was nearest to him, to Cornwall, a slave."

"King's daughter," said Tristan, "No. ... One day two swallows flew, and flew to Tintagel and bore one hair out of all your hairs of gold, and I thought they brought me good will and peace, so I came to find you over-seas. See here, amid the threads of gold upon my coat your hair is sown: the threads are tarnished, but your bright hair still shines."

Iseult put down the sword and taking up the Coat of Arms she saw upon it the Hair of Gold and was silent a long space, till she kissed him on the lips to prove peace, and she put rich garments over him.

On the day of the barons' assembly, Tristan sent Perinis privily to his ship to summon his companions that they should come to court adorned as befitted the envoys of a great king.

One by one the hundred knights passed into the hall where all the barons of Ireland stood, they entered in silence and sat all in rank together: on their scarlet and purple the gems gleamed.

When the King had taken his throne, the seneschal arose to prove by witness and by arms that he had slain the dragon and that so Iseult was won. Then Iseult bowed to her father and said:

"King, I have here a man who challenges your seneschal for lies and felony. Promise that you will pardon this man all his past deeds, who stands to prove that he and none other slew the dragon, and grant him forgiveness and your peace."

The King said, "I grant it." But Iseult said, "Father, first give me the kiss of peace and forgiveness, as a sign that you will give him the same."

Then she found Tristan and led him before the Barony. And as he came the hundred knights rose all together, and crossed their arms upon their breasts and bowed, so the Irish knew that he was their lord.

But among the Irish many knew him again and cried, "Tristan of Lyonesse that slew the Morholt!" They drew their swords and clamoured for death. But Iseult cried: "King, kiss this man upon the lips as your oath was," and the King kissed him, and the clamour fell.

Then Tristan showed the dragon's tongue and offered the seneschal battle, but the seneschal looked at his face and dared not.

Then Tristan said:

"My lords, you have said it, and it is truth: I killed the Morholt. But I crossed the sea to offer you a good blood-fine, to ransom that deed and get me quit of it.

"I put my body in peril of death and rid you of the beast and have so conquered Iseult the Fair, and having conquered her I will bear her away on my ship.

"But that these lands of Cornwall and Ireland may know no more hatred, but love only, learn that King Mark, my lord, will marry her. Here stand a hundred knights of high name, who all will swear with an oath upon the relics of the holy saints, that King Mark sends you by their embassy offer of peace and of brotherhood and goodwill; and that he would by your courtesy hold Iseult as his honoured wife, and that he would have all the men of Cornwall serve her as their Queen."

When the lords of Ireland heard this they acclaimed it, and the King also was content.

Then, since that treaty and alliance was to be made, the King her father took Iseult by the hand and asked of Tristan that he should take an oath; to wit that he would lead her loyally to his lord, and Tristan took that oath and swore it before the knights and the Barony of Ireland assembled. Then the King put Iseult's right hand into Tristan's right hand, and Tristan held it for a space in token of seizin for the King of Cornwall.

So, for the love of King Mark, did Tristan conquer the Queen of the Hair of Gold.

The Philtre

WHEN THE DAY of Iseult's livery to the Lords of Cornwall drew near, her mother gathered herbs and flowers and roots and steeped them in wine, and brewed a potion of might, and having done so, said apart to Brangien:

"Child, it is yours to go with Iseult to King Mark's country, for you love her with a faithful love. Take then this pitcher and remember well my words. Hide it so that no eye shall see nor no lip go near it: but when the wedding night has come and that moment in which the wedded are left alone, pour this essenced wine into a cup and offer it to King Mark and to Iseult his queen. Oh! Take all care, my child, that they alone shall taste this brew. For this is its power: they who drink of it together love each other with their every single sense and with their every thought, forever, in life and in death."

And Brangien promised the Queen that she would do her bidding.

On the bark that bore her to Tintagel Iseult the Fair was weeping as she remembered her own land, and mourning swelled her heart, and she said, "Who am I that I should leave you to follow unknown men, my mother and my land? Accursed be the sea that bears me, for rather would I lie dead on the earth where I was born than live out there, beyond. ..."

One day when the wind had fallen and the sails hung slack Tristan dropped anchor by an Island and the hundred knights of Cornwall and the sailors, weary of the sea, landed all. Iseult alone remained aboard and a little serving maid, when Tristan came near the Queen to calm her sorrow. The sun was hot above them and they were athirst and, as they called, the little maid looked about for drink for them and found that pitcher which the mother of Iseult had given into Brangien's keeping. And when she came on it, the child cried, "I have found you wine!" Now she had found not wine – but Passion and Joy most sharp, and Anguish without end, and Death.

The Queen drank deep of that draught and gave it to Tristan and he drank also long and emptied it all.

Brangien came in upon them; she saw them gazing at each other in silence as though ravished and apart; she saw before them the pitcher standing there; she snatched it up and cast it into the shuddering sea and cried aloud: "Cursed be the day I was born and cursed the day that first I trod this deck. Iseult, my friend, and Tristan, you, you have drunk death together."

And once more the bark ran free for Tintagel. But it seemed to Tristan as though an ardent briar, sharp-thorned but with flower most sweet smelling, drave roots into his blood and laced the lovely body of Iseult all round about it and bound it to his own and to his every thought and desire. And he thought, "Felons, that charged me with coveting King Mark's land, I have come lower by far, for it is not his land I covet. Fair uncle, who loved me orphaned ere ever you knew in me the blood of your sister Blanchefleur, you that wept as you bore me to that boat alone, why did you not drive out the boy that was to betray you? Ah! What thought was that! Iseult is yours and I am but your vassal; Iseult is yours and I am your son; Iseult is yours and may not love me."

But Iseult loved him, though she would have hated. She could not hate, for a tenderness more sharp than hatred tore her.

And Brangien watched them in anguish, suffering more cruelly because she alone knew the depth of evil done.

Two days she watched them, seeing them refuse all food or comfort and seeking each other as blind men seek, wretched apart and together more wretched still, for then they trembled each for the first avowal.

On the third day, as Tristan neared the tent on deck where Iseult sat, she saw him coming and she said to him, very humbly, "Come in, my lord."

"Queen," said Tristan, "why do you call me lord? Am I not your liege and vassal, to revere and serve and cherish you as my lady and Queen?"

But Iseult answered, "No, you know that you are my lord and my master, and I your slave. Ah, why did I not sharpen those wounds of the wounded singer, or let die that dragon-slayer in the grasses of the marsh? But then I did not know what now I know!"

"And what is it that you know, Iseult?"

She laid her arm upon Tristan's shoulder, the light of her eyes was drowned and her lips trembled.

"The love of you," she said. Whereat he put his lips to hers.

But as they thus tasted their first joy, Brangien, that watched them, stretched her arms and cried at their feet in tears:

"Stay and return if still you can ... But oh! that path has no returning. For already Love and his strength drag you on and now henceforth forever never shall you know joy without pain again. The wine possesses you, the draught your mother gave me, the draught the King alone should have drunk with you: but that old Enemy has tricked us, all us three; friend Tristan, Iseult my friend, for that bad ward I kept take here my body and my life, for through me and in that cup you have drunk not love alone, but love and death together."

The lovers held each other; life and desire trembled through their youth, and Tristan said, "Well then, come Death."

And as evening fell, upon the bark that heeled and ran to King Mark's land, they gave themselves up utterly to love.

The Tall Pine-Tree

A S KING MARK CAME DOWN to greet Iseult upon the shore, Tristan took her hand and led her to the King and the King took seizin of her, taking her hand. He led her in great pomp to his castle of Tintagel, and as she came in hall amid the vassals her beauty shone so that the walls were lit as they are lit at dawn. Then King Mark blessed those swallows which, by

happy courtesy, had brought the Hair of Gold, and Tristan also he blessed, and the hundred knights who, on that adventurous bark, had gone to find him joy of heart and of eyes; yet to him also that ship was to bring sting, torment and mourning.

And on the eighteenth day, having called his Barony together he took Iseult to wife. But on the wedding night, to save her friend, Brangien took her place in the darkness, for her remorse demanded even this from her; nor was the trick discovered.

Then Iseult lived as a queen, but lived in sadness. She had King Mark's tenderness and the barons' honour; the people also loved her; she passed her days amid the frescoes on the walls and floors all strewn with flowers; good jewels had she and purple cloth and tapestry of Hungary and Thessaly too, and songs of harpers, and curtains upon which were worked leopards and eagles and popinjays and all the beasts of sea and field. And her love too she had, love high and splendid, for as is the custom among great lords, Tristan could ever be near her. At his leisure and his dalliance, night and day: for he slept in the King's chamber as great lords do, among the lieges and the councillors. Yet still she feared; for though her love were secret and Tristan unsuspected (for who suspects a son?) Brangien knew. And Brangien seemed in the Queen's mind like a witness spying; for Brangien alone knew what manner of life she led, and held her at mercy so. And the Queen thought Ah, if some day she should weary of serving as a slave the bed where once she passed for Queen ... If Tristan should die from her betrayal! So fear maddened the Queen, but not in truth the fear of Brangien who was loyal; her own heart bred the fear.

Not Brangien who was faithful, not Brangien, but themselves had these lovers to fear, for hearts so stricken will lose their vigilance. Love pressed them hard, as thirst presses the dying stag to the stream; love dropped upon them from high heaven, as a hawk slipped after long hunger falls right upon the bird. And love will not be hidden. Brangien indeed by her prudence saved them well, nor ever were the Queen and her lover unguarded. But in every hour and place every man could see Love terrible, that rode them, and could see in these lovers their every sense overflowing like new wine working in the vat.

The four felons at court who had hated Tristan of old for his prowess, watched the Queen; they had guessed that great love, and they burnt with envy and hatred and now a kind of evil joy. They planned to give news of their watching to the King, to see his tenderness turned to fury, Tristan thrust out or slain, and the Queen in torment; for though they feared Tristan their hatred mastered their fear; and, on a day, the four barons called King Mark to parley, and Andret said:

"Fair King, your heart will be troubled and we four also mourn; yet are we bound to tell you what we know. You have placed your trust in Tristan and Tristan would shame you. In vain we warned you. For the love of one man you have mocked ties of blood and all your Barony. Learn then that Tristan loves the Queen; it is truth proved and many a word is passing on it now."

The royal King shrank and answered:

"Coward! What thought was that? Indeed I have placed my trust in Tristan. And rightly, for on the day when the Morholt offered combat to you all, you hung your heads and were dumb, and you trembled before him; but Tristan dared him for the honour of this land, and took mortal wounds. Therefore do you hate him, and therefore do I cherish him beyond thee, Andret, and beyond any other; but what then have you seen or heard or known?"

"Naught, lord, save what your eyes could see or your ears hear. Look you and listen, Sire, if there is yet time."

And they left him to taste the poison.

Then King Mark watched the Queen and Tristan; but Brangien noting it warned them both and the King watched in vain, so that, soon wearying of an ignoble task, but knowing (alas!) that he could not kill his uneasy thought, he sent for Tristan and said:

"Tristan, leave this castle; and having left it, remain apart and do not think to return to it, and do not repass its moat or boundaries. Felons have charged you with an awful treason, but ask me nothing; I could not speak their words without shame to us both, and for your part seek you no word to appease. I have not believed them ... had I done so ... But their evil words have troubled all my soul and only by your absence can my disquiet be soothed. Go, doubtless I will soon recall you. Go, my son, you are still dear to me.

When the felons heard the news they said among themselves, "He is gone, the wizard; he is driven out. Surely he will cross the sea on far adventures to carry his traitor service to some distant King."

But Tristan had not strength to depart altogether; and when he had crossed the moats and boundaries of the Castle he knew he could go no further. He stayed in Tintagel town and lodged with Gorvenal in a burgess' house, and languished oh! more wounded than when in that past day the shaft of the Morholt had tainted his body.

In the close towers Iseult the Fair drooped also, but more wretched still. For it was hers all day long to feign laughter and all night long to conquer fever and despair. And all night as she lay by King Mark's side, fever still kept her waking, and she stared at darkness. She longed to fly to Tristan and she dreamt dreams of running to the gates and of finding there sharp scythes, traps of the felons, that cut her tender knees; and she dreamt of weakness and falling, and that her wounds had left her blood upon the ground. Now these lovers would have died, but Brangien succoured them. At peril of her life she found the house where Tristan lay. There Gorvenal opened to her very gladly, knowing what salvation she could bring.

So she found Tristan, and to save the lovers she taught him a device, nor was ever known a more subtle ruse of love.

Behind the castle of Tintagel was an orchard fenced around and wide and all closed in with stout and pointed stakes and numberless trees were there and fruit on them, birds and clusters of sweet grapes. And furthest from the castle, by the stakes of the pallisade, was a tall pine-tree, straight and with heavy branches spreading from its trunk. At its root a living spring welled calm into a marble round, then ran between two borders winding, throughout the orchard and so, on, till it flowed at last within the castle and through the women's rooms.

And every evening, by Brangien's counsel, Tristan cut him twigs and bark, leapt the sharp stakes and, having come beneath the pine, threw them into the clear spring; they floated light as foam down the stream to the women's rooms; and Iseult watched for their coming, and on those evenings she would wander out into the orchard and find her friend. Lithe and in fear would she come, watching at every step for what might lurk in the trees observing, foes or the felons whom she knew, till she spied Tristan; and the night and the branches of the pine protected them.

And so she said one night: "Oh, Tristan, I have heard that the castle is faëry and that twice a year it vanishes away. So is it vanished now and this is that enchanted orchard of which the harpers sing." And as she said it, the sentinels bugled dawn.

Iseult had refound her joy. Mark's thought of ill-ease grew faint; but the felons felt or knew which way lay truth, and they guessed that Tristan had met the Queen. Till at last Duke Andret (whom God shame) said to his peers:

"My lords, let us take counsel of Frocin the Dwarf; for he knows the seven arts, and magic and every kind of charm. He will teach us if he will the wiles of Iseult the Fair."

The little evil man drew signs for them and characters of sorcery; he cast the fortunes of the hour and then at last he said:

"Sirs, high good lords, this night shall you seize them both."

Then they led the little wizard to the King, and he said:

"Sire, bid your huntsmen leash the hounds and saddle the horses, proclaim a seven days' hunt in the forest and seven nights abroad therein, and hang me high if you do not hear this night what converse Tristan holds."

So did the King unwillingly; and at fall of night he left the hunt taking the dwarf in pillion, and entered the orchard, and the dwarf took him to the tall pine-tree, saying:

"Fair King, climb into these branches and take with you your arrows and your bow, for you may need them; and bide you still."

That night the moon shone clear. Hid in the branches the King saw his nephew leap the pallisades and throw his bark and twigs into the stream. But Tristan had bent over the round well to throw them and so doing had seen the image of the King. He could not stop the branches as they floated away, and there, yonder, in the women's rooms, Iseult was watching and would come.

She came, and Tristan watched her motionless. Above him in the tree he heard the click of the arrow when it fits the string.

She came, but with more prudence than her wont, thinking, "What has passed, that Tristan does not come to meet me? He has seen some foe."

Suddenly, by the clear moonshine, she also saw the King's shadow in the fount. She showed the wit of women well, she did not lift her eyes.

"Lord God," she said, low down, grant I may be the first to speak."

"Tristan," she said, "what have you dared to do, calling me hither at such an hour? Often have you called me – to beseech, you said. And Queen though I am, I know you won me that title – and I have come. What would you?"

"Queen, I would have you pray the King for me."

She was in tears and trembling, but Tristan praised God the Lord who had shown his friend her peril.

"Queen," he went on, "often and in vain have I summoned you; never would you come. Take pity; the King hates me and I know not why. Perhaps you know the cause and can charm his anger. For whom can he trust if not you, chaste Queen and courteous, Iseult?"

"Truly, Lord Tristan, you do not know he doubts us both. And I, to add to my shame, must acquaint you of it. Ah! but God knows if I lie, never went cut my love to any man but he that first received me. And would you have me, at such a time, implore your pardon of the King? Why, did he know of my passage here to-night he would cast my ashes to the wind. My body trembles and I am afraid. I go, for I have waited too long."

In the branches the King smiled and had pity.

And as Iseult fled: "Queen," said Tristan, "in the Lord's name help me, for charity."

"Friend," she replied, "God aid you! The King wrongs you but the Lord God will be by you in whatever land you go."

So she went back to the women's rooms and told it to Brangien, who cried: "Iseult, God has worked a miracle for you, for He is compassionate and will not hurt the innocent in heart."

And when he had left the orchard, the King said smiling:

"Fair nephew, that ride you planned is over now."

But in an open glade apart, Frocin, the Dwarf, read in the clear stars that the King now meant his death; he blackened with shame and fear and fled into Wales.

The Discovery

KING MARK MADE PEACE **with Tristan. Tristan returned to the castle as of old. Tristan slept in the King's chamber with his peers. He could come or go, the King thought no more of it.**

Mark had pardoned the felons, and as the seneschal, Dinas of Lidan, found the dwarf wandering in a forest abandoned, he brought him home, and the King had pity and pardoned even him.

But his goodness did but feed the ire of the barons, who swore this oath: If the King kept Tristan in the land they would withdraw to their strongholds as for war, and they called the King to parley.

"Lord," said they, "Drive you Tristan forth. He loves the Queen as all who choose can see, but as for us we will bear it no longer."

And the King sighed, looking down in silence.

" King," they went on, "we will not bear it, for we know now that this is known to you and that yet you will not move. Parley you, and take counsel. As for us if you will not exile this man, your nephew, and drive him forth out of your land forever, we will withdraw within our Bailiwicks and take our neighbours also from your court: for we cannot endure his presence longer in this place. Such is your balance: choose."

"My lords," said he, "once I hearkened to the evil words you spoke of Tristan, yet was I wrong in the end. But you are my lieges and I would not lose the service of my men. Counsel me therefore, I charge you, you that owe me counsel. You know me for a man neither proud nor overstepping."

"Lord," said they, "call then Frocin hither. You mistrust him for that orchard night. Still, was it not he that read in the stars of the Queen's coming there and to the very pine-tree too? He is very wise, take counsel of him."

And he came, did that hunchback of Hell: the felons greeted him and he planned this evil.

"Sire," said he, "let your nephew ride hard to-morrow at dawn with a brief drawn up on parchment and well sealed with a seal: bid him ride to King Arthur at Carduel. Sire, he sleeps with the peers in your chamber; go you out when the first sleep falls on men, and if he love Iseult so madly, why, then I swear by God and by the laws of Rome, he will try to speak with her before he rides. But if he do so unknown to you or to me, then slay me. As for the trap, let me lay it, but do you say nothing of his ride to him until the time for sleep."

And when King Mark had agreed, this dwarf did a vile thing. He bought of a baker four farthings' worth of flour, and hid it in the turn of his coat. That night, when the King had supped and the men-at-arms lay down to sleep in hall, Tristan came to the King as custom was, and the King said:

"Fair nephew, do my will: ride to-morrow night to King Arthur at Carduel, and give him this brief, with my greeting, that he may open it: and stay you with him but one day."

And when Tristan said: "I will take it on the morrow;"

The King added: "Aye, and before day dawn."

But, as the peers slept all round the King their lord, that night, a mad thought took Tristan that, before he rode, he knew not for how long, before dawn he would say a last word to the Queen. And there was a spear length in the darkness between them. Now the dwarf slept with the rest in the King's chamber, and when he thought that all slept he rose and scattered the flour silently in the spear length that lay between Tristan and the Queen; but Tristan watched and saw him, and said to himself:

"It is to mark my footsteps, but there shall be no marks to show."

At midnight, when all was dark in the room, no candle nor any lamp glimmering, the King went out silently by the door and with him the dwarf. Then Tristan rose in the darkness and judged the spear length and leapt the space between, for his farewell. But that day in the hunt a boar had wounded him in the leg, and in this effort the wound bled. He did not feel it or see it in the darkness, but the blood dripped upon the couches and the flour strewn between; and outside in the moonlight the dwarf read the heavens and knew what had been done and he cried:

"Enter, my King, and if you do not hold them, hang me high."

Then the King and the dwarf and the four felons ran in with lights and noise, and though Tristan had regained his place there was the blood for witness, and though Iseult feigned sleep, and Perinis too, who lay at Tristan's feet, yet there was the blood for witness. And the King looked in silence at the blood where it lay upon the bed and the boards and trampled into the flour.

And the four barons held Tristan down upon his bed and mocked the Queen also, promising her full justice; and they bared and showed the wound whence the blood flowed.

Then the King said:

"Tristan, now nothing longer holds. To-morrow you shall die."

And Tristan answered:

"Have mercy, Lord, in the name of God that suffered the Cross!"

But the felons called on the King to take vengeance, saying:

"Do justice, King: take vengeance."

And Tristan went on, "Have mercy, not on me – for why should I stand at dying? – Truly, but for you, I would have sold my honour high to cowards who, under your peace, have put hands on my body – but in homage to you I have yielded and you may do with me what you will. But, lord, remember the Queen!"

And as he knelt at the King's feet he still complained:

"Remember the Queen; for if any man of your household make so bold as to maintain the lie that I loved her unlawfully I will stand up armed to him in a ring. Sire, in the name of God the Lord, have mercy on her."

Then the barons bound him with ropes, and the Queen also. But had Tristan known that trial by combat was to be denied him, certainly he would not have suffered it.

For he trusted in God and knew no man dared draw sword against him in the lists. And truly he did well to trust in God, for though the felons mocked him when he said he had loved loyally, yet I call you to witness, my lords who read this, and who know of the philtre drunk upon the high seas, and who, understand whether his love were disloyalty indeed. For men see this and that outward thing, but God alone the heart, and in the heart alone is crime and the sole final judge is God. Therefore did He lay down the law that a man accused might uphold his cause by battle, and God himself fights for the innocent in such a combat.

Therefore did Tristan claim justice and the right of battle and therefore was he careful to fail in nothing of the homage he owed King Mark, his lord.

But had he known what was coming, he would have killed the felons.

The Chantry Leap

DARK WAS THE NIGHT, and the news ran that Tristan and the Queen were held and that the King would kill them; and wealthy burgess, or common man, they wept and ran to the palace.

And the murmurs and the cries ran through the city, but such was the King's anger in his castle above that not the strongest nor the proudest baron dared move him.

Night ended and the day drew near. Mark, before dawn, rode out to the place where he held pleas and judgment. He ordered a ditch to be dug in the earth and knotty vine-shoots and thorns to be laid therein.

At the hour of Prime he had a ban cried through his land to gather the men of Cornwall; they came with a great noise and the King spoke them thus:

"My lords, I have made here a faggot of thorns for Tristan and the Queen; for they have fallen."

But they cried all, with tears:

"A sentence, lord, a sentence; an indictment and pleas; for killing without trial is shame and crime."

But Mark answered in his anger:

"Neither respite, nor delay, nor pleas, nor sentence. By God that made the world, if any dare petition me, he shall burn first!"

He ordered the fire to be lit, and Tristan to be called.

The flames rose, and all were silent before the flames, and the King waited.

The servants ran to the room where watch was kept on the two lovers; and they dragged Tristan out by his hands though he wept for his honour; but as they dragged him off in such a shame, the Queen still called to him:

"Friend, if I die that you may live, that will be great joy."

Now, hear how full of pity is God and how He heard the lament and the prayers of the common folk, that day.

For as Tristan and his guards went down from the town to where the faggot burned, near the road upon a rock was a chantry, it stood at a cliff's edge steep and sheer, and it turned to the sea-breeze; in the apse of it were windows glazed. Then Tristan said to those with him:

"My lords, let me enter this chantry, to pray for a moment the mercy of God whom I have offended; my death is near. There is but one door to the place, my lords, and each of you has his sword drawn. So, you may well see that, when my prayer to God is done, I must come past you again: when I have prayed God, my lords, for the last time.

And one of the guards said: "Why, let him go in."

So they let him enter to pray. But he, once in, dashed through and leapt the altar rail and the altar too and forced a window of the apse, and leapt again over the cliff's edge. So might he die, but not of that shameful death before the people.

Now learn, my lords, how generous was God to him that day. The wind took Tristan's cloak and he fell upon a smooth rock at the cliff's foot, which to this day the men of Cornwall call "Tristan's leap."

His guards still waited for him at the chantry door, but vainly, for God was now his guard. And he ran, and the fine sand crunched under his feet, and far off he saw the faggot burning, and the smoke and the crackling flames; and fled.

Sword girt and bridle loose, Gorvenal had fled the city, lest the King burn him in his master's place: and he found Tristan on the shore.

"Master," said Tristan, "God has saved me, but oh! master, to what end? For without Iseult I may not and I will not live, and I rather had died of my fall. They will burn her for me, then I too will die for her."

"Lord," said Gorvenal, "take no counsel of anger. See here this thicket with a ditch dug round about it. Let us hide therein where the track passes near, and comers by it will tell us news; and, boy, if they burn Iseult, I swear by God, the Son of Mary, never to sleep under a roof again until she be avenged."

There was a poor man of the common folk that had seen Tristan's fall, and had seen him stumble and rise after, and he crept to Tintagel and to Iseult where she was bound, and said:

"Queen, weep no more. Your friend has fled safely."

"Then I thank God," said she, "and whether they bind or loose me, and whether they kill or spare me, I care but little now."

And though blood came at the cord-knots, so tightly had the traitors bound her, yet still she said, smiling:

"Did I weep for that when God has loosed my friend I should be little worth."

When the news came to the King that Tristan had leapt that leap and was lost he paled with anger, and bade his men bring forth Iseult.

They dragged her from the room, and she came before the crowd, held by her delicate hands, from which blood dropped, and the crowd called:

"Have pity on her – the loyal Queen and honoured! Surely they that gave her up brought mourning on us all – our curses on them!"

But the King's men dragged her to the thorn faggot as it blazed. She stood up before the flame, and the crowd cried its anger, and cursed the traitors and the King. None could see her without pity, unless he had a felon's heart: she was so tightly bound. The tears ran down her face and fell upon her grey gown where ran a little thread of gold, and a thread of gold was twined into her hair.

Just then there had come up a hundred lepers of the King's, deformed and broken, white horribly, and limping on their crutches. And they drew near the flame, and being evil, loved the sight. And their chief Ivan, the ugliest of them all, cried to the King in a quavering voice:

"O King, you would burn this woman in that flame, and it is sound justice, but too swift, for very soon the fire will fall, and her ashes will very soon be scattered by the high wind and her agony be done. Throw her rather to your lepers where she may drag out a life for ever asking death."

And the King answered:

"Yes; let her live that life, for it is better justice and more terrible. I can love those that gave me such a thought."

And the lepers answered:

"Throw her among us, and make her one of us. Never shall lady have known a worse end. And look," they said, "at our rags and our abominations. She has had pleasure in rich stuffs and furs, jewels and walls of marble, honour, good wines and joy, but when she sees your lepers always, King, and only them for ever, their couches and their huts, then indeed she will know the wrong she has done, and bitterly desire even that great flame of thorns."

And as the King heard them, he stood a long time without moving; then he ran to the Queen and seized her by the hand, and she cried:

"Burn me! rather burn me!"

But the King gave her up, and Ivan took her, and the hundred lepers pressed around, and to hear her cries all the crowd rose in pity. But Ivan had an evil gladness, and as he went he dragged her out of the borough bounds, with his hideous company.

Now they took that road where Tristan lay in hiding, and Gorvenal said to him:

"Son, here is your friend. Will you do naught?"

Then Tristan mounted the horse and spurred it out of the bush, and cried:

"Ivan, you have been at the Queen's side a moment, and too long. Now leave her if you would live."

But Ivan threw his cloak away and shouted:

"Your clubs, comrades, and your staves! Crutches in the air – for a fight is on!"

Then it was fine to see the lepers throwing their capes aside, and stirring their sick legs, and brandishing their crutches, some threatening: groaning all; but to strike them Tristan was too noble. There are singers who sing that Tristan killed Ivan, but it is a lie. Too much a knight was he to kill such things. Gorvenal indeed, snatching up an oak sapling, crashed it on Ivan's head till his blood ran down to his misshapen feet. Then Tristan took the Queen.

Henceforth near him she felt no further evil. He cut the cords that bound her arms so straightly, and he left the plain so that they plunged into the wood of Morois; and there in the thick wood Tristan was as sure as in a castle keep.

And as the sun fell they halted all three at the foot of a little hill: fear had wearied the Queen, and she leant her head upon his body and slept.

But in the morning, Gorvenal stole from a wood man his bow and two good arrows plumed and barbed, and gave them to Tristan, the great archer, and he shot him a fawn and killed it. Then Gorvenal gathered dry twigs, struck flint, and lit a great fire to cook the venison. And Tristan cut him branches and made a hut and garnished it with leaves. And Iseult slept upon the thick leaves there.

So, in the depths of the wild wood began for the lovers that savage life which yet they loved very soon.

The Wood of Morois

THEY WANDERED in the depths of the wild wood, restless and in haste like beasts that are hunted, nor did they often dare to return by night to the shelter of yesterday. They ate but the flesh of wild animals. Their faces sank and grew white, their clothes ragged; for the briars tore them. They loved each other and they did not know that they suffered.

One day, as they were wandering in these high woods that had never yet been felled or ordered, they came upon the hermitage of Ogrin.

The old man limped in the sunlight under a light growth of maples near his chapel: he leant upon his crutch, and cried:

"Lord Tristan, hear the great oath which the Cornish men have sworn. The King has published a ban in every parish: Whosoever may seize you shall receive a hundred marks of gold for his guerdon, and all the barons have sworn to give you up alive or dead. Do penance, Tristan! God pardons the sinner who turns to repentance."

"And of what should I repent, Ogrin, my lord? Or of what crime? You that sit in judgment upon us here, do you know what cup it was we drank upon the high sea? That good, great draught inebriates us both. I would rather beg my life long and live of roots and herbs with Iseult than, lacking her, be king of a wide kingdom."

"God aid you, Lord Tristan; for you have lost both this world and the next. A man that is traitor to his lord is worthy to be torn by horses and burnt upon the faggot, and wherever his ashes fall no grass shall grow and all tillage is waste, and the trees and the green things die. Lord Tristan, give back the Queen to the man who espoused her lawfully according to the laws of Rome."

"He gave her to his lepers. From these lepers I myself conquered her with my own hand; and henceforth she is altogether mine. She cannot pass from me nor I from her."

Ogrin sat down; but at his feet Iseult, her head upon the knees of that man of God, wept silently. The hermit told her and re-told her the words of his holy book, but still while she wept she shook her head, and refused the faith he offered.

"Ah me," said Ogrin then, "what comfort can one give the dead? Do penance, Tristan, for a man who lives in sin without repenting is a man quite dead."

"Oh no," said Tristan, "I live and I do no penance. We will go back into the high wood which comforts and wards us all round about. Come with me, Iseult, my friend."

Iseult rose up; they held each other's hands. They passed into the high grass and the underwood: the trees hid them with their branches. They disappeared beyond the leaves.

The summer passed and the winter came: the two lovers lived, all hidden in the hollow of a rock, and on the frozen earth the cold crisped their couch with dead leaves. In the strength of their love neither one nor the other felt these mortal things. But when the open skies had come back with the springtime, they built a hut of green branches under the great trees. Tristan had known, ever since his childhood, that art by which a man may sing the song of birds in the woods, and at his fancy, he would call as call the thrush, the blackbird and the nightingale, and all winged things; and sometimes in reply very many birds would come on to the branches of his hut and sing their song full-throated in the new light.

The lovers had ceased to wander through the forest, for none of the barons ran the risk of their pursuit knowing well that Tristan would have hanged them to the branches of a tree. One day, however, one of the four traitors, Guenelon, whom God blast! drawn by the heat of the hunt, dared enter the Morois. And that morning, on the forest edge in a ravine, Gorvenal, having unsaddled his horse, had let him graze on the new grass, while far off in their hut Tristan held the Queen, and they slept. Then suddenly Gorvenal heard the cry of the pack; the hounds pursued a deer, which fell into that ravine. And far on the heath the hunter showed – and Gorvenal knew him for the man whom his master hated above all. Alone, with bloody spurs, and striking his horse's mane, he galloped on; but Gorvenal watched him from ambush: he came fast, he would return more slowly. He passed and Gorvenal leapt from his ambush and seized the rein and, suddenly, remembering all the wrong that man had done, hewed him to death and carried off his head in his hands. And when the hunters found the body, as they followed, they thought Tristan came after and they fled in fear of death, and thereafter no man hunted in that wood. And far off, in the hut upon their couch of leaves, slept Tristan and the Queen.

There came Gorvenal, noiseless, the dead man's head in his hands that he might lift his master's heart at his awakening. He hung it by its hair outside the hut, and the leaves garlanded it about. Tristan woke and saw it, half hidden in the leaves, and staring at him as he gazed, and he became afraid. But Gorvenal said: "Fear not, he is dead. I killed him with this sword."

Then Tristan was glad, and henceforward from that day no one dared enter the wild wood, for terror guarded it and the lovers were lords of it all: and then it was that Tristan fashioned his bow "Failnaught" which struck home always, man or beast, whatever it aimed at.

My lords, upon a summer day, when mowing is, a little after Whitsuntide, as the birds sang dawn Tristan left his hut and girt his sword on him, and took his bow "Failnaught" and went off to hunt in the wood; but before evening, great evil was to fall on him, for no lovers ever loved so much or paid their love so dear.

When Tristan came back, broken by the heat, the Queen said:

"Friend, where have you been?"

"Hunting a hart," he said, "that wearied me. I would lie down and sleep."

So she lay down, and he, and between them Tristan put his naked sword, and on the Queen's finger was that ring of gold with emeralds set therein, which Mark had given her on her bridal day; but her hand was so wasted that the ring hardly held. And no wind blew, and no leaves stirred, but through a crevice in the branches a sunbeam fell upon the face of Iseult and it shone white like ice. Now a woodman found in the wood a place where the leaves were crushed, where the lovers had halted and slept, and he followed their track and found the hut, and saw them sleeping and fled off, fearing the terrible awakening of that lord. He fled to Tintagel, and going up the stairs of the palace, found the King as he held his pleas in hall amid the vassals assembled.

"Friend," said the King, "what came you hither to seek in haste and breathless, like a huntsman that has followed the dogs afoot? Have you some wrong to right, or has any man driven you?"

But the woodman took him aside and said low down:

"I have seen the Queen and Tristan, and I feared and fled."

"Where saw you them?"

"In a hut in Morois, they slept side by side. Come swiftly and take your vengeance."

"Go," said the King, "and await me at the forest edge where the red cross stands, and tell no man what you have seen. You shall have gold and silver at your will."

The King had saddled his horse and girt his sword and left the city alone, and as he rode alone he minded him of the night when he had seen

Tristan under the great pine-tree, and Iseult with her clear face, and he thought: "If I find them I will avenge this awful wrong."

At the foot of the red cross he came to the woodman and said:

"Go first, and lead me straight and quickly."

The dark shade of the great trees wrapt them round, and as the King followed the spy he felt his sword, and trusted it for the great blows it had struck of old; and surely had Tristan wakened, one of the two had stayed there dead. Then the woodman said:

"King, we are near."

He held the stirrup, and tied the rein to a green apple-tree, and saw in a sunlit glade the hut with its flowers and leaves. Then the King cast his cloak with its fine buckle of gold and drew his sword from its sheath and said again in his heart that they or he should die. And he signed to the woodman to be gone.

He came alone into the hut, sword bare, and watched them as they lay: but he saw that they were apart, and he wondered because between them was the naked blade.

Then he said to himself: "My God, I may not kill them. For all the time they have lived together in this wood, these two lovers, yet is the sword here between them, and throughout Christendom men know that sign. Therefore I will not slay, for that would be treason and wrong, but I will do so that when they wake they may know that I found them here, asleep, and spared them and that God had pity on them both."

And still the sunbeam fell upon the white face of Iseult, and the King took his ermined gloves and put them up against the crevice whence it shone.

Then in her sleep a vision came to Iseult. She seemed to be in a great wood and two lions near her fought for her, and she gave a cry and woke, and the gloves fell upon her breast; and at the cry Tristan woke, and made to seize his sword, and saw by the golden hilt that it was the King's. And the Queen saw on her finger the King's ring, and she cried:

"O, my lord, the King has found us here!"

And Tristan said:

"He has taken my sword; he was alone, but he will return, and will burn us before the people. Let us fly."

So by great marches with Gorvenal alone they fled towards Wales.

Ogrin the Hermit

AFTER THREE DAYS it happened that Tristan, in following a wounded deer far out into the wood, was caught by night-fall, and took to thinking thus under the dark wood alone:

"It was not fear that moved the King ... he had my sword and I slept ... and had he wished to slay, why did he leave me his own blade? ... O, my father, my father, I know you now. There was pardon in your heart, and tenderness and pity ... yet how was that, for who could forgive in this matter without shame? ... It was not pardon it was understanding; the faggot and the chantry leap and the leper ambush have shown him God upon our side. Also I think he remembered the boy who long ago harped at his feet, and my land of Lyonesse which I left for him; the Morholt's spear and blood shed in his honour. He remembered how I made no avowal, but claimed a trial at arms, and the high nature of his heart has made him understand what men around him cannot; never can he know of the spell, yet he doubts and hopes and knows I have told no lie, and would have me prove my cause. O, but to win at arms by God's aid for him, and to enter his peace and to put on mail for him again ... but then he must take her back, and I must yield her ... it would have been much better had he killed me in my sleep. For till now I was hunted and I could hate and forget; he had thrown Iseult to the lepers, she was no more his, but mine; and now by his compassion he has wakened my heart and regained the Queen. For Queen she was at his side, but in this wood she lives a slave, and I waste her youth; and for rooms all hung with silk she has this savage place, and a hut for her splendid walls, and I am the cause that she treads this ugly road. So now I cry to God the Lord, who is King of the world, and beg Him to give me strength to yield back Iseult to King Mark; for she is indeed his wife, wed according to the laws of Rome before all the Barony of his land."

And as he thought thus, he leant upon his bow, and all through the night considered his sorrow.

Within the hollow of thorns that was their resting-place Iseult the Fair awaited Tristan's return. The golden ring that King Mark had slipped there glistened on her finger in the moonlight, and she thought:

"He that put on this ring is not the man who threw me to his lepers in his wrath; he is rather that compassionate lord who, from the day I touched his shore, received me and protected. And he loved Tristan once, but I came, and see what I have done! He should have lived in the King's palace; he should have ridden through King's and baron's fees, finding adventure; but through me he has forgotten his knighthood, and is hunted and exiled from the court, leading a random life. ..."

Just then she heard the feet of Tristan coming over the dead leaves and twigs. She came to meet him, as was her wont, to relieve him of his arms, and she took from him his bow, "Failnaught," and his arrows, and she unbuckled his sword-straps. And, "Friend," said he, "it is the King's sword. It should have slain, but it spared us."

Iseult took the sword, and kissed the hilt of gold, and Tristan saw her weeping.

"Friend," said he, "if I could make my peace with the King; if he would allow me to sustain in arms that neither by act nor word have I loved you with a wrongful love, any knight from the Marshes of Ely right away to Dureaume that would gainsay me, would find me armed in the ring. Then if the King would keep you and drive me out I would cross to the Lowlands or to Brittany with Gorvenal alone. But wherever I went and always, Queen, I should be yours; nor would I have spoken thus, Iseult, but for the wretchedness you bear so long for my sake in this desert land."

"Tristan," she said, "there is the hermit Ogrin. Let us return to him, and cry mercy to the King of Heaven."

They wakened Gorvenal; Iseult mounted the steed, and Tristan led it by the bridle, and all night long they went for the last time through the woods of their love, and they did not speak a word. By morning they came to the Hermitage, where Ogrin read at the threshold, and seeing them, called them tenderly:

"Friends," he cried, "see how Love drives you still to further wretchedness. Will you not do penance at last for your madness?"

"Lord Ogrin," said Tristan, "hear us. Help us to offer peace to the King, and I will yield him the Queen, and will myself go far away into Brittany or the Lowlands, and if some day the King suffer me, I will return and serve as I should."

And at the hermit's feet Iseult said in her turn:

"Nor will I live longer so, for though I will not say one word of penance for my love, which is there and remains forever, yet from now on I will be separate from him."

Then the hermit wept and praised God and cried: "High King, I praise Thy Name, for that Thou hast let me live so long as to give aid to these!"

And he gave them wise counsel, and took ink, and wrote a little writ offering the King what Tristan said.

That night Tristan took the road. Once more he saw the marble well and the tall pine-tree, and he came beneath the window where the King slept, and called him gently, and Mark awoke and whispered:

"Who are you that call me in the night at such an hour?"

"Lord, I am Tristan: I bring you a writ, and lay it here."

Then the King cried: "Nephew! nephew! for God's sake wait awhile," but Tristan had fled and joined his squire, and mounted rapidly. Gorvenal said to him:

"O, Tristan, you are mad to have come. Fly hard with me by the nearest road."

So they came back to the Hermitage, and there they found Ogrin at prayer, but Iseult weeping silently.

The Ford

MARK HAD AWAKENED his chaplain and had given him the writ to read; the chaplain broke the seal, saluted in Tristan's name, and then, when he had cunningly made out the written words, told him what Tristan offered; and Mark heard without saying a word, but his heart was glad, for he still loved the Queen.

He summoned by name the choicest of his baronage, and when they were all assembled they were silent and the King spoke:

"My lords, here is a writ, just sent me. I am your King, and you my lieges. Hear what is offered me, and then counsel me, for you owe me counsel."

The chaplain rose, unfolded the writ, and said, upstanding

"My lords, it is Tristan that first sends love and homage to the King and all his Barony, and he adds, 'O King, when I slew the dragon and conquered the King of Ireland's daughter it was to me they gave her. I was to ward her at will and I yielded her to you. Yet hardly had you wed her when felons made you accept their lies, and in your anger, fair uncle, my lord, you would have had us burnt without trial. But God took compassion on us; we prayed him and he saved the Queen, as justice was: and me also – though I leapt from a high rock, I was saved by the power of God. And since then what have I done blameworthy? The Queen was thrown to the lepers; I came to her succour and bore her away. Could I have done less for a woman, who all but died innocent through me? I fled through the woods. Nor could I have come down into the vale and yielded her, for there was a ban to take us dead or alive. But now, as then, I am ready, my lord, to sustain in arms against all comers that never had the Queen for me, nor I for her a love dishonourable to you. Publish the lists, and if I cannot prove my right in arms, burn me before your men. But if I conquer and you take back Iseult, no baron of yours will serve you as will I; and if you will not have me, I will offer myself to the King of Galloway, or to him of the Lowlands, and you will hear of me never again. Take counsel, King, for if you will make no terms I will take back Iseult to Ireland, and she shall be Queen in her own land.'"

When the barons of Cornwall heard how Tristan offered battle, they said to the King:

"Sire, take back the Queen. They were madmen that belied her to you. But as for Tristan, let him go and war it in Galloway, or in the Lowlands. Bid him bring back Iseult on such a day and that soon.

Then the King called thrice clearly:

"Will any man rise in accusation against Tristan?"

And as none replied, he said to his chaplain:

"Write me a writ in haste. You have heard what you shall write. Iseult has suffered enough in her youth. And let the writ be hung upon the arm of the red cross before evening. Write speedily."

Towards midnight Tristan crossed the Heath of Sand, and found the writ, and bore it sealed to Ogrin; and the hermit read the letter; "How Mark consented by the counsel of his barons to take back Iseult, but not to keep Tristan for his liege. Rather let him cross the sea, when, on the third day hence, at the Ford of Chances, he had given back the Queen into King Mark's hands." Then Tristan said to the Queen:

"O, my God! I must lose you, friend! But it must be, since I can thus spare you what you suffer for my sake. But when we part for ever I will give you a pledge of mine to keep, and from whatever unknown land I reach I will send some messenger, and he will bring back word of you, and at your call I will come from far away."

Iseult said, sighing:

"Tristan, leave me your dog, Toothold, and every time I see him I will remember you, and will be less sad. And, friend, I have here a ring of green jasper. Take it for the love of me, and put it on your finger; then if anyone come saying he is from you, I will not trust him at all till he show me this ring, but once I have seen it, there is no power or royal ban that can prevent me from doing what you bid – wisdom or folly."

"Friend," he said, "here give I you Toothold."

"Friend," she replied, "take you this ring in reward."

And they kissed each other on the lips.

Now Ogrin, having left the lovers in the Hermitage, hobbled upon his crutch to the place called The Mount, and he bought ermine there and fur and cloth of silk and purple and scarlet, and a palfrey harnessed in gold that went softly, and the folk laughed to see him spending upon these the small moneys he had amassed so long; but the old man put the rich stuffs upon the palfrey and came back to Iseult.

And "Queen," said he, "take these gifts of mine that you may seem the finer on the day when you come to the Ford."

Meanwhile the King had had cried through Cornwall the news that on the third day he would make his peace with the Queen at the Ford, and knights and ladies came in a crowd to the gathering, for all loved the Queen and would see her, save the three felons that yet survived.

On the day chosen for the meeting, the field shone far with the rich tents of the barons, and suddenly Tristan and Iseult came out at the forest's edge, and caught sight of King Mark far off among his Barony:

"Friend," said Tristan, "there is the King, your lord – his knights and his men; they are coming towards us, and very soon we may not speak to each other again. By the God of Power I conjure you, if ever I send you a word, do you my bidding."

"Friend," said Iseult, "on the day that I see the ring, nor tower, nor wall, nor stronghold will let me from doing the will of my friend."

"Why then," he said, "Iseult, may God reward you."

Their horses went abreast and he drew her towards him with his arm.

"Friend," said Iseult, "hear my last prayer: you will leave this land, but wait some days; hide till you know how the King may treat me, whether in wrath or kindness, for I am afraid. Friend, Orri the woodman will entertain you hidden. Go you by night to the abandoned cellar that you know and I will send Perinis there to say if anyone misuse me."

"Friend, none would dare. I will stay hidden with Orri, and if any misuse you let him fear me as the Enemy himself."

Now the two troops were near and they saluted, and the King rode a bow-shot before his men and with him Dinas of Lidan; and when the barons had come up, Tristan, holding Iseult's palfrey by the bridle, bowed to the King and said:

"O King, I yield you here Iseult the Fair, and I summon you, before the men of your land, that I may defend myself in your court, for I have had no judgment. Let me have trial at arms, and if I am conquered, burn me, but if I conquer, keep me by you, or, if you will not, I will be off to some far country."

But no one took up Tristan's wager, and the King, taking Iseult's palfrey by the bridle, gave it to Dinas, and went apart to take counsel.

Dinas, in his joy, gave all honour and courtesy to the Queen, but when the felons saw her so fair and honoured as of old, they were stirred and rode to the King, and said:

"King, hear our counsel. That the Queen was slandered we admit, but if she and Tristan re-enter your court together, rumour will revive again. Rather let Tristan go apart awhile. Doubtless some day you may recall him."

And so Mark did, and ordered Tristan by his barons to go off without delay.

Then Tristan came near the Queen for his farewell, and as they looked at one another the Queen in shame of that assembly blushed, but the King pitied her, and spoke his nephew thus for the first time:

"You cannot leave in these rags; take then from my treasury gold and silver and white fur and grey, as much as you will."

"King," said Tristan, "neither a penny nor a link of mail. I will go as I can, and serve with high heart the mighty King in the Lowlands."

And he turned rein and went down towards the sea, but Iseult followed him with her eyes, and so long as he could yet be seen a long way off she did not turn.

Now at the news of the peace, men, women, and children, great and small, ran out of the town in a crowd to meet Iseult, and while they mourned Tristan's exile they rejoiced at the Queen's return.

And to the noise of bells, and over pavings strewn with branches, the King and his counts and princes made her escort, and the gates of the palace were thrown open that rich and poor might enter and eat and drink at will.

And Mark freed a hundred of his slaves, and armed a score of squires that day with hauberk and with sword.

But Tristan that night hid with Orri, as the Queen had counselled him.

The Ordeal by Iron

DENOALEN, ANDRET, AND GONDOIN held themselves safe; Tristan was far over sea, far away in service of a distant king, and they beyond his power. Therefore, during a hunt one day, as the King rode apart in a glade where the pack would pass, and hearkening to the hounds, they all three rode towards him, and said:

"O King, we have somewhat to say. Once you condemned the Queen without judgment, and that was wrong; now you acquit her without judgment, and that is wrong. She is not quit by trial, and the barons of your land blame you both. Counsel her, then, to claim the ordeal in God's judgment, for since she is innocent, she may swear on the relics of the saints and hot iron will not hurt her. For so custom runs, and in this easy way are doubts dissolved."

But Mark answered:

"God strike you, my Cornish lords, how you hunt my shame! For you have I exiled my nephew, and now what would you now? Would you have me drive the Queen to Ireland too? What novel plaints have you to plead? Did not Tristan offer you battle in this matter? He offered battle to clear the Queen forever: he offered and you heard him all. Where then were your lances and your shields?"

"Sire," they said, "we have counselled you loyal counsel as lieges and to your honour; henceforward we hold our peace. Put aside your anger and give us your safe-guard."

But Mark stood up in the stirrup and cried:

"Out of my land, and out of my peace, all of you! Tristan I exiled for you, and now go you in turn, out of my land!"

But they answered:

"Sire, it is well. Our keeps are strong and fenced, and stand on rocks not easy for men to climb."

And they rode off without a salutation.

But the King (not tarrying for huntsman or for hound but straight away) spurred his horse to Tintagel; and as he sprang up the stairs the Queen heard the jangle of his spurs upon the stones.

She rose to meet him and took his sword as she was wont, and bowed before him, as it was also her wont to do; but Mark raised her, holding her hands; and when Iseult looked up she saw his noble face in just that wrath she had seen before the faggot fire.

She thought that Tristan was found, and her heart grew cold, and without a word she fell at the King's feet.

He took her in his arms and kissed her gently till she could speak again, and then he said:

"Friend, friend, what evil tries you?"

"Sire, I am afraid, for I have seen your anger.

"Yes, I was angered at the hunt."

"My lord, should one take so deeply the mischances of a game?"

Mark smiled and said:

"No, friend; no chance of hunting vexed me, but those three felons whom you know; and I have driven them forth from my land."

"Sire, what did they say, or dare to say of me?"

"What matter? I have driven them forth."

"Sire, all living have this right: to say the word they have conceived. And I would ask a question, but from whom shall I learn save from you? I am alone in a foreign land, and have no one else to defend me."

"They would have it that you should quit yourself by solemn oath and by the ordeal of iron, saying 'that God was a true judge, and that as the Queen was innocent, she herself should seek such judgment as would clear her for ever.' This was their clamour and their demand incessantly. But let us leave it. I tell you, I have driven them forth."

Iseult trembled, but looking straight at the King, she said:

"Sire, call them back; I will clear myself by oath. But I bargain this: that on the appointed day you call King Arthur and Lord Gawain, Girflet, Kay the Seneschal, and a hundred of his knights to ride to the Sandy Heath where your land marches with his, and a river flows between; for I will not swear before your barons alone, lest they should demand some new thing, and lest there should be no end to my trials. But if my warrantors, King Arthur and his knights, be there, the barons will not dare dispute the judgment."

But as the heralds rode to Carduel, Iseult sent to Tristan secretly her squire Perinis: and he ran through the underwood, avoiding paths, till he found the hut of Orri, the woodman, where Tristan for many days had awaited news. Perinis told him all: the ordeal, the place, and the time, and added:

"My lord, the Queen would have you on that day and place come dressed as a pilgrim, so that none may know you – unarmed, so that none may challenge – to the Sandy Heath. She must cross the river to the place appointed. Beyond it, where Arthur and his hundred knights will stand, be you also; for my lady fears the judgment, but she trusts in God."

Then Tristan answered:

"Go back, friend Perinis, return you to the Queen, and say that I will do her bidding."

And you must know that as Perinis went back to Tintagel he caught sight of that same woodman who had betrayed the lovers before, and the woodman, as he found him, had just dug a pitfall for wolves and for wild boars, and covered it with leafy branches to hide it, and as Perinis came near the woodman fled, but Perinis drove him, and caught him, and broke his staff and his head together, and pushed his body into the pitfall with his feet.

On the appointed day King Mark and Iseult, and the barons of Cornwall, stood by the river; and the knights of Arthur and all their host were arrayed beyond.

And just before them, sitting on the shore, was a poor pilgrim, wrapped in cloak and hood, who held his wooden platter and begged alms.

Now as the Cornish boats came to the shoal of the further bank, Iseult said to the knights:

"My lords, how shall I land without befouling my clothes in the river-mud? Fetch me a ferryman."

And one of the knights hailed the pilgrim, and said:

"Friend, truss your coat, and try the water; carry you the Queen to shore, unless you fear the burden."

But as he took the Queen in his arms she whispered to him: "Friend."

And then she whispered to him, lower still:

"Stumble you upon the sand."

And as he touched shore, he stumbled, holding the Queen in his arms; and the squires and boatmen with their oars and boat-hooks drove the poor pilgrim away.

But the Queen said:

"Let him be; some great travail and journey has weakened him."

And she threw to the pilgrim a little clasp of gold.

Before the tent of King Arthur was spread a rich Nicean cloth upon the grass, and the holy relics were set on it, taken out of their covers and their shrines.

And round the holy relics on the sward stood a guard more than a king's guard, for Lord Gawain, Girflet, and Kay the Seneschal kept ward over them.

The Queen having prayed God, took off the jewels from her neck and hands, and gave them to the beggars around; she took off her purple mantle, and her overdress, and her shoes with their precious stones, and gave them also to the poor that loved her.

She kept upon her only the sleeveless tunic, and then with arms and feet quite bare she came between the two kings, and all around the barons watched her in silence, and some wept, for near the holy relics was a brazier burning.

And trembling a little she stretched her right hand towards the bones and said: "Kings of Logres and of Cornwall; my lords Gawain, and Kay, and Girflet, and all of you that are my warrantors, by these holy things and all the holy things of earth, I swear that no man has held me in his arms saving King Mark, my lord, and that poor pilgrim. King Mark, will that oath stand?"

"Yes, Queen," he said, "and God see to it.

"Amen," said Iseult, and then she went near the brazier, pale and stumbling, and all were silent. The iron was red, but she thrust her bare arms among the coals and seized it, and bearing it took nine steps.

Then, as she cast it from her, she stretched her arms out in a cross, with the palms of her hands wide open, and all men saw them fresh and clean and cold. Seeing that great sight the kings and the barons and the people stood for a moment silent, then they stirred together and they praised God loudly all around.

The Little Fairy Bell

WHEN TRISTAN HAD COME BACK to Orri's hut, and had loosened his heavy pilgrim's cape, he saw clearly in his heart that it was time to keep his oath to King Mark and to fly the land.

Three days yet he tarried, because he could not drag himself away from that earth, but on the fourth day he thanked the woodman, and said to Gorvenal:

"Master, the hour is come."

And he went into Wales, into the land of the great Duke Gilain, who was young, powerful, and frank in spirit, and welcomed him nobly as a God-sent guest.

And he did everything to give him honour and joy; but he found that neither adventure, nor feast could soothe what Tristan suffered.

One day, as he sat by the young Duke's side, his spirit weighed upon him, so that not knowing it he groaned, and the Duke, to soothe him, ordered into his private room a fairy thing, which pleased his eyes when he was sad and relieved his own heart; it was a dog, and the varlets brought it in to him, and they put it upon a table there. Now this dog was a fairy dog, and came from the Duke of Avalon; for a fairy had given it him as a love-gift, and no one can well describe its kind or beauty. And it bore at its neck, hung to a little chain of gold, a little bell; and that tinkled so gaily, and so clear and so soft, that as Tristan heard it, he was soothed, and his anguish melted away, and he forgot all that he had suffered for the Queen; for such was the virtue of the bell and such its property: that whosoever heard it, he lost all pain. And as Tristan stroked the little fairy thing, the dog that took away his sorrow, he saw how delicate it was and fine, and how it had soft hair like samite, and he thought how good a gift it would make for the Queen. But he dared not ask for it right out since he knew that the Duke loved this dog beyond everything in the world, and would yield it to no prayers, nor to wealth, nor to wile; so one day Tristan having made a plan in his mind said this:

"Lord, what would you give to the man who could rid your land of the hairy giant Urgan, that levies such a toll?"

"Truly, the victor might choose what he would, but none will dare."

Then said Tristan:

"Those are strange words, for good comes to no land save by risk and daring, and not for all the gold of Milan would I renounce my desire to find him in his wood and bring him down."

Then Tristan went out to find Urgan in his lair, and they fought hard and long, till courage conquered strength, and Tristan, having cut off the giant's hand, bore it back to the Duke.

And "Sire," said he, "since I may choose a reward according to your

word, give me the little fairy dog. It was for that I conquered Urgan, and
your promise stands."

"Friend," said the Duke, "take it, then, but in taking it you take away
also all my joy."

Then Tristan took the little fairy dog and gave it in ward to a Welsh
harper, who was cunning and who bore it to Cornwall till he came to
Tintagel, and having come there put it secretly into Brangien's hands,
and the Queen was so pleased that she gave ten marks of gold to the
harper, but she put it about that the Queen of Ireland, her mother, had
sent the beast. And she had a goldsmith work a little kennel for him, all
jewelled, and incrusted with gold and enamel inlaid; and wherever she
went she carried the dog with her in memory of her friend, and as she
watched it sadness and anguish and regrets melted out of her heart.

At first she did not guess the marvel, but thought her consolation
was because the gift was Tristan's, till one day she found that it was
fairy, and that it was the little bell that charmed her soul; then she
thought: "What have I to do with comfort since he is sorrowing? He
could have kept it too and have forgotten his sorrow; but with high
courtesy he sent it to me to give me his joy and to take up his pain
again. Friend, while you suffer, so long will I suffer also."

And she took the magic bell and shook it just a little, and then by the
open window she threw it into the sea.

Iseult of the White Hands

APART THE LOVERS could neither live nor die, for it was life and
death together; and Tristan fled his sorrow through seas and
islands and many lands.

He fled his sorrow still by seas and islands, till at last he came back to his
land of Lyonesse, and there Rohalt, the keeper of faith, welcomed him
with happy tears and called him son. But he could not live in the peace

of his own land, and he turned again and rode through kingdoms and through baronies, seeking adventure. From the Lyonesse to the Lowlands, from the Lowlands on to the Germanies; through the Germanies and into Spain. And many lords he served, and many deeds did, but for two years no news came to him out of Cornwall, nor friend, nor messenger. Then he thought that Iseult had forgotten.

Now it happened one day that, riding with Gorvenal alone, he came into the land of Brittany. They rode through a wasted plain of ruined walls and empty hamlets and burnt fields everywhere, and the earth deserted of men; and Tristan thought:

"I am weary, and my deeds profit me nothing; my lady is far off and I shall never see her again. Or why for two years has she made no sign, or why has she sent no messenger to find me as I wandered? But in Tintagel Mark honours her and she gives him joy, and that little fairy bell has done a thorough work; for little she remembers or cares for the joys and the mourning of old, little for me, as I wander in this desert place. I, too, will forget."

On the third day, at the hour of noon, Tristan and Gorvenal came near a hill where an old chantry stood and close by a hermitage also; and Tristan asked what wasted land that was, and the hermit answered:

"Lord, it is Breton land which Duke Hod holds, and once it was rich in pasture and ploughland, but Count Riol of Nantes has wasted it. For you must know that this Count Riol was the Duke's vassal. And the Duke has a daughter, fair among all King's daughters, and Count Riol would have taken her to wife; but her father refused her to a vassal, and Count Riol would have carried her away by force. Many men have died in that quarrel."

And Tristan asked:

"Can the Duke wage his war?"

And the hermit answered:

"Hardly, my lord; yet his last keep of Carhaix holds out still, for the walls are strong, and strong is the heart of the Duke's son Kaherdin, a very good knight and bold; but the enemy surrounds them on every side and starves them. Very hardly do they hold their castle."

Then Tristan asked:

"How far is this keep of Carhaix?"

"Sir," said the hermit, "it is but two miles further on this way."

Then Tristan and Gorvenal lay down, for it was evening.

In the morning, when they had slept, and when the hermit had chanted, and had shared his black bread with them, Tristan thanked him and rode hard to Carhaix. And as he halted beneath the fast high walls, he saw a little company of men behind the battlements, and he asked if the Duke were there with his son Kaherdin. Now Hod was among them; and when he cried "yes," Tristan called up to him and said:

"I am that Tristan, King of Lyonesse, and Mark of Cornwall is my uncle. I have heard that your vassals do you a wrong, and I have come to offer you my arms.

"Alas, lord Tristan, go you your way alone and God reward you, for here within we have no more food; no wheat, or meat, or any stores but only lentils and a little oats remaining."

But Tristan said:

"For two years I dwelt in a forest, eating nothing save roots and herbs; yet I found it a good life, so open you the door."

They welcomed him with honour, and Kaherdin showed him the wall and the dungeon keep with all their devices, and from the battlements he showed the plain where far away gleamed the tents of Duke Riol. And when they were down in the castle again he said to Tristan:

"Friend, let us go to the hall where my mother and sister sit."

So, holding each other's hands, they came into the women's room, where the mother and the daughter sat together weaving gold upon English cloth and singing a weaving song. They sang of Doette the fair who sits alone beneath the white-thorn, and round about her blows the wind. She waits for Doon, her friend, but he tarries long and does not come. This was the song they sang. And Tristan bowed to them, and they to him. Then Kaherdin, showing the work his mother did, said:

"See, friend Tristan, what a work-woman is here, and how marvellously she adorns stoles and chasubles for the poor minsters, and how my sister's hands run thread of gold upon this cloth. Of right, good sister, are you called, 'Iseult of the White Hands.'"

But Tristan, hearing her name, smiled and looked at her more gently.

And on the morrow, Tristan, Kaherdin, and twelve young knights left the castle and rode to a pinewood near the enemy's tents. And sprang from ambush and captured a waggon of Count Riol's food; and from that day, by escapade and ruse they would carry tents and convoys and kill off men, nor ever come back without some booty; so that Tristan and Kaherdin began to be brothers in arms, and kept faith and tenderness, as history tells. And as they came back from these rides, talking chivalry together, often did Kaherdin praise to his comrade his sister, Iseult of the White Hands, for her simplicity and beauty.

One day, as the dawn broke, a sentinel ran from the tower through the halls crying:

"Lords, you have slept too long; rise, for an assault is on."

And knights and burgesses armed, and ran to the walls, and saw helmets shining on the plain, and pennons streaming crimson, like flames, and all the host of Riol in its array. Then the Duke and Kaherdin deployed their horsemen before the gates, and from a bow-length off they stooped, and spurred and charged, and they put their lances down together and the arrows fell on them like April rain.

Now Tristan had armed himself among the last of those the sentinel had roused, and he laced his shoes of steel, and put on his mail, and his spurs of gold, his hauberk, and his helm over the gorget, and he mounted and spurred, with shield on breast, crying:

"Carhaix!"

And as he came, he saw Duke Riol charging, rein free, at Kaherdin, but Tristan came in between. So they met, Tristan and Duke Riol. And at the shock, Tristan's lance shivered, but Riol's lance struck Tristan's horse just where the breast-piece runs, and laid it on the field.

But Tristan, standing, drew his sword, his burnished sword, and said:

"Coward! Here is death ready for the man that strikes the horse before the rider."

But Riol answered:

"I think you have lied, my lord!"

And he charged him.

And as he passed, Tristan let fall his sword so heavily upon his helm that he carried away the crest and the nasal, but the sword slipped on the mailed shoulder, and glanced on the horse, and killed it, so that of force Duke Riol must slip the stirrup and leap and feel the ground. Then Riol too was on his feet, and they both fought hard in their broken mail, their 'scutcheons torn and their helmets loosened and lashing with their dented swords, till Tristan struck Riol just where the helmet buckles, and it yielded and the blow was struck so hard that the baron fell on hands and knees; but when he had risen again, Tristan struck him down once more with a blow that split the helm, and it split the headpiece too, and touched the skull; then Riol cried mercy and begged his life, and Tristan took his sword.

So he promised to enter Duke Hoël's keep and to swear homage again, and to restore what he had wasted; and by his order the battle ceased, and his host went off discomfited.

Now when the victors were returned Kaherdin said to his father:

"Sire, keep you Tristan. There is no better knight, and your land has need of such courage."

So when the Duke had taken counsel with his barons, he said to Tristan:

"Friend, I owe you my land, but I shall be quit with you if you will take my daughter, Iseult of the White Hands, who comes of kings and of queens, and of dukes before them in blood."

And Tristan answered:

"I will take her, Sire."

So the day was fixed, and the Duke came with his friends and Tristan with his, and before all, at the gate of the minster, Tristan wed Iseult of the White Hands, according to the Church's law.

But that same night, as Tristan's valets undressed him, it happened that in drawing his arm from the sleeve they drew off and let fall from his finger the ring of green jasper, the ring of Iseult the Fair. It sounded on the stones, and Tristan looked and saw it. Then his heart awoke and he knew that he had done wrong. For he remembered the day when Iseult the Fair had given him the ring. It was in that forest where, for his sake, she had led the hard life with him, and that night he saw again the hut in the wood of Morois, and he was bitter with himself that ever he had accused her of treason; for now it was he that had betrayed, and he was bitter with himself also in pity for this new wife and her simplicity and beauty. See how these two Iseults had met him in an evil hour, and to both had he broken faith!

Now Iseult of the White Hands said to him, hearing him sigh:

"Dear lord, have I hurt you in anything? Will you not speak me a single word?"

But Tristan answered: "Friend, do not be angry with me; for once in another land I fought a foul dragon and was near to death, and I thought of the Mother of God, and I made a vow to Her that, should I ever wed, I would spend the first holy nights of my wedding in prayer and in silence."

"Why," said Iseult, "that was a good vow."

And Tristan watched through the night.

The Madness of Tristan

WITHIN HER ROOM AT TINTAGEL, Iseult the Fair sighed for the sake of Tristan, and named him, her desire, of whom for two years she had had no word, whether he lived or no.

Within her room at Tintagel Iseult the Fair sat singing a song she had made. She sang of Guron taken and killed for his love, and how by guile the Count gave Guron's heart to her to eat, and of her woe. The Queen sang softly, catching the harp's tone; her hands were cunning and her song good; she sang low down and softly.

Then came in Kariado, a rich count from a far-off island, that had fared to Tintagel to offer the Queen his service, and had spoken of love to her, though she disdained his folly. He found Iseult as she sang, and laughed to her:

"Lady, how sad a song! as sad as the Osprey's; do they not say he sings for death? and your song means that to me; I die for you."

And Iseult said: "So let it be and may it mean so; for never come you here but to stir in me anger or mourning. Ever were you the screech owl or the Osprey that boded ill when you spoke of Tristan; what news bear you now?"

And Kariado answered:

"You are angered, I know not why, but who heeds your words? Let the Osprey bode me death; here is the evil news the screech owl brings. Lady Iseult, Tristan, your friend is lost to you. He has wed in a far land. So seek you other where, for he mocks your love. He has wed in great pomp Iseult of the White Hands, the King of Brittany's daughter."

And Kariado went off in anger, but Iseult bowed her head and broke into tears.

Now far from Iseult, Tristan languished, till on a day he must needs see her again. Far from her, death came surely; and he had rather die at once than day by day. And he desired some death, but that the Queen might know it was in finding her; then would death come easily.

So he left Carhaix secretly, telling no man, neither his kindred nor even Kaherdin, his brother in arms. He went in rags afoot (for no one marks the beggar on the high road) till he came to the shore of the sea.

He found in a haven a great ship ready, the sail was up and the anchor-chain short at the bow.

"God save you, my lords," he said, "and send you a good journey. To what land sail you now?"

"To Tintagel," they said.

Then he cried out:

"Oh, my lords! take me with you thither!"

And he went aboard, and a fair wind filled the sail, and she ran five days and nights for Cornwall, till, on the sixth day, they dropped anchor in Tintagel Haven. The castle stood above, fenced all around. There was but the one armed gate, and two knights watched it night and day. So Tristan went ashore and sat upon the beach, and a man told him that Mark was there and had just held his court.

"But where," said he, "is Iseult, the Queen, and her fair maid, Brangien?"

"In Tintagel too," said the other, "and I saw them lately; the Queen sad, as she always is."

At the hearing of the name, Tristan suffered, and he thought that neither by guile nor courage could he see that friend, for Mark would kill him.

And he thought, "Let him kill me and let me die for her, since every day I die. But you, Iseult, even if you knew me here, would you not drive me out?" And he thought, "I will try guile. I will seem mad, but with a madness that shall be great wisdom. And many shall think me a fool that have less wit than I."

Just then a fisherman passed in a rough cloak and cape, and Tristan seeing him, took him aside, and said:

"Friend, will you not change clothes?"

And as the fisherman found it a very good bargain, he said in answer:

"Yes, friend, gladly."

And he changed and ran off at once for fear of losing his gain. Then Tristan shaved his wonderful hair; he shaved it close to his head and left a cross all bald, and he rubbed his face with magic herbs distilled in his own country, and it changed in colour and skin so that none could know him, and he made him a club from a young tree torn from a hedge-row and hung it to his neck, and went bare-foot towards the castle.

The porter made sure that he had to do with a fool and said:

"Good morrow, fool, where have you been this long while?"

And he answered:

"At the Abbot of St. Michael's wedding, and he wed an abbess, large and veiled. And from the Alps to Mount St. Michael how they came, the priests and abbots, monks and regulars, all dancing on the green with croziers and with staves under the high trees' shade. But I left them all to come hither, for I serve at the King's board to-day."

Then the porter said:

"Come in, lord fool; the Hairy Urgan's son, I know, and like your father."

And when he was within the courts the serving men ran after him and cried:

"The fool! the fool!"

But he made play with them though they cast stones and struck him as they laughed, and in the midst of laughter and their cries, as the rout followed him, he came to that hall where, at the Queen's side, King Mark sat under his canopy.

And as he neared the door with his club at his neck, the King said:

"Here is a merry fellow, let him in."

And they brought him in, his club at his neck. And the King said:

"Friend, well come; what seek you here?"

"Iseult," said he, "whom I love so well; I bring my sister with me, Brunehild, the beautiful. Come, take her, you are weary of the Queen. Take you my sister and give me here Iseult, and I will hold her and serve you for her love."

The King said laughing:

"Fool, if I gave you the Queen, where would you take her, pray?"

"Oh! very high," he said, "between the clouds and heaven, into a fair chamber glazed. The beams of the sun shine through it, yet the winds do not trouble it at all. There would I bear the Queen into that crystal chamber of mine all compact of roses and the morning."

The King and his barons laughed and said:

"Here is a good fool at no loss for words."

But the fool as he sat at their feet gazed at Iseult most fixedly.

"Friend," said King Mark, "what warrant have you that the Queen would heed so foul a fool as you?"

"O! Sire," he answered gravely, "many deeds have I done for her, and my madness is from her alone."

"What is your name?" they said, and laughed.

"Tristan," said he, "that loved the Queen so well, and still till death will love her."

But at the name the Queen angered and weakened together, and said: "Get hence for an evil fool!"

But the fool, marking her anger, went on:

"Queen Iseult, do you mind the day, when, poisoned by the Morholt's spear, I took my harp to sea and fell upon your shore? Your mother healed me with strange drugs. Have you no memory, Queen?"

But Iseult answered:

"Out, fool, out! Your folly and you have passed the bounds!"

But the fool, still playing, pushed the barons out, crying:

"Out! madmen, out! Leave me to counsel with Iseult, since I come here for the love of her!"

And as the King laughed, Iseult blushed and said:

"King, drive me forth this fool!"

But the fool still laughed and cried:

"Queen, do you mind you of the dragon I slew in your land? I hid its tongue in my hose, and, burnt of its venom, I fell by the roadside. Ah! what a knight was I then, and it was you that succoured me."

Iseult replied:

"Silence! You wrong all knighthood by your words, for you are a fool from birth. Cursed be the seamen that brought you hither; rather should they have cast you into the sea!"

"Queen Iseult," he still said on, "do you mind you of your haste when you would have slain me with my own sword? And of the Hair of Gold? And of how I stood up to the seneschal?"

"Silence!" she said, "you drunkard. You were drunk last night, and so you dreamt these dreams."

"Drunk, and still so am I," said he, "but of such a draught that never can the influence fade. Queen Iseult, do you mind you of that hot and open day on the high seas? We thirsted and we drank together from the same cup, and since that day have I been drunk with an awful wine."

When the Queen heard these words which she alone could understand, she rose and would have gone.

But the King held her by her ermine cloak, and she sat down again.

And as the King had his fill of the fool he called for his falcons and went to hunt; and Iseult said to him:

"Sire, I am weak and sad; let me be go rest in my room; I am tired of these follies."

And she went to her room in thought and sat upon her bed and mourned, calling herself a slave and saying:

"Why was I born? Brangien, dear sister, life is so hard to me that death were better! There is a fool without, shaven criss-cross, and come in an evil hour, and he is warlock, for he knows in every part myself and my whole life; he knows what you and I and Tristan only know."

Then Brangien said: "It may be Tristan."

But – "No," said the Queen, "for he was the first of knights, but this fool is foul and made awry. Curse me his hour and the ship that brought him hither."

"My lady!" said Brangien, "soothe you. You curse over much these days. May be he comes from Tristan?"

"I cannot tell. I know him not. But go find him, friend, and see if you know him."

So Brangien went to the hall where the fool still sat alone. Tristan knew her and let fall his club and said:

"Brangien, dear Brangien, before God! have pity on me!"

"Foul fool," she answered, "what devil taught you my name?"

"Lady," he said, "I have known it long. By my head, that once was fair, if I am mad the blame is yours, for it was yours to watch over the wine we drank on the high seas. The cup was of silver and I held it to Iseult and she drank. Do you remember, lady?"

"No," she said, and as she trembled and left he called out: "Pity me!"

He followed and saw Iseult. He stretched out his arms, but in her shame, sweating agony she drew back, and Tristan angered and said:

"I have lived too long, for I have seen the day that Iseult will nothing of me. Iseult, how hard love dies! Iseult, a welling water that floods and runs large is a mighty thing; on the day that it fails it is nothing; so love that turns."

But she said

"Brother, I look at you and doubt and tremble, and I know you not for Tristan."

"Queen Iseult, I am Tristan indeed that do love you; mind you for the last time of the dwarf, and of the flower, and of the blood I shed in my leap. Oh! and of that ring I took in kisses and in tears on the day we parted. I have kept that jasper ring and asked it counsel."

Then Iseult knew Tristan for what he was, and she said:

"Heart, you should have broken of sorrow not to have known

the man who has suffered so much for you. Pardon, my master and my friend."

And her eyes darkened and she fell; but when the light returned she was held by him who kissed her eyes and her face.

So passed they three full days. But, on the third, two maids that watched them told the traitor Andret, and he put spies well-armed before the women's rooms. And when Tristan would enter they cried:

"Back, fool!"

But he brandished his club laughing, and said:

"What! May I not kiss the Queen who loves me and awaits me now?"

And they feared him for a mad fool, and he passed in through the door.

Then, being with the Queen for the last time, he held her in his arms and said:

"Friend, I must fly, for they are wondering. I must fly, and perhaps shall never see you more. My death is near, and far from you my death will come of desire."

"Oh friend," she said, "fold your arms round me close and strain me so that our hearts may break and our souls go free at last. Take me to that happy place of which you told me long ago. The fields whence none return, but where great singers sing their songs for ever. Take me now."

"I will take you to the Happy Palace of the living, Queen! The time is near. We have drunk all joy and sorrow. The time is near. When it is finished, if I call you, will you come, my friend?"

"Friend," said she, "call me and you know that I shall come."

"Friend," said he, "God send you His reward."

As he went out the spies would have held him; but he laughed aloud, and flourished his club, and cried:

"Peace, gentlemen, I go and will not stay. My lady sends me to prepare that shining house I vowed her, of crystal, and of rose shot through with morning."

And as they cursed and drave him, the fool went leaping on his way.

The Death of Tristan

WHEN HE WAS COME BACK TO BRITTANY, to Carhaix, it happened that Tristan, riding to the aid of Kaherdin his brother in arms, fell into ambush and was wounded by a poisoned spear; and many doctors came, but none could cure him of the ill. And Tristan weakened and paled, and his bones showed.

Then he knew that his life was going, and that he must die, and he had a desire to see once more Iseult the Fair, but he could not seek her, for the sea would have killed him in his weakness, and how could Iseult come to him? And sad, and suffering the poison, he awaited death.

He called Kaherdin secretly to tell him his pain, for they loved each other with a loyal love; and as he would have no one in the room save Kaherdin, nor even in the neighbouring rooms, Iseult of the White Hands began to wonder. She was afraid and wished to hear, and she came back and listened at the wall by Tristan's bed; and as she listened one of her maids kept watch for her.

Now, within, Tristan had gathered up his strength, and had half risen, leaning against the wall, and Kaherdin wept beside him. They wept their good comradeship, broken so soon, and their friendship: then Tristan told Kaherdin of his love for that other Iseult, and of the sorrow of his life.

"Fair friend and gentle," said Tristan, "I am in a foreign land where I have neither friend nor cousin, save you; and you alone in this place have given me comfort. My life is going, and I wish to see once more Iseult the Fair. Ah, did I but know of a messenger who would go to her! For now I know that she will come to me. Kaherdin, my brother in arms, I beg it of your friendship; try this thing for me, and if you carry my word, I will become your liege, and I will cherish you beyond all other men."

And as Kaherdin saw Tristan broken down, his heart reproached him and he said:

"Fair comrade, do not weep; I will do what you desire, even if it were risk of death I would do it for you. Nor no distress nor anguish will let me from doing it according to my power. Give me the word you send, and I will make ready."

And Tristan answered:

"Thank you, friend; this is my prayer: take this ring, it is a sign between her and me; and when you come to her land pass yourself at court for a merchant, and show her silk and stuffs, but make so that she sees the ring, for then she will find some ruse by which to speak to you in secret. Then tell her that my heart salutes her; tell her that she alone can bring me comfort; tell her that if she does not come I shall die. Tell her to remember our past time, and our great sorrows, and all the joy there was in our loyal and tender love. And tell her to remember that draught we drank together on the high seas. For we drank our death together. Tell her to remember the oath I swore to serve a single love, for I have kept that oath."

But behind the wall, Iseult of the White Hands heard all these things; and Tristan continued:

"Hasten, my friend, and come back quickly, or you will not see me again. Take forty days for your term, but come back with Iseult the Fair. And tell your sister nothing, or tell her that you seek some doctor. Take my fine ship, and two sails with you, one white, one black. And as you return, if you bring Iseult, hoist the white sail; but if you bring her not, the black. Now I have nothing more to say, but God guide you and bring you back safe."

With the first fair wind Kaherdin took the open, weighed anchor and hoisted sail, and ran with a light air and broke the seas. They bore rich merchandise with them, dyed silks of rare colours, enamel of Touraine and wines of Poitou, for by this ruse Kaherdin thought to reach Iseult. Eight days and nights they ran full sail to Cornwall.

Now a woman's wrath is a fearful thing, and all men fear it, for according to her love, so will her vengeance be; and their love and their hate come quickly, but their hate lives longer than their love; and they will make play with love, but not with hate. So Iseult of the White Hands, who had heard every word, and who had so loved Tristan, waited her vengeance upon what she loved most in the world. But she hid it all; and when the doors were open again she came to Tristan's bed and served him with food as a lover should, and spoke him gently and kissed him on the lips, and asked him if Kaherdin would soon return with one to cure him ... but all day long she thought upon her vengeance.

And Kaherdin sailed and sailed till he dropped anchor in the haven of Tintagel. He landed and took with him a cloth of rare dye and a cup well chiselled and worked, and made a present of them to King Mark, and courteously begged of him his peace and safeguard that he might traffick in his land; and the King gave him his peace before all the men of his palace.

Then Kaherdin offered the Queen a buckle of fine gold; and "Queen," said he, "the gold is good."

Then taking from his finger Tristan's ring, he put it side by side with the jewel and said:

"See, O Queen, the gold of the buckle is the finer gold; yet that ring also has its worth."

When Iseult saw what ring that was, her heart trembled and her colour changed, and fearing what might next be said she drew Kaherdin apart near a window, as if to see and bargain the better; and Kaherdin said to her, low down:

"Lady, Tristan is wounded of a poisoned spear and is about to die. He sends you word that you alone can bring him comfort, and recalls to you the great sorrows that you bore together. Keep you the ring – it is yours."

But Iseult answered, weakening:

"Friend, I will follow you; get ready your ship to-morrow at dawn."

And on the morrow at dawn they raised anchor, stepped mast, and hoisted sail, and happily the barque left land.

But at Carhaix Tristan lay and longed for Iseult's coming. Nothing now filled him any more, and if he lived it was only as awaiting her; and day by day he sent watchers to the shore to see if some ship came, and to learn the colour of her sail. There was no other thing left in his heart.

He had himself carried to the cliff of the Penmarks, where it overlooks the sea, and all the daylight long he gazed far off over the water.

Hear now a tale most sad and pitiful to all who love. Already was Iseult near; already the cliff of the Penmarks showed far away, and the ship ran heartily, when a storm wind rose on a sudden and grew, and struck the sail, and turned the ship all round about, and the sailors bore away and sore against their will they ran before the wind. The wind raged and big seas ran, and the air grew thick with darkness, and the ocean itself turned dark, and the rain drove in gusts. The yard snapped, and the sheet; they struck their sail, and ran with wind and water. In an evil hour they had forgotten to haul their pinnace aboard; it leapt in their wake, and a great sea broke it away.

Then Iseult cried out: "God does not will that I should live to see him, my love, once – even one time more. God wills my drowning in this sea. O, Tristan, had I spoken to you but once again, it is little I should have cared for a death come afterwards. But now, my love, I cannot come to you; for God so wills it, and that is the core of my grief."

And thus the Queen complained so long as the storm endured; but after five days it died down. Kaherdin hoisted the sail, the white sail, right up to the very masthead with great joy; the white sail, that Tristan might know its colour from afar: and already Kaherdin saw Britanny far off like a cloud. Hardly were these things seen and done when a calm came, and the sea lay even and untroubled. The sail bellied no longer, and the sailors held the ship now up, now down, the tide, beating backwards and forwards in vain. They saw the shore afar off, but the storm had carried their boat away and they could not land. On the third night Iseult dreamt this dream: that she held in her lap a boar's head which befouled her skirts with blood; then she knew that she would never see her lover again alive.

Tristan was now too weak to keep his watch from the cliff of the Penmarks, and for many long days, within walls, far from the shore, he had mourned for Iseult because she did not come. Dolorous and alone, he mourned and sighed in restlessness: he was near death from desire.

At last the wind freshened and the white sail showed. Then it was that Iseult of the White Hands took her vengeance.

She came to where Tristan lay, and she said:

"Friend, Kaherdin is here. I have seen his ship upon the sea. She comes up hardly – yet I know her; may he bring that which shall heal thee, friend."

And Tristan trembled and said:

"Beautiful friend, you are sure that the ship is his indeed? Then tell me what is the manner of the sail?"

"I saw it plain and well. They have shaken it out and hoisted it very high, for they have little wind. For its colour, why, it is black."

And Tristan turned him to the wall, and said:

"I cannot keep this life of mine any longer." He said three times: "Iseult, my friend." And in saying it the fourth time, he died.

Then throughout the house, the knights and the comrades of Tristan wept out loud, and they took him from his bed and laid him on a rich cloth, and they covered his body with a shroud. But at sea the wind had risen; it struck the sail fair and full and drove the ship to shore, and Iseult the Fair set foot upon the land. She heard loud mourning in the streets, and the tolling of bells in the minsters and the chapel towers; she asked the people the meaning of the knell and of their tears. An old man said to her:

"Lady, we suffer a great grief. Tristan, that was so loyal and so right, is dead. He was open to the poor; he ministered to the suffering. It is the chief evil that has ever fallen on this land."

But Iseult, hearing them, could not answer them a word. She went up to the palace, following the way, and her cloak was random and wild. The Bretons marvelled as she went; nor had they ever seen woman of such a beauty, and they said:

"Who is she, or whence does she come?"

Near Tristan, Iseult of the White Hands crouched, maddened at the evil she had done, and calling and lamenting over the dead man. The other Iseult came in and said to her:

"Lady, rise and let me come by him; I have more right to mourn him than have you – believe me. I loved him more."

And when she had turned to the east and prayed God, she moved the body a little and lay down by the dead man, beside her friend. She kissed his mouth and his face, and clasped him closely; and so gave up her soul, and died beside him of grief for her lover.

When King Mark heard of the death of these lovers, he crossed the sea and came into Brittany; and he had two coffins hewn, for Tristan and Iseult, one of chalcedony for Iseult, and one of beryl for Tristan. And he took their beloved bodies away with him upon his ship to Tintagel, and by a chantry to the left and right of the apse he had their tombs built round. But in one night there sprang from the tomb of Tristan a green and leafy briar, strong in its branches and in the scent of its flowers. It climbed the chantry and fell to root again by Iseult's tomb. Thrice did the peasants cut it down, but thrice it grew again as flowered and as strong. They told the marvel to King Mark, and he forbade them to cut the briar any more.

The good singers of old time, Beroul and Thomas of Built, Gilbert and Gottfried told this tale for lovers and none other, and, by my pen, they beg you for your prayers. They greet those who are cast down, and those in heart, those troubled and those filled with desire. May all herein find strength against inconstancy and despite and loss and pain and all the bitterness of loving.